paper

Hanna Peach writing as

sienna blake

SB Publishing

Paper Dolls: a novel / by Sienna Blake. – 1st Ed.
First Digital Edition: April 2016
Published by SB Publishing
Copyright 2016 Sienna Blake

ISBN-10: 1544135319
ISBN-13: 978-1544135311

To Emma,

Because you were the first to believe in Aria's story.

Contents

Prologue

In the end, my life came down to two people – two faces, two pairs of hands that have pushed aside tears, two pairs of arms that have protected me, held me despite the darkness, despite the pain that threatened to pull me under. And now these two people, the two people I loved the most, were tearing me apart.

"Choose, Aria!" my sister cried at me, her sharp voice echoing over the expanse of the gorge and the sound of water crashing onto rocks.

My hand holding the gun felt heavier and heavier, the muzzle dipping, sweat rolling from where my palm wrapped around the grip, my tendons trembling and crying out in a discordant harmony along with the weighted, fractured wailing of my heart.

I shifted my weight, trying to stand in a way that would keep me upright, even as my legs were trembling so hard I thought I might collapse, my feet crushing dried, withered leaves that had swept onto the bridge as if they were bones or pieces of my shattered self. The smell of my own sweat and fear mixed in with the pine and the tang of moist earth.

Choose. The rest of my life came down to this. One choice. Two faces.

In moments like these, everything slowed. Salem always joked that it was life's way of making sure you didn't miss the turning points, the important bits. As if gravity sank heavier and heavier with the weight of the moment until the world was too heavy to turn and everyone held their breath.

It certainly felt like that now. My next action, my next word, would change all of our lives.

"Aria," Clay's deep voice reached my ears. "Whatever happens…I love you." The usual assuredness and authority was gone. Instead, strain and hurt had crumpled up and shoved into his throat. *Choose me. Save me. Love me.*

Before him my life had felt like a stack of old movies: frames missing or out of order, muted crackling sound, flickering and shuttering away, unloved and unseen in an old unused cinema, dank carpets and the smell of stale cigarettes in the musty air.

Then I found him. Or he found me.

He created a warm shield around me where I could be safe. He coaxed away all my layers and shed all my masks and his love soaked right into my skin, right into the very soul of me. He pulled out the fossil buried inside that had been my heart and breathed life into me.

How could I give up the man I loved? The one who loved me with a fierce and unwavering passion, the man who made me feel like I could defeat demons as long as he was by my side.

Winking in the threads of sunlight piercing through the solemn grey clouds, seed fluff twirled about me like swirling, dancing couples. Spinning around like Salem and I used to do in our backyard, hands clasped together tightly, turning round and round, eyes to the sky, our twin voices giggling and floating into the air like dandelions.

She had been my shield before Clay.

"I'm nothing without you, Aria," Salem's voice trembled, desperation leaking into the breaths between her words. *Choose me. Need me. Love me.*

How could I end her? I just got her back. For so long we shared almost everything, and she protected me. Her whole life had been about protecting me. Because she loved me that much.

How could I turn against her, toss her away like an old broken toy?

But I had to choose.

Several weeks ago there was one small, stupid moment, after

I had her back and I had Clay, where I believed I could be happy.

Damn, girl, are you actually smiling?

Oh Flick, everything is just perfect.

One stupid moment.

But that's the thing about us humans: we're resilient. Hope is so hard to snuff out. Even if we've been kicked and beaten down and trod on, hope flares. It rises to the top like oil on water.

Even now as I stare between Clay and Salem, trying to digest our impossible situation, Hope is still there, that terrible pixie, fluttering on my shoulder, whispering.

Maybe it doesn't have to end this way?

Maybe Flick will show up and sort this out in the way only she could do, clear and stern but with a whole lot of sass.

Maybe the police will come storming through the trees, their flashlights and guns upon us, forcing us all apart.

Or a knight riding on a white horse…

Fuck you, Hope. Here's the truth.

Nobody is coming.

No one will save us.

And someone isn't going to make it out of this forest today.

I could see us now, the three of us making a chain like when I was a kid, folding pieces of coloured paper into rectangles, cutting out an arm, a leg, and half a head, and unfurling my new patterns in the light to reveal a line of paper dolls. Clay, Salem and I – we were all just paper dolls in a paper chain, me in the middle, each end pulling tighter and tighter until something had to tear.

Who would I rip apart?

"Choose," my sister screamed. "It's either him or me."

My fingers tightened around my gun in a reflex. This was it. I either ended her. Or destroyed Clay.

I squeezed my eyelids shut for a moment, just for a moment of peace. Just for an instant I could shut out the inevitable, and in this blessed darkness I believed I could conceive a way that both could exist in my life. A way that I could choose Salem *and* Clay.

You can't have both.

You tried.

You.

Can't.

Have.

Both.

Choose now.

But how?

What do you do when someone puts a gun to your head? Clay's words came back to me, echoing as loud in my mind as if he had just spoken them. *You refuse to bend. You push back. You find another way. You take that gun off him and put it back in his face. But you do* not *give in.*

Find another way…

I knew what I had to do. A kind of peace settled on my skin, as delicate as gossamer, as light as silk.

I opened my eyes to a world of bright light until my vision adjusted. The torn and pained faces of the two people I loved came into focus. The only two people I've shared air with while we slept, the same two people I'd crawl into Hell to be with, and the only two people I would die for. I forced the ghost of a smile forward.

And turned the gun on myself.

Chapter One

Four weeks earlier…

"I still can't believe you won." I chanced a glance up to Clay, hiking a few metres in front of me. He had impossibly long legs but he never walked so fast that I couldn't keep up. His dark t-shirt was fitted enough to show off the wide V of his torso, a patch of dampness on his shirt sticking to the middle of his shoulder blades. Damn. That was a great back.

His voice, deep and rumbling, called back to me. "I can't believe you made me work so hard just for a date."

"I doubt you've ever had to work for a date before so don't think for a second I feel one bit sorry for you."

"That is true. Most women can't resist my charms."

I snorted. "I'm not most women."

He glanced back at me over his shoulder, his dark blue eyes sparkling with intensity. "Indeed, you are not." It felt like his words hid another meaning from me.

Leaves crunched under my feet like tiny old bones and small lizards rustled away from the sounds of our footfalls. The path we were walking on, through the National Park in the Sunshine Coast hinterland, was skinny and barely visible at times, the green outstretched hands of ferns hiding the toes of tree roots, and moss stretched across slippery rocks. Despite being at the start of a

Queensland summer, the air was cool under the trees.

"You know what I'm still trying to decide?" he asked.

"What?"

"Whether you're worth all that work."

I let out an indignant noise.

He laughed. "I'm joking, angel. You're worth it, even if I had to wait another three months just to get you on a date."

"Then you'd have given up?"

"Then I'd have to seriously rethink my strategy."

Truthfully, his strategy was perfect; he put me at ease almost immediately and never pushed too hard, happy to let our friendship develop first for as long as it took. It had been *me* that was the problem.

But he had been patient until he found a tiny crack in the wall I built around myself, just a crack but it was wide enough for him to begin to pry me open. And now I was here, hiking with him, alone, on a date.

Clay's tanned calves flexed into diamonds as he walked. I sighed internally. He even had great calves. My eyes continued to travel up, entranced as his muscles flexed and coiled with latent power. Suddenly I found myself staring at his butt, firm and rounded in his dark maroon knee-length shorts. I sighed again. That was one hell of an ass. Perhaps the most amazing ass in the world. Not that I had ever spent much time dissecting the characteristics of a great ass. But I just knew instinctively this was a good one. I knew because every time I stared at it I got this urge to grab it. My cheeks heated. Lord help me. What was I thinking? I wasn't like this. I better look away before I...

...tripped. Dammit. My arms flew out in the air as my toe caught on a root or a rock or something. I managed to catch myself before I fell into the dirt.

"You alright?" Clay stopped and turned.

"Fine." I straightened up, trying to pretend that my ogling him had not been the cause of my near fall, my eyes darting everywhere except at him. "I just tripped."

"I know it's hard but try not to be so distracted walking behind me."

My mouth dropped open and my eyes darted involuntarily to him. He grinned at me, a twinkle in his eye.

I lowered my face, letting my long auburn hair hide my hot cheeks. Or, at least I hope it hid them. I could never seem to hide anything from Clay. "Just turn around," I demanded, "keep walking."

"God, I love it when you get bossy."

"Clay!"

"I love it when you say my name."

I fought the rising flush. Damn him. He enjoyed making me blush. He almost made a game of it. But that's all it was. Just a game to him. A man like Clay couldn't possibly be interested in a girl like me in *that* way. Right? "Just…just," I spluttered, "just shut up and keep going."

"Yes, ma'am."

"How did you find out about this spot, anyway?" I asked as we started off again.

"I grew up in the area. I used to come out here as a boy with my father."

We hiked in silence, deeper and deeper into the forest, the air thick of the smell of eucalyptus. Friendly bugs flitting about, flashes of ruby and vibrant blue. The undergrowth, skinny ferns and thick velvet bushes, shook with the scatter of small rodents and lizards, scurrying away from our footfalls.

Finally we came out to the jagged, rocky edge of a small lake, a clear jewel amongst the surrounding forest. I stopped and wiped away the sweat that had mixed with the sunscreen on my forehead and was beginning to sting my eyes. I squinted across the lake at a flash of sunlight glinting off something…glinting off Salem's long red hair.

"Watch me. Watch me," she screamed, her girlish voice bouncing off the insides of the trees that lined a different lake, a secret magical pool we had discovered in the nearby forest the summer of our thirteenth birthday. She stood dressed in nothing but her white cotton underwear on the tip of a large rock that jutted out over the water, budding prepubescent breasts, her skinny legs like pale stalks.

"Be careful," I called out as I sat, fully dressed, in the shade of the trees, far enough from the bank that there was no chance I'd fall in.

She took a short run and leapt off the edge of the rock, flipping over in the air. My heart jammed into my throat as she arced over, then hit the water with a crash and disappeared. Droplets landed all across my skin and my body broke out in a chill. Salem had always been the adventurous one.

I held my breath, as I always did when she was underwater. Habit.

As the seconds ticked over I began to feel a growing pressure in my chest.

Where was Salem? Why hadn't she come up yet?

The skin of the lake remained unbroken, ripples stretching out to the edges, the only proof she had ever gone in the water. My voice broke through like a gasp around her name as I expelled the stale air in my lungs. She hit her head at the bottom. Oh God. She had hit her head and now she was going to drown. I told her it was dangerous but she never listened to me.

I crawled over to the edge of the lake so there was no chance that I would fall in too, my fingers scratching against the stone, scuffing my knees as my shorts rode up. I leaned over the rock, holding my breath again, imagining her lying like a pale dead fish along the rocks on the bottom.

Instead I saw her face peering back at me through the water. She reached out for me as I reached out for her. Our hands grabbed each other and I tugged backwards, falling on my butt. She broke through the water's surface and pulled herself up to sit on a rock on the edge of the lake, droplets shaking off her long hair turned the dark colour of old blood from the water, laughter falling from her lips.

I glared at her, teetering for a second between fury and relief that she was alright. Relief won out. I lunged at her, wrapping my arms around her. "Salem," her name lodged in my throat, "you scared me. I thought…I thought…"

"I'm fine, silly."

"But you were under for ages. And I thought you'd—"

She shushed into my hair. I gripped her tighter, not caring that my clothes were soaking up water from her wet body. "You know I'd never, ever leave you."

She had lied.

But then again, so had I.

Clay dropped the small pack from his shoulder, jolting me back to the present.

I glanced back over to the rock where Salem had been standing. But Salem wasn't there. I wasn't wet from her body. My arms were empty. It had been a memory playing out before my eyes. Just a memory. Not real.

"Last one in is a rotten egg." Clay pulled his shirt off over his head and dropped it onto his pack without a hint of self-consciousness to his graceful motion. For a second I was struck dumb. I don't think I had ever been this close to a shirtless man before, firm planes of his chest, perfect six-pack, thick forearms, all covered in smooth golden skin so different from my milky skin. I wished my skin took the sun like his did. His china-blue eyes twinkled with mischief under thick, heavy brows and the shock of dark hair that fell over his forehead and often caught between his lashes.

Last one in is a rotten egg. I looked down into the lake. Salem's pale figure, her hair like seaweed, lay prone along the bottom. I gasped, stepping back from the edge, and squeezed my eyes shut. *Salem isn't there, Aria. She isn't real.* I forced my eyes open and looked again. Sure enough the bottom of the lake was empty.

"You okay?"

I jolted at Clay's voice, hoping he hadn't noticed my strange behaviour. *This is why you don't date.* "I, er...didn't bring anything to swim in."

One side of his mouth lifted up. "So don't wear anything."

I turned my head to hide the heat in my cheeks. "I'm not going in without clothes on."

"Why not?"

I glanced over and caught him sliding off his shorts, revealing slim hips and thighs, legs in a pair of dark grey boy leg briefs, a

17

large bulge in his−

Oh. My. God.

I turned my head again, this time my face igniting into twin flames.

Thankfully he didn't seem to notice my embarrassment. Or perhaps he just chose not to point it out. "So go in with clothes on. It's warm enough that they'll dry."

I shook my head. "I mean, I'm not going in. At all."

"Are you serious?"

I nodded, still staring at the glassy lake surface, glinting at me like broken glass. Who knew what lay beneath the surface? What dark things lay waiting? People died in lakes.

I didn't see Clay coming towards me until he grabbed me. For a brief second I felt a lashing of fear through my body as a very different pair of arms grabbed me. I gasped and this unwanted presence faded, leaving behind Clay's strong and warm body curled around me, trapping me in his arms, but making me feel safe. I became aware of the strength in his forearms and his arms, the way that he used them to keep me against him and a very different emotion coursed through me, something hot and electric. I fought a shudder.

I looked right, his face sitting just over my shoulder. There was a wicked glint in his eyes as they held my stare for one moment, then he looked out. I followed his gaze and found the water.

Realisation struck me. "You wouldn't dare."

He lowered his lips to my ear, the softness brushing against my lobe, causing my thighs to tremble. "Wouldn't I?"

He began to walk us forward. I struggled against him, a rush of adrenaline coursing through my veins, shaking off the gathered cobwebs and bubbling out into giggles. "Oh my God, Clay. I have no other clothes. My shoes. Everything will get wet."

"You had your chance to undress." His deep voice, full of amusement, tickled down my neck making me shiver.

He dragged me all the way to the lake's edge onto a flat rock jutting out over the water. Through the surface was the rocky lake bed and several pale fish swimming about.

He paused. I exhaled. He was just bluffing. Of course he was just bluffing. He wouldn't really do it.

He picked me up and my feet kicked out automatically. "No! Don't!"

With his laughter in my ear, I was tossed forward. I inhaled, squeezing everything shut, and waited for the water to swallow me up.

He didn't release me. My body jerked against his arms as he tugged me back and my legs pulled back in. He placed my trembling legs back on the rock and his arms loosened around me. It took me a second to realise that he had been bluffing.

"You ass." I turned and slapped his chest. It was like hitting granite. "I hate you."

He grabbed my wrists to stop me from hitting him again and pulled me towards him, this time face to face. One of his arms wrapped around me to trap me against him, my arms between us. My fingertips fluttered on his chest. His bare torso was so warm in contrast to the cool air that it sent shivers through me.

"No you don't," he said. "You love me." I could still see amusement in his eyes, but joining it now was a seriousness.

I swallowed hard. "You arrogant ass. Keep telling yourself that."

"I will. Just until you figure it out."

He was too close and almost naked and his skin was too warm and he smelled too damn good, hints of cedar but it was tempered with a warm musk and some kind of spice. I couldn't think of anything clever to say back. It wasn't fair of him to do this to me. His brain seemed perfectly functional whenever I was near. Why couldn't I have this same effect on him?

My gaze moved across his face, deep-set blue eyes that always cut right through me like a white-hot blade, his lashes enviously thick and black, carved cheekbones, stubble that was constantly shading his jaw. Then finally to his mouth that was just a tad too wide and his top lip that pouted out just a touch farther than his bottom lip, the epitome of perfect imperfection and I wanted so badly to see whether they felt as good as they looked. I groaned before I could stop myself, then came a lash of embarrassment. What was wrong with me? I was groaning just *looking* at his mouth. God help me if he ever decided to kiss me.

As if he heard me thinking the word kiss, his gaze dropped down to my mouth. I inhaled sharply as my lungs tightened, and my lips parted. Dammit. I knew what it must have looked like. A sign that I wanted him to kiss me.

I didn't.

Not really.

Male voices called out, ricocheting across the lake. "Woot. Kiss her! Go for it, mate!"

Other hikers had seen us. Hikers who weren't helping this awkward situation. I grew hot from my centre out to the edge of my skin.

I pushed at Clay and he let go of me. I turned my head left and right trying to find the source of my embarrassment. I spotted them, a group of three boys, young, perhaps only fifteen or sixteen, moving past the lake, their black and blue shirts flashing through the tree trunks. They continued to whistle and tease before their voices faded as they moved out of range.

Clay didn't seem fussed like I was, that damn lazy grin of his sitting easily on his beautiful face. "Aria," he said quietly. "I *am* going to kiss you."

I froze. My heart went from pleasant thud to stampeding beast in two seconds flat. Was this it? After twelve weeks of his friendship, after twelve weeks of seeing him almost every day, twelve weeks of this growing curiosity, eventually becoming a hot, aching tightness in my gut every time he got too close, was this where we were going?

His smile widened.

My chest tightened with panic. Clay always seemed to know what I was thinking. I could never seem to hide anything from him. I wasn't safe from his probing eyes. I wasn't safe from what I had begun to feel for him.

"I am going to kiss you," he repeated. "But not now."

I let out a breath that I hadn't realised I had been holding. I had a reprieve. At least for now. Twisting around my relief was a bitter disappointment. One of these days I may have to admit to myself how much I wanted Clay.

"One day I will kiss you. On the day you beg me for it.

Until then…"

"I'll never beg."

"Never say never."

He took a step away from me, turned, and dove into the water, his beautiful body arcing like a golden bird before diving into the crystal liquid with barely a splash and disappearing from sight. While he was under I found myself holding my breath as I used to do with Salem so many years ago.

…seven…eight…nine…

He broke up through the surface of the water and I let that breath go, relief relaxing my body.

"Come on in. The water's amazing."

I wanted to. But it was safer on the edge. I lowered myself to sitting and pulled off my shoes, dipping my toes into the cool water. "See, I'm in."

Clay flicked water at me. I flinched back as the droplets hit my face. "Hey, cut that out."

He continued his assault. I yanked my feet out of the water and pushed myself to standing, backing up until his droplets couldn't reach me anymore, dirt squeezing up between my toes.

"Life starts in the deep end, angel. Don't spend the rest of your existence just watching from the edge."

His words cut through me. "I have a life," I said in self-defence. "Just because I won't to jump in with you…" I trailed off. But I hadn't ever jumped in, had I? I had always just watched from the side.

I stared at Clay, swimming through the water with powerful cuts of his arms and felt a strong tug towards the glittering lake. What had started out a sliver of discontent several weeks ago had steadily grown into this…inner rebellion. The safety on the shore was beginning to feel stifling and boring. I wanted something more than safety. I wanted to jump in there with him. I wanted to brave the deep end.

Without allowing myself a moment to second-guess myself, I ran forward and jumped. For a second I was airborne, the feeling of flying coursing through me, a feeling of weightlessness. I hit the water, so cold in contrast to the humid air that it made my lungs spasm. I gasped before I shut my mouth against the invading water that covered me completely. I felt it catch me in its warm arms and slow my descent. Under the water there was a kind of silence. A womb-like sensation of being safe and surrounded. What had I ever been scared of?

My feet found the uneven lakebed. I kicked off and shot back up, my face breaking through the surface of the water. The warm air stung against my frigid cheeks. I inhaled and felt a rush of thankfulness that I was alive. Sometimes I forgot how good it felt just to be alive. Clay always seemed to find ways to remind me. To push me into places and feelings where I didn't want to go at first, but then I did, and every time it felt like shooting stars under my skin.

"I knew you had it in you."

I spun to face Clay, his face all grin and perfect, straight teeth. He was standing partly out of the water, his taut pecs just above the waterline, and droplets on his tanned skin. His fractured reflection underneath him was a beautiful inversion.

I was staring.

Of course, he had noticed me staring, a half-grin pulling up at the corner of his mouth. I looked away trying to pretend that he didn't stun me the way he always did. He was so beautiful it hurt to look at him, burning the backs of my eyes like I had been staring into a flame for too long. I always had to rip my gaze away from him, but it was only ever temporary, my eyes just drawing back to him like moths.

Clay pushed back along the surface of the lake, forcing the water out of his way, until he slowed to a stop and lay on his back just floating there. With his body partially out of the water, I could see the scattering of dark chest hair plastered to his chest, a tiny pool of water between his firm chest and those ridges of his abdominal muscles. I never used to understand women's fascination with the male body, but now I did. There was a coiled power promised in each muscle, a seductive heat that seemed to radiate from each fibre that drew me closer, fingers itching to run along those firm lines and sharp edges. And I wanted to suck the water out from every place that it pooled.

"Hey, what do you think that looks like?"

I flinched at his voice. Had he caught me drooling over him?

No, he was still floating on his back, staring directly up, his right arm now outstretched.

"What are you looking at?" I lifted my face to the heavens. The sky was a perfect Queensland summer dark blue, a few scattered clouds ambling their way across.

"You have to come here."

I waded towards him and stopped a metre away. My eyes found his torso, golden and firm and perfect, rising up out of the water like a golden island.

"Closer."

I moved half a metre away from him. If I lifted my arm I could touch him.

But it was he who touched me first. His right hand wrapped around my arm and tugged me to his side; where he was touching me felt like it was on fire. "Get on your back, like me."

I did as he asked. I almost sank from disappointment when he took his hand from me and lifted it up to the sky to point again.

"That cloud. What do you see?"

"What?"

"In that cloud, what do you see?"

I frowned. "A cloud."

He laughed. "Come on, angel. You can do better than that."

I sighed quietly and stared at the cloud that he was pointing at. It was misshapen and fluffy and I didn't see a damn thing in it other than a cloud. But I know Clay wouldn't let up if I didn't say *something*. "A rabbit."

I felt his eyes on me, then he hummed as he studied the cloud. "A rabbit. Yeah, I can see that. There's his ears and his teeth and his tail."

I frowned. I didn't see a rabbit. Trust Clay to see things in the clouds that I couldn't. I started to drift away from him across the water. I was going to let us drift apart but I felt his hand finding mine just under the surface of the water. His fingers pushed their way through my fingers and he tugged me so that I floated right up against him, his thick corded arm pressing right up along mine.

I was too surprised to protest.

It felt so good, just floating there with Clay, staring up to the sky and watching the cluster of condensed air that people called clouds, even though a voice inside of me warned me not to let him get too close. It was a habit now, I guessed, after three long years of being alone, moving every few months, of searching for a sister who didn't want to be found.

"What about that one?" He pointed to another, this time with his left hand, his right hand firmly curled into mine.

"A…baby rabbit?"

"There are more than rabbits in the clouds."

I sighed. "That's why you're the artist and I'm just a checkout chick."

"Don't say that. What you do and who you are are two different things. Anyone who judges who you are by what you do is short-sighted."

"Some of us weren't destined for big things. It is in the stars," I said. "The stars above us, govern our conditions."

"Perhaps…but men at some time are masters of their fates: The fault, dear Aria, is not in our stars, but in ourselves…"

I lashed out and righted myself, blinking rapidly as I heard a memory of Salem's voice, speaking those exact words to me, her young voice reverberating and quivering with emotion.

"What's wrong?" Clay righted himself too, but he did it smoothly, barely making a splash, while the ripples were still widening from my clumsy efforts.

"You just quoted Shakespeare."

"So did you. *King Lear*."

"And you quoted *Julius Caesar*."

He grinned. "You know Shakespeare?"

"*Know* Shakespeare." Salem and I used to read out his plays. We could assign each other roles and recite our lines in fake British accents, and run and jump around the garden play-fighting with sticks as our swords. I sighed dramatically. "I don't just know Shakespeare, he and I have a relationship."

"Well, this is awkward. Because *I* have a relationship with the old Bard."

"No."

"Yes. And I'm a year older than you so my relationship has been going on longer. Mine trumps yours."

"Length of time does not equal a depth of connection. My connection with Shakespeare is deeper. I *love* Shakespeare. Mine trumps yours."

"You might think you love Shakespeare but you couldn't possibly love Shakespeare more than me."

"I bet I do."

"I bet you don't." His eyes twinkled. "Let's play a game."

The very thing I lost which forced me on this…confusing and utterly unadvisable date in the first place. "Gee, I didn't see that coming."

"I'll have to work on being more surprising, then. So are you in? Or are you chicken."

"I'm not chicken."

"So you're in."

"I haven't heard this game yet."

"We'll do Shakespeare quotes. Whoever guesses wrong first, loses, and the other wins."

"Wins what?"

"Same as always."

A request from the other. I shuffled, nervous as hell. "What will you pick if you win?"

"Ladies choose their prize first."

"Fine. If I win, you get to be my chauffeur. Drive me wherever I want."

"You already have a car."

"I have a tin box with an engine of a lawn mower held together with rust. When I win−"

"*If* you win."

"Fine. If I win you'll be my driver."

"For a week."

"For a month."

"Fine." A smile began to crawl across his face. "*When* I win you owe me…our first kiss."

"A kiss?"

"So it's settled." He grinned as if he already won. "I'll be kind. I'll even let you go first."

"I…" I had to swallow to unstick my throat. He wanted a kiss? "I didn't agree to the game yet."

"Afraid you'll lose?"

"I won't lose this game." I found a section of the lake where I could actually feel the bottom and raised myself up as tall as I could. "I'm not going to lose." My chin was only barely out of the water, but I felt more stable.

"Put your money where your mouth is."

"I'll start." I just knew this was a bad idea. What did they say? Pride comes before the fall… *Things without all remedy should be without regard: what's done is done.*"

He gave me a look. "Really? Aren't you even going to make this hard for me?"

"You haven't even answered yet."

"*Macbeth.*" He smirked at me, knowing that he got it right.

I shrugged, pretending like I didn't care, while inside my heart began thudding just a little faster. Maybe he did know what he was doing?

"My turn," he said, his voice resounding with gravity. "*Doubt thou the stars are fire;*
Doubt that the sun doth move;
Doubt truth to be a liar;
But never doubt I love."

My skin prickled as he spoke, each word of his spoken with passion. "The answer is *Hamlet.* You're good. But you're not as good as me."

"You haven't won."

"Yet. *Our doubts are traitors and make us lose the good we oft might win, by fearing to attempt.*"

"*Measure for Measure.*"

I sank slightly back in the water. "You're good," I conceded.

He grinned. "I know."

I swallowed. "It's your turn."

"*Did my heart love till now? forswear it, sight! For I ne'er saw true beauty till this night.*" He spoke his line with effort and reverence, as if he were really Romeo, his lips trembling as said the word *ne'er*. His gaze ripped through me and I felt naked, the temperature of the water seeming to drop, making me shiver, and yet at the same time, my insides began to glow like embers.

He raised an eyebrow at me. "Don't tell me that one has you stumped."

"No," I growled, cursing myself for losing my brain over a silly quote. It had just seemed so real. It had seemed like he was speaking to me. "*Romeo and Juliet.*"

He smiled. "Correct."

I was silent as I considered my next move. Finally I spoke, "*Why, this is very midsummer madness.*"

He only paused for a second before he spoke, a small smile teasing his full lips. "Most people would naturally assume that this quote comes from *Midsummer Night's Dream* because of the reference to midsummer."

Dammit. That was what I had been hoping. "But you think you know better?" I tried to bluff.

"But I know better."

"You still haven't answered."

"This line is from *Twelfth Night*, spoken by...Olivia, actually."

I shrugged, growing more and more uneasy at the ease at which he seemed to be recognising my quotes. He was good. He was very good.

I pushed these thoughts aside. But I was better. I knew Shakespeare's lines like they were the very breaths of my life, the very words of my soul. "Your go."

He spoke again, his eyes never leaving mine, "*My bounty is as boundless as the sea,*
My love as deep; the more I give to thee,
The more I have, for both are infinite."

I swallowed as the thick, ropy knot tightened in my throat. "Stop doing that," I said, my voice barely squeezing out.

"Doing what?"

"Choosing *those* kinds of quotes."

"What kind of quotes?"

He was going to make me say it. "You know...the love ones."

"I like the love ones. And as far as I'm aware there were no rules about what kinds of quotes we could or couldn't use, were there?"

No. There weren't. But it seemed to me that I had no rules around Clay. He stripped me of all of them.

"Answer," he said. "That is, if you know it."

"*Romeo and Juliet*. Again," I said, and he nodded.

It was my turn. I paused, letting my mind filter through all of Shakespeare's plays. He wouldn't win. I wouldn't let him. I knew the further we went, the more he would use those love quotes to mess with my head and the more likely I'd mess up. I needed to end this. Now.

Finally, I found a quote so obscure that he couldn't possibly get it right. I tried to hide my grin. I cleared my throat. "*Men's evil manners live in brass; their virtues we write in water.*"

I watched his eyes widen, then his features hardened into a frown. I wanted to run my fingertips across his forehead to smooth out the heavy lines that I had caused.

Finally he broke eye contact with me, his eyes glancing up to the sky as if the answer was somehow written amongst the rabbits in the clouds.

I had won. He didn't know the quote. I'd get my prize; him at my beck and call to drive me where I wanted. *It means you'll spend more time together.* Not that he ever needed an excuse. I had won. But that would mean, he wouldn't get his kiss. I wouldn't get *my* first real kiss. A wave of sadness rose over me so suddenly it made my eyelashes flutter. I wanted to take back my quote, to give him something that was less obscure. But I remained silent.

His face broke out in a knowing grin, that cheeky, arrogant grin that I had come to know *very* well in these last twelve weeks since we met. I knew in an instant, he had been faking. *Gotcha*, it was written all over his face. The face I now wanted to slap.

"That line," he began, "just happens to come from one of my favourite plays."

"Which...which one then?" He could still get it wrong.

"*Henry VIII.*"

I sank back down into the water as if it could hide me. But

there was never anywhere I could hide from those eyes, not those eyes that sought my insides out and forced me, the real me, to the surface. Me and all my fears, all my hidden worries, all the baby-skinned hopes that I hid from the world. Hid from everyone, except for him. And Salem. Salem used to know me, the real me, too.

He moved around me in the water as I remained frozen where I was, the very tips of my toes anchoring against the gritty rocks at the lakebed. I was prey, his prey. Every ripple of water that circled out from him as he moved lapped against my body, rocking against me so that it almost felt like skin slapping against skin. I stifled a shiver.

"Tell me something honestly, angel," I heard his voice behind me. Then there was a silence. I felt his exhale of breath against my neck and realised that he had come up behind me. I caught my inhale in my lungs. "Did you feel disappointed when you thought you were going to win?"

I hated how he seemed to see right into me. I hated that I couldn't seem to hide from him, ever. And yet, I loved it. There was something completely exhilarating in the knowledge that he saw me – the real me – and chose to inch ever closer. He liked me, in spite of me.

"It's your go," I said, my voice sounding weak even to my own ears. He knew what I had felt. He didn't need me to tell him. He just wanted to torture me by letting me know that he knew.

He made no sound. No movement. It went on for so long that my neck began to prickle. Was he even still there?

I turned around. He was right there. Right there where he had always been. Waiting for me to turn to him. His brilliant eyes stood out even more under dark wet lashes, as they studied me, peeling away every single layer of me, my armour turning to lace under his gaze.

"It's your go," I repeated. It was the only thing that was safe to say.

"I'll let you off this time," he said, his voice so low I could just barely hear it over the rustle of the small creatures that tread the edge of the lake and the splashing of water by the birds that flew down to drink. "But one day, you'll have to admit to yourself how you feel."

No, I didn't. I could be perfectly happy for the rest of my life behind this wall of denial. Right? "It's your turn," I said, my voice cloudy with bravado. "Or have you run out of quotes already?"

He smirked. "Oh little angel, I'll have you know, I could go all day and all night long if you let me." The look in his eye held a promise. Suddenly I wasn't sure whether he was talking about quoting Shakespeare.

"Okay," he spoke before I could say anything, "I have a hard one for you. A long, hard one. Are you ready for it?"

My flush deepened. We were definitely not talking about Shakespeare quotes anymore. I gathered as much bravado as I could. Two could play at this game within a game. "I can take whatever you have."

"Really. I can't wait to see if that's true."

"Then give it to me, Clay. Show me what you've got."

"What made me love thee? let that persuade thee there's something extraordinary in thee. I cannot: but I love thee; none but thee;" The tip of his tongue darted out to wet the middle of his top lip, that thick top lip that was so deliciously unbalanced and yet so mesmerisingly perfect. "*...and thou deservest it.*"

My mind went blank.

I knew that one. I knew it, I just…

It was his tongue. His stupid tongue on his stupid lip. This wasn't fair. Ref! "I know it."

"Then give it to me, angel." His voice was low, throaty and his breathing rushed out heavily as he said it. Heat trickled like lava down the insides of my body to pool in between my legs. All this innuendo. It was making my brain sticky. I couldn't think. I knew this quote but damn it if it wasn't buried under all this deep breathing and these thoughts of his tongue and the sinful promises his words held.

"Come on, angel. I want it." Every word became his hands against my body, rubbing across my skin and yanking my hips closer to him. "Let me have it. Don't hold back."

"*Othello*," I blurted out because I couldn't think of anything else. I knew as soon as I said it that I was wrong.

The smile that stretched out across his face was triumphant. "I'm afraid it was *The Merry Wives of Windsor*."

I knew that. I friggin' knew that. But his stupid tongue and his words and his damn games made my mind short-circuit. Damn him. Damn my recalcitrant body.

His smile faded, replaced with a look so serious it razored me in two. "I believe you owe me."

He moved towards me, only his head above the water, like a predator, a crocodile, cutting through the water towards me with his eyes fixed on his target.

He gripped my upper arms and pulled me flush against him, my chest against his naked form, only the flimsy cotton of my pale blue shirt between us. My skin broke out in goosebumps as if I were cold. But I was far from it. My insides heated, parching my throat. I tried to swallow and found I couldn't.

My feet no longer touched the bottom. I was tethered only to Clay. The silence became heavier, hotter. Only a few bird calls and the drops of water falling off our bodies into the lake's surface disturbed it.

"Shall I take my prize now…or later?" The way he was staring at my mouth, his own lips parted, leaning in closer to me until the desert skies of his eyes were all I saw, my horizon and my world, curving around me like the shape of the Earth. I felt his warm breath blowing around on my cheeks. He was going to kiss me.

Close your eyes and relax your mouth.

But his lips didn't touch mine.

My eyes flew open. He was peering at me, a slight crease in between his brows. "You look terrified."

"I…" He didn't realise how close he was to the truth. I was. I was terrified. But not because of him.

I had never kissed anyone.

No, that's not quite true…

"He likes you," Salem teased, then giggled as she bounced on the bed in our bedroom.

I leaned against the far wall with my legs across the blanket and picked at the hem of my skirt. "No, he doesn't."

"He does. Which means he's going to kiss you." She made

wet sucking noises through her puckered lips. I picked up a pillow from next to me and shoved it into her face. She laughed as she grabbed it and dropped it into her lap.

I chewed my lip. "I don't know how to kiss."

Her grey eyes went round; so did her pink mouth. "What if you're bad at it?"

I gasped. "What if I'm bad?"

"What if you're really, really bad?"

"Oh God, what if I'm horrible?"

"You need to practice."

"Practice? On who?"

"Practice on me."

"On you? But you're a girl!"

She rolled her eyes. "So? Would you rather practice on a dry yucky pillow?" She shoved the pillow in my face and it was my turn to push it out of the way.

"Ew. I guess not."

She scooted over on the bed until we were flush side by side, her thigh against mine as we leaned against the wall. "Close your eyes and relax your mouth."

I did. I felt her warm breath blowing around on my cheeks before I felt her soft lips on mine.

Nothing ever happened with that boy I had liked. I can't even remember his name now, just that he had dusty blonde hair that curled close to his head and lovely pale shell-shaped ears.

And I never told anyone about that kiss.

Clay pulled back and my heart thudded *no* in protest. Even the water seemed to sigh as he pulled away. "Aria, I'm not going to force a kiss on you if you don't want it."

But I did want it. How could I explain to this gorgeous man who had probably known the feeling of a hundred lips on his that I had *never* been properly kissed? Let alone properly kissed by a man who made my insides tremble, a man whose mere name on my lips made my heart flutter, a man who coloured my paper-thin life.

"It's okay if you don't want me to kiss you. I'm not mad." He pouted. "I may need a bowl of Ben and Jerry's and a hug later, but it's okay."

His arms dropped from me and my body relaxed with relief. Yet underneath it, distinctly, was a roar of disappointment. A call to speak up for once. I just couldn't let him pull away thinking I didn't want it.

"I've never done it before," I blurted out.

He frowned. "What?"

"I've never kissed anyone before." I winced. "Not properly."

He blinked. "No one has ever kissed you before?"

"No."

"Ever?"

"No."

"Like, never, ever?"

"Jesus. Like never ever, okay?" I snapped. My own patheticness causing my cheeks to heat. "No one has ever even tried."

"Oh, Aria," he breathed as he slid closer to me through the water. His hand came up to slide against my cheek, his thumb pressing ever so lightly into the flesh of my bottom lip. Sparks cascaded down my body like a waterfall. "If you let me kiss you, I'll make up for each of those eighteen years without kisses."

"That's a big call."

"I'm prepared to put my money where my mouth is."

"What if I'm horrible?" I said in a whisper.

"A kiss is only ever horrible if it's between two people who don't truly want it. Do you want it?"

I nodded, my throat too closed to speak.

His eyes darkened and he leaned in closer. "You don't know how much I want it."

"But…I don't know how."

"You will. Do you trust me?"

"No."

He snorted. "Yes, you do. Otherwise you wouldn't be here alone with me in a lake in the middle of the woods."

He had me there. I stared at him. *Trust me*, his stare said. And I was surprised to find something inside me responding, *yes.*

In that moment I wondered what it took for trust to develop.

It was hard to quantify, trust. And sometimes it wasn't logical. Like with Clay. Somehow I had felt at ease around him even from the first time we met. Then at some point I had chosen to trust him.

Or perhaps it hadn't been a choice. I'd slipped into trusting him the way his presence slipped around me with safety and warmth when he was near, like a woollen rug and a lit fireplace on a cold winter's night. He made trusting him so easy for me, easing into my body like breath. However it had happened, the trust was there. I could *feel* it hugging me.

Then I realised, I had only ever trusted Salem like this.

"Aria?"

I nodded, then held my breath. He shifted closer, the only sound in my ears the swishing of water as it hurried out from between us.

"A nod is not good enough," he said as his fingers found my face. "You have to tell me what you want."

"You know what I want," I breathed.

"Pretend that I don't."

"You already won, Clay. Just do it."

"I haven't won. I'm still trying to figure out whether I can even win with you."

"What is that supposed to mean?"

"If you want me to kiss you, you have to say it." His eyes drilled into mine, his mouth inches away, and my body felt a tug towards him stronger than any pull I've ever felt. "I won't until you say it."

I wanted to.

I wanted to say it.

I parted my lips, his eyes dropped to them. Say it.

Say it.

Be brave.

You jumped in the deep end, Aria. You can do this. You want this.

But I couldn't.

I closed my mouth again.

The corners of his mouth drew down. I had disappointed him. His fingers slid out from my jaw as he pulled away.

"Kiss me," I blurted out. And my stomach lurched as if I were free-falling. "I want you to kiss me."

He paused, his eyes darting up to mine, surprise clear on his face. I'd surprised him. I'd surprised myself. When have I ever done that?

A smile pulled up at one side of his mouth as he slid closer to me again, his hand absently coming out to tug at one of the stands of my hair, floating in the water like copper seaweed. "I don't think I heard you."

"Yes, you did." I pouted. The bastard was going to make me say it again.

"Pretend I didn't."

Why did he have to push me like this? All the time, relentlessly, pressing me further and further out from behind my wall. Every time I thought he had pushed me far enough, he would nudge me again. "Your hearing seems to have gone to shit."

He laughed. "You know, you only ever swear when you're nervous. Are you nervous, angel?"

Damn. You. Clay Jagger.

"I'm not nervous."

"Then tell me−"

"Kiss me, damn you. And you better make it worth it."

He chuckled the way he always chuckled, with his whole body, his eyes crinkling and his shoulders shaking slightly and his chest making the water surface ripple. He partially lifted himself out of the water, just to his chest line. I couldn't help but stare. He was all I could see. A freckle, small and brown sitting on his left pec. The pink new skin of a strange round scar. His dark chest hairs coiled happily against him.

He slid his hands around my jaw again and tilted my face up. I inhaled his smell of cedar and musk. Heaven help me, this was it. Excruciatingly slowly, he leaned down, pausing with his mouth inches from mine.

What was I doing? What was I about to let him do? I couldn't let this man-God kiss me. I didn't know how to kiss him back. He would laugh when he realised how inexperienced I was. Aria Adams, the most pathetic eighteen-year-old girl in all of Australia, no, the world. I started to panic and I knew it was seconds before

I pushed him away.

I didn't want to push him away.

I squeezed my eyes shut and held my breath. Hoping, praying it would be enough to keep this panic inside, inside long enough for him to kiss me.

But he didn't. Yet again, there was just a pause and the rush of our breaths.

What was wrong? Why wasn't he kissing me?

"Angel."

My eyelids fluttered open, only to be consumed by blue orbs like the clear Queensland sky stretching out to the horizon, a rich sapphire radiating out to a pale dusty robin's egg blue. "Yes?"

"I told you I'd make you beg," he said into my mouth. Before I could protest, he closed his lips over mine. The chatter in my brain stopped. The panic that had risen up inside me stilled before exploding into dust.

His lips were soft and warm as they parted around my bottom lip, sucking it gently. I heard a moan before recognising the vibration in my throat meant that it was coming from me. His tongue brushed against the entrance to my mouth, begging for me to part my lips. I did and he slipped inside me, his warm tongue rubbing against mine, slowly at first then firmer, more insistent.

And just like that. I was kissing him back. My tongue and lips dancing with his to a song as old as humanity itself. My hand went up to his neck and held on for dear life.

He tilted his head, and without thinking I followed his lead, tilting the opposite way so our mouths locked like two pieces of a puzzle. Fissures and sparks melted tracks through my body, trickling down until they ended in a heated puddle between my legs.

He was right.

I knew what to do. I knew it just like I knew how to breathe, or how to sing. Perhaps a kiss was sown into our very fabric as humans, perhaps the way our mouths fused and our tongues danced was written in our blood, our DNA. Or perhaps, this instinct only took over when you kissed the right one.

Chapter Two

After we got out I lay out on a large flat rock, the warmth from the sun seeping up through my back. Clay lay beside me and the side of his hand lightly touched mine, sending all my awareness to it.

In the comfortable silence of the afternoon, punctuated by the occasional cry of a bird of prey finding its mark and the rustling of wind through the trees, I felt his finger shift.

I looked over to him, trying to be discreet. Sometimes the light hit him in a certain way and he looked like a painting done by one of the old masters, ethereal in beauty and so unreal.

Right now his eyes were closed, his lashes almost touching his cheekbones. He seemed to be asleep, his chest rising and falling steadily.

He moved again and this time I knew he had meant to do it, his finger curling around mine, tucking securely around me, a small sign of possessiveness, one that I relished. I let my finger curl around his too. Even though it was the only place we were joined, in that moment I felt an utter contentment.

A muffled musical tune broke through the peace, making me frown. He sat up, searched around in his bag and pulled out his mobile just as the call ended.

I recognised that tune. It was one of my favourites from a band called Evanescence. "Is that 'Bring Me to Life'?"

He grinned. "Top five bands, ever."

"Best band ever." I sighed. "Amy Lee's voice is so…haunting. It's like she's singing *to* me."

"Should I be jealous?"

"I'll let you come to our wedding."

A beep sang out from his phone, signalling a text. He tapped his phone, his eyes scanning the screen, and his face fell to a frown.

I lifted myself up onto my elbows. "What is it?"

He shifted. Did he just tilt the screen so I couldn't see the message? "Nothing."

"It doesn't look like nothing."

He tucked the phone back into his backpack. "We should go," he said. "The light's beginning to dim." He got up, pulling me up behind him but he wouldn't meet my eyes.

Back in the car, we drove through the outskirts of town, the radio playing low. I stared out the window, watching the passing Queenslanders, the weatherboard houses raised on stilts, the open front lawns, neighbours keeping boundaries through flower beds and bushes. Or brickworkers' cottages, squat amongst the ghostly trunks of the gum trees, the smell of eucalyptus on the air coming in through my partially open window.

We drove past a hunched cramped-looking car the colour of dried mustard. Without thinking I spun towards Clay and smacked my fist against his upper bicep, yelling, "Punch buggie baby vomit." My hand just bounced right off him. It was like hitting a wall. It probably hurt my knuckles more than it did his arm.

He glanced over at me, a questioning look clear on his face. "You have a bit of a violent streak, don't you?"

"I'm not being violent. It's punch buggy."

"You can call it a widdle punchie-wunchie and it doesn't make it any different."

"I didn't hit hard enough to hurt you." I doubted a cannonball could hurt him.

"No, you didn't. But you still *hit* me. It's always the quiet ones who have the secret violent streak," he teased.

This, for some reason, twanged on my nerve as if it were an out-of-key guitar string. "You don't know punch buggy?"

"Is that a cartoon character?"

"It's a game. Salem and I would play all the time. The first person who sees a Volkswagen Bug gets to call it and to hit the other one."

"And...baby vomit?"

"That's our own version. You couldn't just say the colour - yellow, green, blue - you had to make up the weirdest colour reference you could think of."

"You were close with her, weren't you?"

I sank back into my seat. "Yes."

"Tell me about her."

That's when I stopped listening. My eye was stuck on the dark sedan that I could see in the rear-view mirror. We turned right down another street and the car behind us did too. A creeping sensation trickled through my body.

"Aria?" Clay's voice broke into my thoughts.

"That car is still there."

"What car?"

"That dark one with the solo driver."

I spun in my seat, hiding my face as I peered around the headrest to the car following behind us. Even as I squinted I couldn't see the driver well enough that I could make out whether it was a man or a woman. I couldn't see the make or model from here but it was such a common car anyone would have just brushed it off. But not me. The hairs on my arm rose. "They're following us."

"Who would be following us?" I could hear the disbelief in his voice.

My eyes darted to the side mirror. How could I possibly explain it to Clay without revealing the truth? I couldn't tell him. Even if I wanted to explain myself, how would I do it without sounding crazy?

My fingers gripped at the seat and my seatbelt. The car accelerated behind us. My scream lodged in my throat. It was going to ram us from behind. My nails dug into the seat and I grabbed the handle above the door, bracing for the hit.

It swerved around us at the last minute into the opposing traffic lane and zoomed around us. As it passed us I could see the driver, an older woman with dark sunglasses on. She didn't even glance at me as she passed.

Not following us. Not after me. Just some crazy bitch who needed to be somewhere.

She turned off at the next left and I let out a sigh of relief. The rush of air into my lungs made the ends of my fingers tingle and I only realised then that I had been holding my breath. As we drove past the intersection, I spotted the dark sedan roaring away.

Paranoid or what, Aria? Careful, or you'll become just like Salem.

I sat focusing on steadying my breath and calming my heartrate down. Keep it inside.

"Aria." I felt a hand slip onto my knee. I snapped my head towards Clay only to see him glancing at me, concern crinkling through his features. Concerned for my mental health. If only he knew. *I'm not the crazy one.* "Are you okay?"

"Fine." I sat there, fists tight in my lap. "Just…I was stupid enough to watch a scary movie last night. Had a nightmare from it. I think that's why I'm jumpy." I forced a laugh. "It's nothing." *I'm just being paranoid.* "Do you have any siblings?" I asked him, just to change the topic. I don't know why I picked siblings. I didn't want to talk about Salem.

Or maybe, I did.

His jaw twitched. "Um, no. It was just me and my dad… mostly."

"What about your mother?"

"She was sick most of my childhood."

"Oh, sorry. Is she okay now?"

"She's…dead."

"I'm sorry."

"It's fine. It happened years ago."

"My mother died suddenly when Salem and I were young, really young." I remembered hiding in the cubby house, curled into a tight ball, holding my mother's necklace in my hand, Salem's warm body wrapped around my back. *It's okay. We have each other. Only each other. We'll be okay.*

"It sucks," he said. "But you grow up and move on, right?"

"It still hurts though," I said quietly. "Everyone you lose is a piece of you gone that you'll never get back."

He didn't say anything but his hands tightened on the wheel, his fingers going white. Then he answered, his voice sliding into the air like water across glass. "How many pieces do you have to lose before there's nothing left?"

He pulled up in front of my apartment and turned off the ignition. For a second we both just sat there in silence.

"Thank you for—" We both started at once.

He smiled. "Ladies first."

"Thank you for today. I had a really good time."

"No worries."

"Even if you did blackmail me into coming."

"It wasn't blackmail. I won the right to take you out, fair and square."

"And even if you did blackmail me into kissing you."

"That I won as well." He made a pursing motion with his mouth. "Lucky I have such a healthy self-esteem or I'd start developing a complex over you."

I rolled my eyes. A healthy self-esteem was something he didn't need any more of. "What were you going to say?"

"Thank you for letting me take you. It's the first time I've ever taken anyone there. It's the first time…I've wanted to."

Oh. The way his voice took on a hushed tone made me realise how much that spot must have meant to him. "You're welcome."

The silence grew heavy and every time I glanced at him he was staring at me intently like he had something more to say. The inside of the car grew hotter and hotter until I could barely stand it.

"Okay, then," I said, pressing the buckle to my seatbelt loose.

His large palm slid over mine. "Wait." His voice was low and full, weighted with a sound I didn't recognise.

I turned to face him. This time he didn't wait for me to tell him to kiss me. Or perhaps I begged for it in the way my breath hitched when I saw his face move in closer. Or the way my lips parted, drawing in breath so hard it was like I was trying to suck him closer.

His mouth moved across mine, crushing my lips. This time the kiss was harder, the softness from earlier was gone. Tenderness replaced with something...hotter...more intense. Darker. Like there was life in my lips that he was trying to drink from. Like it had been months or perhaps years since our last kiss and he wasn't sure whether we would ever get another one. His desperation poured into my mouth, his tongue pushing between my lips, fighting with mine.

I kissed him back just as hard, startled at how quickly this wanting turned to an ache. I found the hem of his shirt and I pushed my hand up along his warm body, thrills rushing through me as my fingers explored every hard bump and dip of his stomach, then his wide chest. Only when I heard him moaning, did a shiver of hesitation shoot through me. What were we doing? This was too much. Too fast.

I pulled away. And he let me go. We sat in our seats, our chests moving in and out, our unsteady breaths filling the car with hot, sweet air. What had just happened? I had been groping him like a woman of no morals. Two kisses and he was turning me into an animal.

My fingers found the car door handle. "Thanks again for today." I had to get out of the car. It was too hot in here.

"Aria..."

I paused at the longing in his voice and looked back at him. *Don't go,* his face said.

"I...I'll see you tomorrow. Okay?"

I nodded.

I slid out of his car, a deep red older-model Mustang, and walked up my driveway, feeling his eyes on me the whole way inside.

* * *

When I first wake it's like I'm born again, unburdened by life, new and fresh and unfettered behind fluttering eyes and cotton mouth, until the memories reorder themselves, falling into place like frames in a movie, and the flickering ghosts from the past reach out to grip me in their bony fingers again.

And her face. Always her face. Always Salem.

Salem rising out of the depths of the lake water to greet me, laughing at my fear and tear-streaked face. Salem's defiant glare, fierce eyes and her sharp promises. And Salem's pleading gaze, her glassy pupils, and her trembling bottom lip, the only sign of the broken doll within.

And of the last time I saw her…

Six months ago, in front of the Starbucks in Broadbeach, getting into a strange black sedan, my protests stuck in my throat, separated from her by a busy street, cars flashing between us so that she flickered in and out of my sight like she was under a strobe light. Had she seen me, across the road yelling and waving and ignoring stares from passersby?

Did she see my frantic dash across the street, cars braking, angry horns blaring and loud cusses from the open driver-side windows?

But by the time I had reached the other side, Salem was gone. And I was left, a grey speck on the sidewalk as the sounds of the city and the crush of the pedestrians and my grief swallowed me up.

Since that sighting in Broadbeach, I had followed my instincts north, taking a cheap overnight bus up along the Queensland coast. All I had to go on was the crumpled shred of paper, torn from a journal, left in the ashtray of the table that I had last seen Salem at. The shred of paper I still have, that I carry in my wallet with me:

rage Falls Mirage Falls Mirage Falls Mirage Falls Mirage Falls Mira

This was how I ended up a few months ago in this Sunshine Coast hinterland town called Mirage Falls. I hadn't seen a sign of her since.

You and me. My words to Salem rang out in my mind like a taunt. *It'll always be you and me. We'll protect each other.*

What a liar I had turned out to be.

* * *

If this woman knew that I, the girl who was pointing out the different features and benefits between the two brands of vibrators she couldn't decide over, had never had sex, would she laugh or just walk out?

"It really just depends on what you like," I said. "Do you prefer clitoral stimulation which the Aphrodite provides with this vibrating surface or do you prefer a G-spot stimulation which the Paris will give you because of its curved end?"

The customer was in her mid-forties I guessed, coarse hay-coloured bob framing her plump cherry-flushed cheeks. She had been in here a few times before, only ever browsing the lingerie, but I had noticed her eyes flashing more than once to this section up the back, the one hidden behind a partitioned wall of black and white damask wallpaper.

She hadn't been game enough to ask for what I knew she really wanted but I had taken a chance and had casually mentioned our latest offer: buy an underwear set and get ten percent off our range of boutique toys. She had stammered, trying to repress the excitement I could see twinkling in her eyes, before saying, "I guess it wouldn't hurt to look."

She stared at both display items in either of her hands, chewing her lip. Aphrodite versus Paris. She was already sold, the hungry look in her eyes saying everything she wasn't. She just needed a little push.

"They're both different but wonderful sensations," I said. "Although if you can't decide, there is always our greater discount for more than one item…"

She bought both. I rang her purchases up and packed the items into a glossy pink and black striped carry bag, a tiny whip hanging off one of the silk handles.

The Whip & Flick was the only boutique lingerie (and a little bit more) store in the small forest-hugged town of Mirage Falls. The store was well lit by crystal chandeliers, and furnished with plush satin damask-covered armchairs, elegant black glass display tables and red satin display pillows carrying Indian silk blindfolds and real Italian leather whips, giving it a distinct boudoir feel.

"Thank you. I hope you enjoy your purchases," I said before

she tottered off.

Flick walked up to the counter from the back room, a box of the latest Agent Provocateur shipment in her arms. "Thanks again for stepping in today on your day off," she said. "You're a life saver."

"Not a problem." It wasn't like I had anything planned.

Flick's dark exotic features were the best blend of her Mauri father and Australian mother: high cheekbones, sweetheart face, deep-set eyes and caramel skin. I guessed her age to be early thirties but her official stance was 'real ladies never tell their age' category and unofficially 'don't ask unless you want a punch to the face'.

Her real name was Felicity Grace; the only way I even knew that was because I read her name on the store lease that I spotted once on the office desk ready to be renewed. Only her mother called her Felicity Grace. She said that her parents named her that because they were qualities they'd hoped their child would have. It turned out they jinxed themselves instead.

She rested her box on the counter as she snatched the latest sale receipt from my hand and eyed the total price. She whistled. "Nice work. For someone who hasn't *actually* experienced the joys of sex, you sell it damn well."

I laughed to cover up the thread of discomfort in my belly. I might not know sex. But I knew people. I had learned quickly when I had been suddenly homeless and alone at fifteen how to read people; who they were, who they weren't, what they *really* wanted from me…

"I guess that's a compliment?"

"Tell me," she tapped her chin, "what are you waiting for again?"

"For the knight on his valiant horse wearing shiny armour." This was a running joke between us. Only because I never wanted to talk about my reasons why. I wasn't waiting. I had just been occupied with more important things for the past three years…like trying to find Salem.

"A knight? Puh-lease, just give me his long, thick lance."

I laughed at her crude joke.

"Or maybe," Flick said, her voice lowering, "you're waiting for Mr Dark and Delicious to make his move. He doesn't have a horse but I bet he's got something you could ride."

I hid my blazing cheeks and waved at her. "This isn't break time. Stop standing around and go unpack your panties."

"I can't remember," she said, shaking her head as she picked up her box again, "exactly *who* is the boss here?" She spun, her thick ebony hair swirling around her head like a shampoo commercial. God, how I envied her hair, falling in rich dark waves the colour of ravens. Not like my straight-as-a-curtain, auburn hair.

She sashayed towards the front display table, her ample curves swaying hypnotically. Ample curves – something else I would never have. Despite what I ate I remained slim as a beanpole.

When I had arrived here several months ago, Flick had taken one look at me, loitering on the sidewalk outside her store one early morning, a map in one hand, a single backpack slung over my shoulders, and hauled me into her store and her life despite my initial resistance. She agreed to hire me and house me without references and without a contract, which meant I could leave at any time if I wanted to. Although without any sign of where Salem had gone, I had nowhere else to go.

I fussed with one of the racks of clothes… Actually 'clothes' might not be the right word. They were thin strips of leather, studded or braided, or with indecent cut-outs making them look like lace. I would never wear one of these outfits, but I was there to work, not to judge. "Whatever floats their boat, and we cater for all kinds of boats," Flick always said with a wink.

A shadow fell across the store window and the hairs on the back of my neck rose to attention. I was being watched.

My gaze shot up. Clay stood leaning against the glass front of the store, peering in, partially silhouetted in the afternoon light, with his arms overhead like he was stretched out on a beach. His torso fanned out even more with his arms like that, his biceps straining against his shirt sleeves, and the bottom hem lifted so that there was a strip of taut stomach showing above the pale stonewashed jeans that showed off his strong legs.

He had no qualms about being seen staring into a lingerie store.

But that was Clay. He didn't care what people thought of him. I liked that, envied it a little. It wasn't that I cared what people thought of me, it was more that I wished they didn't think of me at all. Mostly I got my wish; for most people I faded away, but not to Clay. Never to Clay.

I tried to swallow, my pulse suddenly beating in my throat. I got a flash of him above me, his powerful arms like a wall on either side of me, shutting the rest of the world out, his necklace swaying like a hypnotist's pendant as he−

I shook that image off but the heat it left behind remained. Two kisses and I was turning into…Flick.

Through the store window, I saw the grin stretch across his face when his eyes found me. He looked at me as if nothing or no one else existed. My stomach flipped the way it always did when I was caught in his gaze. It could have been seconds or even hours that we were staring at each other, I don't know. Time does funny things when I'm around Clay.

He pushed off the glass and walked to the entrance. The doorbell dinged as he stepped inside, joining the clanging of my heart.

He weaved through the display tables and stopped before me. I'm tall, five-eleven, but he still towered over me, his shoulders hanging like outcrops of a cliff. His hand reached out and picked up a strand of hair from the top of my blouse. Where his fingers brushed my skin, tingling shards showered down through my body. He twirled a strand of my hair and grinned.

"Hey, angel," he said. His deep voice easing around his nickname for me ran up and down my back like fingers, causing small shivers.

"Why do you call me angel?" Even though he wasn't touching me, just that strand of my hair, I could almost *feel* his fingers. Just knowing he held a part of me in his hands was enough to make the roots of my scalp prickle.

He smiled. "Because you're as pure and innocent as one."

I frowned at his assessment of me.

"You can't have her yet," Flick called out from the other side of the store, bursting this invisible bubble around us and letting the rest of the world back in. "She's still mine for the next thirty minutes."

Clay winked at me before responding to Flick. "She's always been mine, Flick. I'm just lending her to you."

His.

He always said that I was his, even before he kissed me. I had feared that things would be weird between us because of our kiss yesterday. But here he was just being Clay. I shouldn't have worried.

"Do you want to wait outside?" I asked him. "I won't be long."

"Nope."

"No?"

"I can see you better from in here."

Before I could answer, I saw a shadow move in front of the store window. I looked up, frowning, because the only man who ever stood at that window was standing next to me. But it wasn't a man leaning against the glass, silhouetted in the afternoon sun.

It was Salem.

Chapter Three

I found her. I found Salem.

After three long, lonely years…

Or, more like, she found me.

For a second I just stared at the mirror reflection of me in my twin sister. Her auburn hair was just as long as mine but where mine fell straight down my back, hers was wild around her head like a fiery halo, like she had just gotten out of bed.

Whose bed did she get out of?

I saw the porcelain skin of her hands pressed against the glass, her cherry mouth which, if I wasn't mistaken, carried the same pout that only I had learned to soften. But mostly I saw her fierce doe-eyes which I knew were the colour of a stormy sky. They weren't looking back at me. They were glaring at Clay.

Before I could move, before I could blink or even mouth the first syllable of her name, she disappeared out of sight, slipping past the edge of the window and letting the light stream back in where she had stood as if she had never been there in the first place.

"Wait," I cried.

"What's wrong?" I heard Clay asking, but for once he couldn't control my attention like he usually did. I shoved my way through the store, ignoring Flick's startled cry and the clattering of hangers that I'd knocked off the racks. I didn't stop to pick them up or even to yell out an apology. The only thing I could think of was Salem.

Getting to Salem, throwing my arms around Salem. To yell at her that I hated her for leaving me behind, and that I loved her and I would never ever let her leave me again.

I hit the door with my palms and tumbled out onto the sidewalk of the Mirage Falls main street, a wide thoroughfare of mainly stores and shops, the bell jangling like an alarm above my head. Where was she? Where did she go?

I spun wildly, staring up and down the street, ignoring the pedestrians, some of them giving me a wide berth, some with quizzical looks on their faces.

I couldn't see her. Not the flick of her auburn hair or the black crop top and ripped black skinny jeans she had been wearing. Nothing. She was gone.

She must have slipped into one of the many side streets that angled off from this main road. But which one?

I grabbed a man walking past, a man I didn't recognise. "Sir, please, did you see a girl? She looked just like me but she was dressed in all black. She was just here."

He shook his head, grumbling, yanking his arm away from me before he hurried away, glancing back at me with wide eyes as if I were mad.

I'm not mad. She was here. I saw her.

But now she's gone. Salem's gone.

I almost had her. But she's gone.

What if I never find her again?

"Aria!" The bell jangled again as Clay came running out after me, stopping at my side. "You okay? You look like you've seen a ghost."

I might as well have.

I'd only seen glimpses of Salem since she ran away. But it's been enough to let me know that she was still alive. And enough of a trail of breadcrumbs to know when she'd moved on.

That's why my trail had stopped cold here. Salem was still here in Mirage Falls.

She knew I was here.

She knew I was looking for her.

Why hasn't she let me find her?

50

She saw me in that store, I know she did. So why had she disappeared instead of coming in?

Because you failed her…

I shut my eyes as the familiar feelings of guilt rose up to lash open the scars that lined my insides. I could make it up to her. I could. If she'd just let me find her. If she'd just come back to me. The hole in my soul, the one shaped and looking exactly like me, throbbed without her presence, like a phantom limb.

"Aria?" Flick joined us both on the sidewalk. "What's going on?"

"Didn't you see her?"

"See who?"

Clay was just staring at me, the furrow between his brows the only sign of emotion on his face.

Neither of them knew that I was trying to find Salem. Nobody did. I never talked about her to anyone. Firstly, because why bother trusting anyone if I was just going to move away? Secondly, and more importantly, I couldn't risk anyone talking to the police.

Except yesterday I had told Clay about our punch buggie game…

"No one. It was nothing."

Flick gave me a clear look of disbelief. "Don't give me that. You ran outta there like the place was on fire. Didn't she, Clay?"

Clay remained silent. Just watching me.

I had to diffuse this situation before they started asking too many questions. "It's nothing. I just thought I saw someone I knew. But it was no one." Before Flick or Clay could ask anything more, I brushed past them towards the store. "I'll fix up those hangers."

In the reflection of the store glass window I saw them glance at each other.

* * *

After my shift ended Clay and I walked along the sidewalk towards my apartment. It was mid-November in Queensland, which meant perfect blue skies and the coming of long summer days, our shadows long and skinny in front of us.

Our footsteps always fell into a comfortable pace, side by side, like we'd been walking beside each other for years, walking so close that our arms would sometimes brush.

As close as Salem and I used to walk.

As much as I had tried to push her to the back of my head, there she was. So near I felt like she was right behind me. Salem *was* in Mirage Falls. I had been right. After three months of nothing she had reappeared. Why now?

Did it matter? She was back.

Why didn't she come inside the store? Why did she run away?

Maybe she's still mad at you?

I'd apologise. I'd make it right. I just had to find her. It's a small town. I'd find a way. Besides, she had to eat, live somewhere and work. Now that I knew I was in the right place, all these things gave me avenues to start hunting again.

"Earth to Aria."

I shook my head of Salem-shaped thoughts and glanced over to Clay. "Sorry. I'm here."

"What were you thinking about?"

"Salem," I said without thinking. I flinched, surprised at myself. Something about Clay just drew things out of me without my control. I wasn't sure whether I liked this effect that he had on me.

I glanced at him, biting my lip, the same caution riveting under my skin as when he first started walking me home. It was faded now, worn down by Clay's persistence, but it was still there, hidden underneath my trust and the comfort I felt around him.

"Salem. Your sister?"

I nodded.

"Was that who you thought you saw today?"

I stumbled on a crack in the sidewalk but Clay caught my arm before I could fall, holding me with such ease like I was as light as a doll. "Thanks," I muttered.

"So was it?"

"What?"

"Was that your sister who you thought you saw today?"

"Yeah." I let out a huff of breath. There was no getting away from this conversation. "I've…I've been looking for her."

"Why?"

There was something so easy about being with Clay that made me want to let go and just open up to him. But I shouldn't. I shouldn't talk about Salem.

"You don't have to tell me," he said. "We can talk about something else if you like."

I nodded, and felt release. His small kindness in allowing me not to talk about it meant everything to me. Perhaps that's why I felt it was so easy to be around Clay. He pushed me, but he knew when not to push. Perhaps it was this that made me want to open up to him.

"She ran away three years ago. Since then I've been looking for her. I *had* been looking for her, until I arrived in Mirage Falls and lost her trail."

He whistled. "Three years is a long time, Aria."

"I know."

"Why did she run away?"

You're so tight. I flinched and batted away the memories that threatened to bubble back up to the surface. I felt Clay's reassuring arm around my shoulder. "I'm sure her reasons were good ones."

I nodded, biting back tears, thankful for his steadying presence, for his warmth and for knowing exactly when I didn't want to talk. No one had known me quite like this…not since Salem.

"So…what happens if you find her?"

"*When* I find her."

"Okay. *When* you find her, then what?"

"Then she can be in my life again. I can try and…help her."

"Someone has to want to be helped to be helped."

"She wants my help."

"Are you sure about that?"

A hot blustering anger rose up inside me and I shrugged Clay's arm off my shoulder. "What are you saying?"

"I'm saying that maybe you should let it go."

"Let it go? I'm not just going to abandon her."

"The way you describe it, she abandoned you."

She had good reason to. "It wasn't like that."

"Maybe she doesn't want to be found."

"That's not true. She wants to be found. That's why she keeps appearing."

"Then why would she run away today?"

"Because…" because she doesn't trust me. Because when she needed me, I failed her. "She has her reasons. You don't know her like I do."

"I might not know her but I know you–"

"You don't know *anything* about me," I hissed. I broke out into a jog to get away from him.

"Aria," he called out after me. "Aria, stop. I'm sorry," he said. He grabbed my arm and spun me.

The anger coursing through me made me yank it from him. "Don't touch me."

His face crumpled. "I'm sorry. I didn't mean to upset you. That's the last thing I ever want to do to you. Please, Aria." His voice was so pained it struck a nerve in me even through my anger.

I tried to speak, but a sob came out instead. My anger broke into the icy, bitter shards of guilt. I buried my face in my hands.

I heard him curse. His arms folded around me, his hands sliding across my back, warming me from the outside in. I stood there letting his presence and his touch calm me.

"It's my fault she ran away," I mumbled. "I've been trying to find her to…make it better. I miss her so much. I'd do anything to get her back. When I decided to stop looking for her a few weeks ago it was the hardest decision I ever made. And now I saw her – I know I saw her – and she's here and I almost had her back and…" I trailed off. I must have sounded like a lunatic.

"I get it, Aria. You might not think I do, but I get it. I know what it's like to miss someone who was a big part of your life. I know what it feels like…the guilt you hold inside when you know that part of what caused them to go away was because of something you did and you swear and you pray that if you just got one more chance, just one more chance with them, then you wouldn't screw it up a second time. You'd make it right."

Stunned at his insight, I just nodded against his chest, pressing my nose into his cotton grey shirt and inhaling his scent into my nose. He held me tighter, his hand running through my hair, his lips on my forehead, sending waves of calm through my body. But there was something that bothered me about what he had said.

I pulled back to look at him. "When you said all that, you sounded like you were talking from experience."

His jaw flinched and a pained look came over his face. "Aria, I don't ever want to lie to you about anything. But I'm not ready to talk about…*her* yet."

Her. The way he said it sounded so pained. A deep abscess barely covered by a new knit of skin. Who she was? What had she meant to him? What did she still mean?

I was so caught up in my thoughts that I barely noticed when Clay began to sway, softly at first. He was humming under his breath. His feet began to shuffle and his humming grew louder until I recognised the melody of Jeff Buckley's 'Hallelujah' in the bassy rumble of his voice.

"Clay, what are you doing?"

"Ah." He looked down at me, a soft smile on his face. "What do you think I'm doing?"

"You're dancing."

"Am I?" He made a show of darting his face around in various angles as if to inspect our situation, all the while still humming and shifting both our weights from side to side. "Hmmm, I believe I am. And you appear to be dancing with me."

We were dancing. In the middle of this sidewalk. His humming turned to singing. His hands brushed down the sides of my arms making me shiver and he caught my hands, turning me out as I stifled a giggle again, then spinning me back in. A man walking his dog walked around us and I caught a curious look on his face. I pressed my face into Clay's cotton shirt. "Clay, we're in public."

He hummed into my hair. "That didn't seem to bother you yesterday."

The reminder of our fiery kiss in his car made my body heat again. I shivered. He chuckled before placing a kiss on my forehead. "Come on. Let's get you home."

With his arm still around me he began to walk us down the sidewalk. I clung onto him, my arm wrapping around his wide back and settling into his side to where I could feel the firmness of his V muscle. I sighed and leaned further into him, a cascade of thrills running through my arm when he squeezed my shoulder and smiled down at me. We fit so perfectly. A lightness seemed wrapped around me, and my heart floated on a warm bed. Was I… could I possibly be…happy?

I was. Happy. The world could break apart in this moment and I wouldn't care. I couldn't remember the last time I felt this way. But I knew I hadn't felt this way since Salem left.

"Wanna play a game?" he asked, pulling me out of my thoughts.

I eyed him warily. "The last two times I played games that you suggested with you I was forced to go on a date with you and also give up my first kiss."

He grinned. "Scared at what else I may take from you?"

I tried to ignore that lascivious look in his eye and the tremor his words caused down my spine. "I'm just saying, maybe I should have a go at suggesting games."

He made a face. "The last time we played a game that you suggested, I was pummelled under a fit of violence."

I frowned until I remembered punch buggy. I laughed. "You wuss."

"Call me what you want. I'm still choosing the game. It's called 'would you rather…?'"

You wanna play a game?

Sure, Salem.

It's called 'would you rather…?'

I swallowed the knot in my throat and pushed aside that memory. "I know how to play."

"Ladies first. I'm nothing if not a gentleman."

We walked for a few moments in silence, my mind going over all the questions I could ask him. What did I want to know about him?

Who is the woman you lost? Would you rather her or me?

I shook this thought away. Clay said he wasn't ready to speak about her yet. But he would. I had to trust that he would. Right?

"Come on, Aria," he probed. "I'm sure that inquisitive mind

of yours has a million things to ask me."

"I'm just not sure whether I want to uncover the real Clay," I teased. "Lord knows what kind of dark, depraved secrets you keep."

He was silent and I caught the flash of something in his eyes and his brows furrowed.

I nudged him. "I was joking."

His face melted into a smile. "Of course."

That was odd. But I brushed it aside and blurted out the first question I could think of. "Would you rather live in only daytime or only night time?"

He grinned and the momentary tension from before seemed like it may have been a product of my imagination. "That's easy. Night time."

"Really? Why?"

"Night time's the best time. The world is finally quiet so I can actually think. I draw better at night. You know many famous artists did their best work at night. Toulouse-Lautrec, Proust, Kafka…"

"I knew it."

"Knew what?"

"You're a vampire."

"Shouldn't I be sparkling then?"

I rolled my eyes. "*That* is not a vampire. Dracula, Anne Rice's Lestat de Lioncourt, *those* are vampires."

"Then shouldn't I be burning up into flames or something?" He held out his arm, the lazy afternoon sun glistening against his golden hairs.

"True," I acquiesced before sighing dramatically. "I guess you mustn't be a vampire then."

"Plus you have garlic breath and I wouldn't be around you if I was a vamp."

My hand shot up to my mouth. "I don't have garlic breath." My mind raced over what I had had for lunch; my standard ham and salad sandwich, a Pink Lady apple and a diet soda. But no garlic.

Wait a minute.

When I turned my head to glare at him, he was already grinning.

"I don't have garlic breath," I repeated.

"You have lovely breath."

"Hmmpft, not a vampire, maybe just some sort of zombie."

"Are you calling me undead?"

"I was thinking more brainless."

It was his turn to glare at me.

I laughed. "Don't dish it if you can't take it."

His glare broke and the lines across his mouth relaxed into a soft smile. "What about you? Daytime forever or live in the dark side with us zommmbies." He raised his free arm out, walking stiffly for a few seconds before he broke effortlessly back into a walk.

"Daytime."

"Why?"

I hate the dark. "I like the sun." I lifted up a pale arm and let the sunlight shine off my light hairs. "I guess you can tell that the sun doesn't like me, but I need the light. The world is already too dark a place."

"But fun things happen in the dark." He waggled his eyebrows.

"Bad things happen in the dark," I said quietly.

A strange silence fell over us, the sun falling behind the cloud for that moment, and I shivered.

"It's in the darkest of nights, that the stars shine brightest," he said quietly.

I swallowed, hard.

"Okay," he continued, "so I can't convince you to come over to the dark side with me. Looks like we have a problem."

"What's that?"

"We couldn't see each other anymore because we'd be in two different worlds. Or on the same world that didn't spin so that half the world was always in daylight and the other half always in darkness."

The thought that I might ever have to go without seeing Clay again made my heart wilt. Without meaning to, I had let him become so much a part of my day, my life… "We could still visit each other."

"Really? Would you brave the dark for me?" he asked, an edge of seriousness to his voice.

"Only if you were there with me."

"Always. I'd never let you face the dark alone."

"Would you risk sunburn for me?" I said, trying to lighten the mood.

"I'd risk anything," he said quietly. "Everything."

I swallowed hard. "Why do you always say things like that to me?"

"Because they're true."

My heart thudded in my chest. I could feel his eyes on me but I couldn't make myself meet his gaze.

"Maybe we could build a house that sat on the dividing line," he said. "Half day, half night."

"That'd work."

"We'd keep the garden on your side."

"We'd have the bedroom on your side." I sensed rather than saw him grinning. "What?"

"You do realise," he said slowly, "you just admitted that you wanted to sleep with me."

"I did not," I exclaimed in horror. But I did. I said *the* bedroom, not the bedroom*s*, my inner desires made clear. The thought of sleeping next to Clay in the dark made shivers run up my arm.

"And that you just admitted to wanting to live with me," he continued. "Soon you'll be begging me to marry you." He winked.

I rolled my eyes, trying to brush off the heat that was coiling about in my stomach. "It's your turn to ask a question."

"Are you trying to deny you want me?"

"It's your turn to ask a question," I repeated through gritted teeth.

"That was a question."

"That was not a *game* question."

"One of these days, Aria…" he muttered. "Fine. Would you rather have loved and lost than never to have loved at all?"

My stomach tightened as I thought of Salem, the only person I had ever loved. And I had lost her. I thought of the three years

I had gone trying to find her, chasing a ghost, chasing a woman who didn't want to be found. I let myself feel the empty aching hollow pain in my stomach that used to be filled with her presence. Somehow in the last six months, it had gotten worse. But I had learned to ignore it. To cover it up. "Never at all. I'd rather not love anyone. It hurts too much when they leave."

He was silent before he answered. "I don't think you mean that."

"You don't know what I mean. You've only known me three months."

"I know that you loved your sister and it hurts you that you lost her. But I've lived in a world without *any* love. And I can tell you, it's worse. Don't wish for a loveless life, Aria."

"You think the pain of losing the person you love is worth it?"

"It is."

"Then you've never lost someone you truly loved."

"Yes, angel." His voice weighed heavily and it made me look at him with sadness. "I have."

And I remembered, *her.* The woman.

This time he didn't stop at my sidewalk. He walked me all the way up to my front door.

Up to my front door. Of my apartment.

My feet wobbled in my sneakers and my mouth felt like cotton. I stood with my back to the door and faced him. He seemed to cast a shadow over me as he stepped in close. He lifted up his fingers and I could barely move. I stopped breathing as he brushed my cheek before pushing the hair back behind my ear and tracing down my neck, then twirling a strand of my hair. My mouth parted, ready to taste him again.

But he didn't lean in. He cleared his throat. "See you around, angel."

My heart sank into my toes. "Okay."

But he didn't pull away as he usually did…

I don't know if he moved first or I did, but suddenly we were against each other, lips on lips, chest to chest, hip to hips, kissing with the fire that we lit yesterday. All that existed of me was contained in our mouths and under his hands, now moving from my waist and up my sides and dragging sections of my clothing along with it so that the cool evening air rushed in. My back banged against my front door but I didn't care. His thigh moved in between my legs as he leaned against me with his weight and pressed up against the ache that was already shouldering for him. I moaned and pushed my hips farther into him, sending a wave of pleasure through me unlike anything I've ever experienced. I felt the vibration of his groan against my tongue as he hardened against my hip.

I didn't care who saw us. I just didn't care.

Suddenly he wasn't there anymore. The cold air rushed in between us as he stood, arms straightened, holding himself away from me, his fingers on my shoulders still holding me to the door. We were both panting. My head spun and if it weren't for him holding me up, I may have slithered to the ground into a puddle.

"Why did you stop?" I whispered.

"Need a second," he muttered. "And a cold shower." He looked at me, lust still clouding his eyes like a troubled sky.

All I could think of was that just beyond this wooden door was my living room and a few more steps and there was my bedroom and my bed. Clay Jagger, in my bed. The thought made a sharp ache lash through my body.

"Do...do you," I paused to lick my lips, which had suddenly gone dry, "do you want to come in?" My voice warbled at the end of my sentence.

His eyes widened for a second, letting me know that I had surprised him with my question.

"I want to," he breathed out. "But I can't...not tonight."

My heart squeezed so hard it hurt. "Oh. Right. Why...why not?" I asked, hoping that I didn't sound so disappointed.

"I have things to do...a comic deadline. And I know if I go inside, that..." he turned on his gorgeous half grin, a mix of lust and cheekiness and a hint of danger in his eyes, "we won't leave for days."

We won't leave for days. I shuddered at the promise.

"One day. One day soon, angel. I want to do this properly with you. You make me want to make up for...the times I haven't done it properly. I want to make it right, with you."

His words trickled into my chest and pooled into my heart. It didn't ease the ache for him, if anything, it just enflamed it. I shut my eyes, just listening to his breath and my breath, both heavy, both, I realised, pleasantly in time with each other. I felt the outline of his wide palms and his strong fingers on my shoulders and tried not to imagine that same feeling down further across my skin. I tried not to imagine what it would feel like to have those large hands across the rest of my body.

He cleared his throat. "I should go now, angel. I have a deadline."

I opened my eyes and he was peering at me with slight concern. I nodded, trying to ignore the ache in my core, trying to feign coolness. "Of course. You know, I want to see your work one day. If you're happy to show me?"

He raised an eyebrow. "You want to see all the nerdy comics I draw?"

I smiled. "I'd love to see you geek out."

"It wouldn't bore you? It'd bore most girls."

"It would be the most interesting thing in the world to me to see what you're passionate about."

He grinned. "Don't suppose you'd come to the next comic-con with me?"

"Sure."

"Dressed up."

"Now you're pushing it."

He laughed and tugged my hair again. "See you around, angel." He turned and sauntered away down the sidewalk, leaving me staring after him.

I closed my door behind me, turning the key all the way before I leaned against it with my forehead on the glossy surface. This desire for him had faded to a barely tolerable ache. What was he doing to me? A few kisses and I was turning into a sex maniac. Apparently innocent little Aria didn't want to stay innocent little Aria anymore. This wasn't me. Was it?

Or perhaps it was. A piece of myself I had ignored. Hidden. Underneath my carefully constructed façade. Clay was just the catalyst. He was doing things to me, revealing parts of me I never knew I had, igniting desires in me I never thought I'd want.

Oh Clay, you'll be the death of me one day.

* * *

I woke up the next morning like always, newborn and fresh, staring at blankness, before an image of two dark and intense eyes, and a certain pair of soft, inviting lips cast across the backs of my eyelids. I stretched and shifted under my sheets and my mouth carried the lightness of a soft smile.

My mind turned to our kiss yesterday. The way the temperature had heated, the way the kiss turned aggressive, almost violent, as he crushed me against the door and held my mouth to his with his fingers twisted in my hair. My body heated, the fissures appearing like molten cracks under my skin, making my lungs open, seeking more air.

I shivered at the promise of more…intimate things with Clay. Of his fingers seeking places never before explored, of his lips painting kisses on my skin new as blank canvas, of letting him into my body.

A realisation lashed through me, causing me to bolt upright, clutching the sheets to my chest.

Salem.

I didn't think of Salem first. I thought of Clay.

What did this mean?

You're forgetting her. A tiny thread of guilt wormed its way through me.

Never. I would never forget her. I would never stop missing her.

You're replacing her.

I couldn't. I could never replace her…

A knock sounded on my front door, snapping me out of my thoughts. I glanced over at the clock on my bedside table. It wasn't even 8:30 a.m. Who would be knocking?

Clay.

It could only be Clay. Perhaps he forgot that I was starting later today. I threw on a terrycloth dressing gown over my shorts and thin camisole and tied it up as I padded barefoot to my front door, my heart skipping with joy at the thought of seeing him so early. I only wish I was wearing something more…sexy. Perhaps I should take advantage of the staff discount at Flick's boutique.

I unlocked the door and swung it open, a smile on my face as I squinted against the sun. My eyes adjusted and the world outside came into focus as did the person standing at my door.

My breath lodged into my throat and I made a wheezing noise. My heart, thudding inside my ears, drowned out the sounds of calling birds and a distant lawn mower. I stumbled back, blinking, trying to clear my vision. I must be seeing things. Hallucinating.

It wasn't Clay standing there, on my threshold.

It was Salem.

Chapter Four

My mirror image, my twin, the very woman I had been searching for the last three long and lonely years, stood right there in front of me. Feelings so convoluted and overwhelming slammed into my body like a wave and I was left barely standing and choking like I was underwater.

"Heya, sis. What's crackin'?" Her voice, sounding so much like mine but rougher and with a hard edge, forged by the one experience we didn't share when we were together.

"S-Salem," I managed.

Why? Where? How…? Everything I had wished to say to her over the last three years crammed up into my throat, turning itself into a barricade. All I could do was gasp.

She raised an eyebrow. "So, you gonna invite me in or what?"

Right. Invite her in. That would be a good first step. I nodded and stepped aside, barely feeling the cool tiles underneath my feet. She moved past me, a black scuffed duffel bag over her shoulder. Some sort of sweet perfume hit my nose like a thick incense, dragonsblood and musk, but underneath I recognised the sour sharpness of whiskey. I don't remember her ever smelling like that.

I shut the door and turned the key in the lock, the cheap keychain, half a silver heart on the end swaying as I stared at it. And stared at it. They had come in pairs. I had bought them hoping that one day I'd be able to give Salem the other half of my heart, the other half that she already owned.

Would this be that day?

When I turned around, would she really be there? Did I dream that Salem showed up? Did I imagine this? Wishful thinking? Temporary insanity after three desperate years of searching?

You stopped searching, remember?

Did Salem know that I gave up on her? I turned slowly as if I were facing a firing squad.

But Salem wasn't there.

Holy shit. I was going mad.

I heard movement in my bedroom. Moments later she appeared, walking back into the living room.

I wasn't going mad.

Salem was here.

She was here.

In my apartment.

She dumped her bag on the floor of my small living room. "Nice place." She plopped down on my couch and lifted her booted feet up on my coffee table.

That was Salem.

"You gonna offer me a drink or what?"

"Drink. Right. Water?"

"Coffee."

"Milk? Sugar?"

"You have any whiskey?"

"In your coffee?"

"It's called an Irish coffee."

"But…" I blinked, staring at the lime-coloured digits on my microwave. Yes, it was still morning. It was 8:36 a.m. No, the numbers weren't flicking around like crazy so this wasn't a dream. I had read somewhere that was how you knew whether something was a dream; if the clock numbers spun or if you couldn't read words. Or was that a movie I saw? I don't know. My memory had never been any good. "But it's still morning."

When I looked back at her, Salem gave me a searing look. After all this time I recognised that look. It was the 'chill out, man, stop being so uncool' look. It was the look she used to give our neighbours behind their back when the old bat told me off for stealing the cherries out of her tree. I would never be game enough to climb any trees, it was always Salem that did it. But somehow I was always the one who got in trouble. I would never rat Salem out though. I would never tell on her. I just took the scolding.

When did I become uncool?

You were never cool. You were only cool because you were with Salem.

"Fine," Salem drew that word out and combined it with a long-suffering sigh. "I'll just have it black. Like my heart."

I somehow made it into the kitchen and fumbled around with cups and spoons and a half-empty container of instant Nescafe Gold, as the water roared away in my shitty plastic kettle.

Fuck. I didn't drink but damn if I needed one now. Whiskey at 8 a.m. didn't sound half bad. I kept sneaking glances over to Salem, now flicking through one of the magazines from under the coffee table that I think Flick must have left one time.

As I poured the water into the mugs I watched the granules dissolve under the heat, turning the water to mud. I added milk to mine, disguising the darkness, and left hers black. The spoon dinged sharply into the thick silence broken only by the rustle of pages.

Salem is back.

I tried that again, saying it slower in my head.

Salem. Is. Back.

She came back to me. I let her down. But she still came back to me. I gave up on her. But she came back to me.

I carried the two coffee cups over to the living area, walking slowly, trying not to spill the contents or my sanity onto the carpet. Salem dropped her feet from the table and threw the magazine aside. It skidded on the side table before coming to rest, partly flopped over one edge.

I sat her cup down on the low table, placing my own aside hers, twin red mugs, one with the lip chipped from that time it was knocked down, hers rolling with steam.

I sat down on the other side of the couch, grabbing one of the cushions to place in my lap and began to play with one of the corner fringes, the space between us, like the last three years, yawning open like a canyon.

She nudged her chin towards her mug. "Thanks, Rosey."

Rosey. I hadn't heard that nickname in years. When we were children she started calling me Rosey because my cheeks would turn into red roses whenever I got embarrassed. They still did. Salem never had that problem. Nothing ever embarrassed her.

Something crawled up my spine and seized my chest. Suddenly I couldn't breathe, my lungs held in an iron grip. Everything over the last three years bubbled up into a thick hot mess and I couldn't hold it back. I began to cry, my vision blurring with tears so that I could barely see the outline of my twin sitting before me, my Salem, sitting on my couch.

I heard her tsk as if my tears were a nuisance but she shuffled up to my side and slipped a gentle arm around my shoulders, shushing me like she used to do when we were kids. "It's alright." Her soft lips pressed a kiss to my forehead. "No need to cry."

I leaned into her, resting my head in the warm crook of her neck, ignoring her harsh cloying perfume and letting the comfort of her presence wash over me, easing the tightness in my chest and brushing down the source of my tears like a sandcastle returning to nothing under the persistent wash of waves.

She began to hum under her breath. It was a song that Mama used to hum to me when I was sick or upset. It calmed me. I remember the tune, "A Sailor's Lullaby", lilting and soft like an old ballad. When Mama died, Salem took over humming to me. I was safe. She would protect me. Always. And from anything. I wasn't alone anymore.

For some reason, Clay's face broke through into my mind. *You weren't alone anymore.*

My sobs subsided and her humming faded. We just sat there, my sister and I, leaning into each other.

"I...I missed you," I squeezed those words out of my constricted lungs. "I missed you so much."

"Missed you, too, sis."

I pulled back, wiping under my eyes, and my twin's image became clearer. Her arm stayed around my shoulders and I treasured the weight of it. I studied her face and her sharp grey eyes stared back at me. The last time I had a chance, a real chance to study her face, we had been fifteen.

God, it was like looking in a mirror, but…not. She wore more eyeliner than I ever would, and her mouth wore a permanent scowl. She had no extra scars, no new piercings that I could see, and she still wore her hair long and loose like I did.

She wore waist-high skinny jeans, which her slim legs looked great in, a midriff top that came just to her beltline, giving me flashes of her slim pale waist. I knew she was studying me too, seeing how I'd grown, seeing how we now differed after three years apart.

"Where have you been?" I tried not to sound so needy. I'm not sure I succeeded.

She shrugged a shoulder. "Around."

"I've been looking for you."

"I know."

"You knew?"

She nodded. "Yeah. Although you stopped looking, didn't you?"

I swallowed down the knot of guilt. "Why didn't you come back sooner?"

She shifted and her arm drew back to lean instead along the back of the couch. "I had some stuff I had to do. Didn't want to involve you."

"But…you're my best friend, Salem. We do everything together."

"Not everything," she said, and I swear I could hear the hint of bitterness in her voice. "I see you gotta boyfriend now."

Clay. She'd seen Clay in the store.

My cheeks flushed and a tiny flutter of happiness fluttered in my chest. Clay's smiling face, his gorgeous lips and the sexiest dimple ever became clear in my mind. "I don't know if I'd call him my boyfriend."

"I would."

We did kiss in the woods. And we shared more kisses since then. Like the one yesterday as he crushed me against my front door and knotted his fingers in my hair and my body became a furnace and my legs became so weak I nearly slid down to his feet. I was lost for a second in the memory of his mouth on mine.

Salem's voice broke through that, "You wouldn't share *him* with me, would you?"

"No!" A fierce possessiveness stabbed through my body and the material of the cushion in my lap strained against my fists.

"Calm down, it wasn't a suggestion. I was just making a point. We don't share *everything* anymore."

It was true. Salem and I had grown up. We were no longer joined at the hip, no longer mirror-dressing shadows of each other. We had grown apart, into two adults, with two lives and…our own sets of secrets.

"You gonna tell me about him or what?"

I had wanted to tell Salem all about Clay since I met him. I ached to tell her. I dreamed of sharing my growing happiness with her. But now that she was here right in front of me, I felt… hesitant. And I wasn't sure why.

"His name is Clay. Clay Jagger." I paused.

What was wrong with me? This was Salem, my sister, my twin, my soulmate, the other half of my soul. I could tell her anything.

I used to tell her everything.

A lot had happened in three years. People can change in three years.

"Is that it?" She leaned back to study me. "All I get is a name?"

I shuffled on the couch. It suddenly came to me, the reason why I didn't want to talk about him. He was *mine*. He was the first thing I cared about in my life that I wouldn't share with her. When it came to Clay and me, Salem was on the outside. And I knew she would hate that. "What do you want to know?" I asked, just to stall.

"Is he good to you?"

"He's wonderful."

"So far."

"What's that supposed to mean?"

She shrugged. "What's Mr Wonderful like? Apart from,

obviously, wonderful."

This was ridiculous. This was Salem. I could tell Salem all about Clay and she'd be happy for me if he made me happy. I forced myself to speak, "He's…very sure of himself. In fact, apart from you he's the most confident person I know. He's a deeply passionate person, which can get intense sometimes. Too intense for some people but for me, it's perfect. He has a killer sense of humour. He makes me laugh all the time. And…" It struck me that I could have been talking about Salem. I felt lightheaded all of a sudden. Wasn't that so funny, that Clay and Salem were so alike.

"And?"

"Oh, um. And he likes to play games."

"*Games?*" Salem gave me a look.

I flushed. "Not like that, not kinky games if that's what you're thinking."

"Since when do you know what I'm thinking anymore?"

Touché. "I mean, silly games, word games, little competitions."

"Like *we* used to play." Was it just me or did Salem's voice tighten?

I brushed this off. "He…he makes rash decisions. Impulsive. But when he wants something, when he really wants something, he won't stop…" I swallowed hard, "until he gets it." *Like he did with me.*

"Sounds like a keeper."

"He is."

"Do you love him?"

I laughed because my nerves jangled. "You can't ask me that."

"I just did."

"What does love even mean?"

"It means…that it doesn't matter what they have or haven't done, who they are or aren't, you'll be there for them anyway."

Like Salem. She loved me. And I loved her.

But she wanted to know if I loved someone else other than her.

I studied her face, searching for the repressed jealousy, the buried accusation that I may have found myself someone like her to replace her, the hidden anger that I may have made something of a life for myself without her. I couldn't see it. At least, I didn't think I could see it.

"He's someone I could love," I said truthfully.

She cracked a half-smile in the 'I care, but not so much that it's uncool' way that she had perfected. "Good for you."

I let out a soft sigh of relief. She wasn't mad. She didn't hate me.

I reached out, taking my cup in my hands and sipped, tasting warm sweet milk with a hint of coffee. I didn't know how Salem could drink hers black. I glanced at her cup still sitting there. She hadn't even touched it.

"You gonna invite me to stay or what?"

"Here? But I only have one bed."

"We used to share a bed."

"I know…" But that was years ago when we were just kids.

"You don't want me to stay?"

"No, it's not that…"

"Spit it out. What's your deal?"

"Are you…? Are the police…?"

She scowled and a familiar darkness clouded her face. I hated when her face would look like that. "Nobody's going to come busting in here into your perfect little world, if that's what you're worried about." There it was again. The hint of bitterness in her words. The shard in her tone. Or was I just being paranoid?

"My life's not perfect."

"Nice place, *wonderful* boyfriend, decent job…looks pretty perfect from where I'm sitting."

"I'm not worried about the police. I'm worried about you."

"Don't worry about me."

"How could I not? Salem," now my voice was rising, "you ran away, no note, no goodbyes, nothing."

Her voice became hard like bullets. "There were some extenuating circumstances, if you remember?"

Pieces of that night flashed across the backs of my eyes and I flinched. I remembered. I didn't want to, but I remembered. How could I ever forget that night? "But you disappeared for three years. I looked for you for three years, chasing after you for three years.

Now you just knock on my door and waltz back into my life, no explanations and expect me to just accept it?"

"Yeah. That's what I'm asking you to do." She stared levelly back at me, the air between us buzzing like an angry cloud of wasps.

I let out a long slow breath, my frustration leaking out. Salem never withheld anything from me before. "Don't I deserve some answers?"

She rolled her eyes. "Never mind. I'll find somewhere else to stay."

"No." I grabbed her arm, stopping her from standing. Maybe I was being too hard on her too soon. Maybe she just needed time before she told me what she'd been doing all these years, and what she was hiding. I just needed to give her time. "Stay."

"I wouldn't want to be a burden."

"You wouldn't. I want you to stay."

She inhaled then exhaled slowly. "I suppose I *could* stay for just a little while."

I almost laughed. Somehow in the space of thirty seconds she had gone from asking me for a favour to making me feel like she was doing *me* a favour. Some things never changed.

"I'll go make some space in the cupboards for you." I eyed her duffel bag. "Is that all you have?"

"It's all I need."

I stood up but this time she grabbed my arm before I could walk away. She stood, facing me, her eyes narrowed. "You wouldn't be thinking of…turning me in, would you?"

"How could you even think that?"

"I notice you haven't denied it."

I yanked my arm from her grip and faced her front-on so she could see me. *Here I am Salem. I'm the same girl you left behind. I'm not hiding anything. You are.* "I'm not going to turn you in. I'm insulted you'd even suggest it. But if you think I will, then you should go. The door's right there."

She raised an eyebrow, tilting her head. I recognised the mild surprised on her face at the way I stepped up to her challenge.

"You've changed, sis," she said softly.

Maybe I wasn't the same girl she left behind. "You haven't."

* * *

When I left for work later that morning I was surprised to see that Clay wasn't waiting for me as usual until I remembered that he said he had a deadline. I felt partly naked as I walked without him at my side. But I almost didn't mind today. I missed him, yes, the way I always missed him when he wasn't around. But today I was almost glad to walk alone to work. Alone with my thoughts, alone with my delirious knowledge that Salem was back.

Salem was back.

My other half was back. I couldn't help the lightness in my step.

"Damn, girl," Flick said, as I strode through her boutique to the back room to drop off my bag, "are you actually smiling?"

I grinned, showing my teeth.

"Oh my God," Flick's mouth dropped open.

"What?" I glanced around me looking for her source of shock. When I looked back at her she was staring at me.

"You got laid last night."

I rolled my eyes. "Trust you to go straight to sex."

Flick grabbed my arm. "Spill it. And don't leave out a single sordid detail."

I couldn't help the bubble of happiness that tumbled around inside me. "Oh Flick, everything is just perfect."

Just perfect.

I had my sister back, after three years of being apart. And I had Clay, the most wonderful man in the world.

Everything was just perfect.

* * *

"Hey, sis," Salem called to me from the bedroom after I had gotten home from work that evening. My stomach fluttered with butterflies at the sound of her voice. My sister was here waiting for me.

I called back a greeting as I locked the door behind me. Before I took two steps in, my eyes rested on the coffee mug in the living room. It was her coffee mug from this morning. She hadn't even bothered to even take it to the sink.

I walked over to it and saw it was still filled to the brim, now cold. She hadn't even taken one sip of it even after I had left the house, late because I had been making space for her in my room.

I wouldn't clean up after her. She was an adult now. I left the cup even though it nagged at my consciousness, and I walked to the open doorway to my bedroom – *our* bedroom. She was lying on her stomach on the bed reading a magazine. I spotted her duffel bag still on the chair, unopened, unpacked, exactly where I had placed it up out of the way this morning before I ran out for work. She hadn't even bothered to unpack. What the hell had she been doing all day?

A roll of agitation went through me. I opened my mouth to say something but... I snapped it shut and spun, walking into the living room instead. I couldn't get mad at her the very first day she was back. It was her first day back. So what if she didn't tidy up her cup. Or unpack. Right?

"How was work?" she called from the room. "Sell any plastic dicks today?"

"Work was fine," I called back to her, dropping onto the couch and leaning back against the cushions, my irritation easing. It was good to hear her voice again. It was good to have her to come home to again, to tell her everything about my day again. I shouldn't be getting annoyed at her. "We had a girl in who couldn't get her vibrator to work so I had to lend her a hand, pardon my pun. It got a bit messy. But all in all, a good day's work."

She appeared from the corridor. "You *what*?"

"Kidding," I sang out. I noticed her peering at me strangely. "What?"

"You've developed a sense of humour."

I snorted. "Gee, thanks."

"And a bit of a backbone. Nice work, Rosey."

I rolled my eyes. "Trust you to make a compliment sound

exactly like it's *not.*"

There was a hard glint to her eyes. "So this is loverboy's influence, is it?"

My cheeks warmed as Clay's face came to mind. A giggle bubbled up out of me as I thought of the last few months that I had known him. "Yeah," I said around a breath, "I guess so."

* * *

Later that night, Salem and I stood in my room staring at the double bed that we would share.

"Which side are you going to take?" I asked her.

She nodded to the far side of the bed where my mobile phone charger and side lamp sat. "Your shit is on that side so I guess I'll take this one. Nearest the door. That *was* my usual spot, wasn't it?"

My body turned cold. All that old guilt, cold and weathered with age, began to seep back in. "I can take this side if you–"

"Don't worry about it." She shrugged as if it was nothing, but she didn't meet my eyes. "It doesn't matter anymore, does it?"

We changed into bedclothes in silence. I couldn't help but sneak glances at her out of the corner of my eye. Her body had grown into a woman's body, just like mine: modest breasts, slim hips and legs, auburn hair between her legs.

It surprised me that she hadn't gotten any tattoos or piercings. For some reason I had always expected that she would go down that route. She had always been the more rebellious one. Then again, Salem was never one for standard acts of defiance. She would more likely *not* get tattoos because everyone else was doing it.

I got into bed first. She zipped up her duffel bag, still on the chair. I stifled the urge to tell her to put her things away now. I had, after all, made room for her in my closet. But it was late. She could unpack tomorrow. She slid into bed next to me and I turned off the side lamp.

For the first time in three years I had someone I loved next to me filling that space that had lain empty for so long. The sheer presence of her body beside mine brought tears to my eyes. I swallowed a sob. "I missed you, Salem," I whispered. I felt her tense beside me but I kept going. "There wasn't a day in the last three years that went by without me thinking of you."

Her voice slid to me through the dark, "I missed you too."

I turned my head towards her and stared at her silhouette in the dark. "You ran away from me. You kept running." I tried not to let the anger out through my voice but I failed.

She was silent for a time before speaking, "I stayed away because I wanted to keep the attention away from you, to let you try and live a normal life. If they found you… I couldn't stand it if you got into trouble."

"They?"

"You know…"

They. The police. They would have been looking for us since that night.

"But it's been long enough now that I thought it was safe to come back. I thought you might need me now."

She had stayed away to protect me. Like she had always protected me. How could I ever have thought she didn't want me with her? "I'm sorry for getting mad earlier."

"'Sokay."

"I'm glad you're home."

"Me too."

"Never leave, okay?"

In the dark I felt Salem's hand reach out over the sheets and grab mine.

I gripped onto it, as tightly as I could, the only thing I could do.

Don't watch, she whispered.

I shoved that memory away. And cleared my throat. "Before I forget, you should give me your mobile number, just in case."

"Just in case I run away again?"

"I mean like if I'm at the store and want to ask you if you want me to pick you anything up."

She made a funny noise. "Thanks for the sentiment, Rosey, but I don't have a mobile."

"You don't have a mobile? Who doesn't have a mobile?"

"I don't. Is that a crime?"

I cringed at her choice of words. "No." I chewed my lip in the dark. "Why don't you have a mobile?"

"They can track you using your mobile."

I worried my lip with my teeth. In our time apart Salem had grown paranoid. Doesn't she have reason to be paranoid? "So you've spent all this time without a mobile."

"Spent all this time without a lot of things."

"Did you…work or something?"

"Something."

"I don't understand."

I heard her huff loudly and I smelled her minty toothpaste. She shifted in the sheets, pulling her hand from mine. Like my questions were annoying her. My questions shouldn't be annoying her. She should *want* to tell me all this stuff. She used to tell me everything. And now…it felt like my asking her to share herself was like prying. I was supposed to be her sister. Her other half.

Relax, Aria, it's her first night. Give the girl a break.

Her voice came out, bitterness seeping from her every syllable. "It's pretty hard for *me* to get a job, isn't it? Considering… everything. It's not like I've bought a fake identity to fall back on."

What the hell was that supposed to mean? "But you have to have done something to support yourself over the years…" I trailed off as a realisation grew in my belly.

I remembered one of the motel rooms where I had tracked her once. I remembered my stomach dropping as I scanned the room, empty of her. The bed unmade, an old dark stain on the threadbare carpet. The air sour with the scent of sweat and cheap aftershave. Even then I think a part of me guessed what she had been doing to get by but…

"Trust me, you don't want to know." Even in the dark of my bedroom, I could hear the sneer underneath her words. Innocent little Aria. Knows nothing of the world and of having to struggle. Screw her. I knew. I knew about struggle.

"You don't have to keep things from me. You never kept things from me."

"You can't handle the truth."

"I can."

"No, you can't. You never have. That's why you have me to protect you from them."

"But–"

"Just go to sleep." She turned her back on me, signalling the end of the conversation.

* * *

I woke up feeling a comforting presence next to me.
Clay.

I rolled over to face him, a smile on my face and my body already heating up in his presence, before slowly opening my eyes.

I flinched back. It was Salem's back that I was staring at. Not Clay's. Disappointment flooded me. Then a sharp wave of guilt.
You'd rather Clay was in this bed, not her.

I was a bad sister. I was a bad person. How could I even think that? How would Salem feel if she knew…?

I would never tell her. I couldn't.

The secrets between us were piling up, it seemed.

I slipped my legs out of bed and crept to my bedroom door.

"Hey."

I spun. Salem was already awake and staring at the wall. My cheeks flushed. Had she known I had thought that she was Clay?

Don't be stupid. You're close but she can't read your mind.

I croaked when I tried to speak. I had to clear my throat before I could get anything out. "Hey. How did you sleep?"

She shrugged.

"Do you want breakfast?" I asked, trying to inject as much cheer as I could into my voice. "I have some time before work. I could make us banana pancakes?"

I caught her eye and a small smile came across her face. I knew she was remembering too…

"Banana pancakes," a young Salem shrieked as she jumped all over me, her tiny fingers pressing all over my face. "Ba-na-na-na-na-na-na-na-na-na, make those bodies siiiiiing."

I groaned at my over-enthusiastic alarm clock. Only this one didn't have an off button. Salem never seemed to sleep. "Go away, it's still dark out."

I heard her snort and she bounced out of bed, the mattress springing behind her. She grabbed my sheets and I tugged them tighter over my head.

I knew it wasn't the end of it. I felt her fingers against the end of the blanket. I gripped on tighter, preparing myself for what came next, tucking my feet up against my butt and pulling my knees into my chest so that I was as small as possible. It never worked, though.

She scrambled up the bottom of the mattress and found my toes, the only part of my body that was ticklish. I began to scream.

Near the entrance to my bedroom I smiled at the now grown-up Salem pushing herself up in bed.

She stretched her arms above her. "I never thought I'd see the day when you actually woke up earlier than me."

"Some things change."

"Some things never do."

I stopped dead when I stepped out into the living room. That damn coffee mug was still there. Before I could stop myself, I snapped. "Jesus Christ, Salem."

"What?" Her voice called back to me from the open bedroom.

"I asked you to clean up your mug. But it's still there." I grabbed the cup and stormed into the kitchen, dumping it into the sink, black liquid pouring out from the mug on its side and disappearing down the drain.

"Relax, Rosey. It's just a mug. Shit, you're even more uptight than I remember."

"It's not just a mug. I'm not here to do everything for you."

"No," her cold voice came from behind me. "I wouldn't expect *you* to do anything for me.

You have to do this for me, Rosey. I can't take it anymore. I'll go crazy. She had only ever asked me to do one thing for her. And I had failed her, hadn't I?

I spun to face her as this familiar guilt clawed at me. Salem stared at me as she leaned on the bedroom door frame, her face hardened, but there were flashes of hurt in her stormy eyes.

There was so much I wanted to say to her. I had rehearsed everything I would say to her over the lonely nights while I'd been searching for her. Now that she was here, none of the words would come. They were too swollen and painful to be able to purge without also ripping myself apart. "I'm sorry." It was all I could say. I'm sorry. Sorry for failing you. Sorry for what you had to endure. I'm sorry…for everything.

Her mouth softened but her eyes remained dark clouds. "It's fine."

But we both knew it wasn't. The past was unchangeable and it remained silent and trapped between us, a tension that had been building ever since she returned. This was a small release, just enough to keep it from exploding. For now.

You'll have to face it soon.

I'm not ready.

I shoved these thoughts away and took a deep breath. I had to do something to dissipate this lingering awkwardness. "So, do you want pancakes?" I bent down to look inside one of the kitchen cupboards. The large frypan was down here somewhere. I hadn't bothered with fancy breakfasts before, just a bowl of cereal was enough for me, but now that Salem was back…

"I'm not hungry."

"What?" I shot up and smacked my head on the underside of the cupboard, a smarting pain shooting through my skull. I rose to standing more carefully this time as I rubbed my head. "What do you mean you're not hungry?"

"I mean, I'm not hungry."

"When are you *not* hungry? God, you used to eat *everything* while…" There I was, stuck in the past again. We weren't kids anymore. We had both changed. "What about when you *do* get hungry?"

"I can feed myself, you know."

Of course she could. She has been feeding herself for the last three years without my help. Here I was trying to take care of her, for what? In a hope that it would make up for…*everything*.

I winced. *She never needed you. You were the one that needed her.*

I closed the cupboard and opened a different one, finding my usual bowl and box of cereal and assembling my usual breakfast, finishing it off with a sliced banana and milk. I sat on the couch and ate my breakfast.

"What do you wanna do tonight?" Salem asked as she dropped down on the couch beside me.

"Oh, um, yeah, about tonight…" I rubbed the back of my skull where a tension headache was starting to work its way into my brain, "I forgot I had plans with Clay tonight."

"Well, don't let me stop ya."

"I can cancel plans with him if you want me to stay."

"It's fine. We'll hang out another time when you and loverboy aren't busy."

"It's not a big deal if I cancel him. He'll understand."

"All good. I think I need a day home alone. Get a break from all your nagging."

That stung. I ignored the annoyance that comment arose in me.

"So, how did you and Mr Wonderful meet, anyway?"

I flinched and prayed that she didn't notice. Salem had always been overprotective. She would hate it if she knew the truth. I really didn't feel like arguing with her. Again. And not about Clay. "I… We… He's a friend of a friend. A friend of my boss's actually." I cringed internally when my voice came out a little too tight at the end of my sentence. I glanced over to her to see if she had noticed. She was nodding slowly but there was a strange look in her eye. For a second I thought she had caught me out.

Then she grinned, showing a little too much of her teeth. "A friend of your boss's. A good friend?"

"Yeah, pretty good." Please stop asking questions.

"How long have they known each other?"

I rubbed my itching neck. Probably karma getting ready with the beginnings of a huge rash for all my lies. "Um, I think they go back to high school. Yeah, I think so." Liar, liar, liar.

"So he's not some weirdo stranger who just spotted you on the street then waltzed into your sex store so he could meet you.

Good to know. Wouldn't want my Rosey-girl getting involved with the wrong guy."

It was like she knew. Did she know? She always seemed to know when I tried to lie, even as a kid.

"No, of course not." Unable to take any more of her scrutiny, I stood up and walked into the kitchen, placing my empty bowl and spoon into the sink.

When I turned around she was standing there staring at me from the edge of the kitchen.

She grabbed my arm as I tried to walk past her. "It's good to be back," she said, but her eyes were hard as steel as she stared at me. "Good to be back with my sis. The only one who'd never lie to me. Right?"

"Right."

"The only one I could ever count on. I can count on you, can't I? Sis?"

"Of course." I forced a smile back at her even though my skin was prickling. "I...I need to go to the bathroom." I pulled my arm out from her too tight, almost painful grasp. When I turned my back on her the hairs on my neck rose.

As I closed the door to the bathroom, I caught her staring at me from the living room, something close to menace in her eyes.

Chapter Five

"Are you sure you'll be okay here by yourself?" I asked Salem for like the fiftieth time.

"Go, be with loverboy. I'll be fine." She waved at me from the couch, her eyes focused on the flashing images, some animated movie that was showing on Friday night TV.

"Are you sure?" I said as I paced the living room, checking the clock, making sure I had everything in my bag – keys, wallet, phone, lip balm, and at Flick's insistence, condoms – then checking the clock again. "I can cancel. He'll understand."

She snorted. "What, and have to spend a night with you wishing you were with him getting some? No thanks."

I flushed. "I am not going to *get some*, as you so eloquently put it."

"Whatever."

"I have fresh groceries." I opened the small fridge and stared inside. "Veges, chicken, some cheese. And I have sauce for a stir fry in the cupboard or there's wholemeal pasta."

"Ew, who eats wholemeal pasta?"

I spun around, slamming the fridge door shut. "I eat wholemeal pasta."

She made a face.

I walked to the couch and stood there, worrying my lip. "Will you be alright for dinner?"

"Yup, I know the local number for pizza delivery by heart."

"Salem, pizza's not good for you."

"What are you, my mother?"

I was about to reply but I heard three sharp blasts of a horn from the street. "Okay, that's him."

"He's not going to come up?"

"Um, no." I turned to grab my bag from the kitchen counter, hoping she didn't see the flush that was most definitely on my face given how hot my cheeks had gone.

"You haven't told him I'm here, have you?"

"No, but I will."

"Are you ashamed of me?"

I gasped and spun, my hand still stuck in my handbag. "I'm not ashamed of you. Clay and I, we're just… I'm just waiting for the right time."

"Uh-huh." She jumped off the couch and stalked over to the window.

"Get back from there. He'll see you."

Salem just kept staring outside through the blinds. "Please, even if he does, he'll think I'm you." She sniffed. "It's too dark for me to get a good look at him anyway." She returned to her couch and the movie.

I found what I was looking for in my bag. "I almost forgot. Here." I held out a key. It was a copy of mine and at the end was the other half of my key-chain pair, the other half of my heart. "I had a second key cut for you."

She laughed at something on-screen. "Just put it down on the table." She made a nudging motion with her chin.

I shoved away a sliver of rejection and slipped it on the table before straightening. "Okay, I'm off."

Salem made a solemn Queen-wave at me, her eyes still on the TV.

"How do I look?"

"Does it really matter what clothes you're wearing if he's just going to tear them all off anyway?"

"Salem!"

She tore her eyes away from the screen and graced me with a brief once-over. "You look great. Now leave."

"Okay, then," I muttered to myself, "don't miss me too much."
I turned and walked out of my apartment, my bag slung over my
shoulder.

I paused just outside the door and worried my lip.

What was I doing?

I should stay here with Salem. Hang out with Salem. After all,
I haven't seen her in three years.

I stuck my head back into my apartment. "Are you sure you
don't want me to−"

"Oh my God, get out!"

I shut the door before the pillow she threw at me could hit me
in the face.

Outside, Clay was leaning against his Mustang, waiting for
me, outlined in the fading afternoon sunlight. Me. This gorgeous
man, dressed in dark denim that hugged his strong thighs, and a
white shirt, was waiting for *me*. My worry over Salem faded at the
sight of him.

He grinned as I walked up to him. "You are gorgeous."

I looked down at myself. I was wearing skinny jeans teamed
with silver ballet flats and a white cotton top threaded with silver,
giving it a subtle shimmer. "You're biased."

He pulled me into his arms, leaning down so his nose rubbed
against mine. "Maybe. But it doesn't change the fact that you're
gorgeous."

"What if…I were wearing a potato sack?"

"That's a very lucky potato sack." He rubbed the end of his
nose along my cheekbone and towards my ear.

"What if…I were tarred and feathered."

"Then you'd be the sexiest chick in the world."

"What if…I were wearing a grey cow onesie?"

He hummed against my ear, sending shivers down my spine.
"Then you'd be udderly irresistible?"

I slapped him lightly on his chest, hard like granite.

He laughed, the sound rolling into my body, and he pulled me
flush against him. "You can play the What If game all you like, but
you'll still be the most beautiful thing to me, whether you were
wearing a sack, a grey cow onesie, or…nothing at all under all

those feathers."

His breath against my ear made me shiver.

When he covered my lips with his, my whole world silenced, fading like a ballet chorus behind a velvet curtain as the spotlight fell upon just Clay and me. We became my whole world and everything in it, my nose filling with his scent of cedar and a hint of warm spice. His lips parted as he tilted his mouth and he brushed the seam of my lips with his tongue. I opened my mouth to let him in and offered him a sigh in return. His strong hands slid around my back, holding me firmly to him. I seemed to melt further and further into his unyielding body, melding to him like I was made to. My fingers fluttered over his chest and his neck, too scared to land anywhere, almost disbelieving that he was real at all.

Clay Jagger was real and he was kissing me.

Finally and yet all too soon, he pulled away. "Let's go," he whispered. "Before we do something on your street that your neighbours wouldn't appreciate."

My skin tingled as my thoughts rolled over exactly what he had meant by *something*.

He let go of me and his eyes flicked to something over my shoulder. "You know, it looks like you left the TV on."

I spun. The space between the living room window curtains was flashing with lights from inside. I forced a smile. "It's to discourage burglars." I wasn't ready to explain about Salem yet. Tonight was just supposed to be about us.

He nodded, seeming to accept my answer. I glanced back to my apartment. Did the curtain just move? Was that Salem at the window again? My heart stabbed a little with guilt. It wasn't fair that I was leaving her tonight to be with Clay. I shouldn't have left her there alone.

"Look, twins."

I turned sharply towards him. "*What?*" Had he seen Salem?

"Twins." He pointed down to the two of us. "We're practically wearing his and her outfits."

We were both in dark denim and white tops. I laughed, partly in relief. "Aren't couples supposed to start doing that after they've been together *too* long?"

He grinned at me.

"What?"

"You just acknowledged that we're a couple."

"Did I?"

He pulled me in for another slow and lingering kiss. "About damn time, Aria Adams," he murmured against my mouth.

* * *

I stepped out of the car after Clay had parked it on the side of a thin road surrounded by trees. He had driven us out of town along one of the hinterland roads that looped up the mountain range that Mirage Falls was nestled in.

A few street lights dotted sickly pools of light over the nearby bridge, the sound of water drumming off rocks and the air moist with misty drops. There were no other cars parked here and for the last fifteen minutes until we stopped, none had passed us. We were definitely alone here for miles. Why would he bring me out here?

Wouldn't want my Rosey-girl getting involved with the wrong guy. A trickle of fear dripped down my spine.

Clay's door slammed shut, making me jump. I shoved my apprehension aside. "Clay, where are we?"

He stared towards the bridge. "The Mirage Gorge. This is where Mirage Falls gets its name."

"Why are we here?"

He didn't answer. He walked around to my side of the car and slammed my door shut. The noise was like a gunshot in my ears, sending another jolt through me. The sky was turning a brilliant fiery colour, sunset was almost upon us.

"Clay, why are we here?"

"I want to show you something."

This was ridiculous. I trusted Clay. He would never hurt me. So why did my body shiver as we made the short walk to the bridge? The sound of gravel crushed under our feet like a death march.

The bridge crossed over a deep narrow gorge, a waterfall dropping from behind it. Wooden slats lined an iron structure that was wide enough for one brave car; thin poles and strung wire to the height of my hipbone were the only things to stop someone from falling into the abyss. I kept to the middle of the bridge, my feet clattering over the wooden slats, and Clay walked closest to the railing. I wondered how old this bridge was and hoped to God it would hold us.

I was being ridiculous. Of course it would hold us. It was designed for cars to pass over.

He paused at the centre of the bridge, leaned against the railing and looked out, his back to the waterfall. We were high enough that we could see the burning sun just about to dip under the sea of forest across the mountains. I stood next to him and tried to enjoy the view, trying to ignore all these jumbled feelings churning inside me. For a time all that I could hear was the drumming of the waterfall crashing down upon all those jagged rocks below.

Finally he turned to look at me, an odd look in his eyes. "Beautiful, isn't it."

I nodded.

"Have you been here before?" he asked.

"No."

His face became serious, almost pained, and his eyes took on a faraway look, as if he was looking straight through me. As if I wasn't there at all. I shivered. "What is it?"

He shook his head. "Just remembering something."

"Remembering what?"

He looked out again, his eyes becoming unfocused. "Remembering…the last time I was here."

A fear ricocheted through me. This was why I had strange feelings about this place. It was like I could feel the ghost of someone's past hovering about my shoulder. It was the ghost of Clay's past.

"What happened here?"

He didn't answer for a long time. Then his next words were almost a whisper, "I almost died here."

Chapter Six

I almost died here.

"What?"

Clay stared at his hands, the tips of his fingers running along the grooves of the top of the railing. "When I was eighteen, my world fell apart. My mother was my whole world and she just… she died. My father couldn't handle it so he just left. I was left all alone. I couldn't cope. I came here to…" he trailed off.

He came here to end his life.

My voice was barely a whisper. "You were going to jump?"

He nodded.

Dear God. I stared at the abyss over the edge of the railing. I saw Clay almost three years ago as his fingers curled over the railing and he pulled his legs up and over. I shook this image away. "Why didn't you?"

"An angel came to me, right here on this bridge. She wore a white dress and her halo shone brighter than anything I'd ever seen."

I froze. An angel? Was he serious?

Then I realised. He saw things too. Just like me. Post-Traumatic Stress Disorder after his mother died. How brave he was to share his hallucination with me. I wouldn't make light of this gift. I wouldn't judge him. "And she saved you?"

He nodded. "If I lived she promised me…" He looked up and his eyes burned into mine. "She promised me *you.*"

I swallowed, hard. "What?"

He smiled softly. "Don't misunderstand me; she didn't actually promise me *you*. I didn't know you then. She promised me that I wouldn't always be alone. She promised me that if I could make my way through this darkness, I'd find my light again."

My head spun as I tried to process everything he was saying.

His eyes bored into me. "Do you think I'm crazy?"

I shook my head. No crazier than me.

He looked out over the gorge, leaning his hands on the railing. "Sometimes we need to crumble to nothing before we can rebuild ourselves into someone better. Sometimes we need to start again at nothing."

"You are nothing." I thought I heard *his* voice behind me and jumped. I stared back at the road I had just walked up but there was no one else here. This place. There was something about this place. It felt like the past was a ghost here and he was reaching for me with his hands. A wind shook the trees that lined the road and there it was, that voice hissing through the leaves and over the sound of thundering water. *"Why couldn't it have been you?"*

Oh God, not here. I clamped my hands over my ears. Keep it inside.

"Why didn't you die and not her?" His large hand wrapped around my wrist. I tried to pull my hand from his. "Go away," I hissed. But he wouldn't let go. He began to drag me forward, stumbling, farther and farther forward to the edge of the bridge. Below me the gorge gaped down and the dying light caught off the splashing water. *"It should have been you."* I felt myself tipping.

An arm went around me and I smelt cedar and musk. Clay. Suddenly I was tethered between the past and the present, a paper doll being pulled from both sides.

"Let go of me!"

But neither of them would. Two pairs of hands, one from the past, one from the present, just gripped me tighter and pulled.

"Come back to me." Clay's voice was like the morning light, breaking through the mist clouding my reality. He shushed into my hair, his gentle whispers drowning out the other voice. "I'm real. I'm here. Focus on me."

I slipped out of the grip of the hand from the past and it faded into the dark shadows. For now.

Clay held me securely in his arms, and rocked me gently. It was like he knew instinctively what to do. Why wasn't he running? After seeing me in the midst of a post-traumatic stress hallucination, acting as if it were real? "Why are you still here?" I spat out.

He turned me to face him, grabbing my shoulders. "Aria," he said fiercely, "do you believe in signs?"

"Signs? Like what?"

"Signs. Messages from God–"

"I don't believe in God. No God would allow such horrible things to exist…" I trailed off.

"I do. You shine to me, Aria. Brighter than anything in my whole wretched life. I knew after I saw you that you were my Northern Star."

I choked on a laugh that had no humour in it. "Can you get a refund for faulty goods?"

"There is nothing faulty about you."

Flashes of black memory flapped across my eyes like angry crows and I felt sick to my stomach. "You don't know everything about me," I whispered.

"I know enough."

"No, you don't."

Clay held my chin gently and lifted. "There's *nothing* you could tell me that would make me love you less."

My mind stuttered over his words. Did he say what I thought he said? He couldn't possibly…

"You love me?"

"I love you. All of you, every piece of you. Even the pieces that are torn or smudged. Especially them."

My heart clenched so hard that it physically hurt. I swear it just cracked open. A warmth soaked out and into my bones.

In that very moment, how could I not fall in love back with Clay Jagger?

I fell against his chest, my legs still not working properly. I opened my mouth to speak. To say…something.

You're saving me.
Thank you.
I love y…

But all words failed me. So I spoke the only way I could. I leaned up and pressed my mouth to his and clutched him to me as if he were my only lifeline in this storming grey world. Perhaps he was.

Our mouths moved. He clung to me as well, as if we were both lost in a storm. Every part of me felt like it was spinning, falling, sinking into love with him.

And yet, as I dropped, I was submersed in a growing terror. Only in the face of love can you comprehend just how destructive its loss could be. Love dug roots into you and the deeper they went, the more would be ripped away when they left.

His hands gripped me tightly to him, hands that I knew like my own, strong fingers, warm palms and smooth nails, the masculine dusting of hair on each knuckle.

As we kissed our bodies pressed into each other like we couldn't get close enough. Could it be possible that two bodies could become the same person? I pushed my hips up and against his growing hardness. He groaned into my mouth. I wanted this. He wanted this.

And I saw us stripping each layer of clothing off, and him sitting me onto the railing, the waterfall drumming in the background, and sliding in between my thighs.

Instead he pulled away, his breath heavy and uneven, and he glanced around the darkened sky, beginning to fill out with stars. "Come on, it's getting late. Let's get you home."

We were driving through the edges of Mirage Falls when Clay suddenly pulled the car over, the tires screeching like a chorus of screams. My heart thundered in my chest. "What's wrong?"

He grabbed me and crushed his lips to mine. My head spun, half lost in the feel and the smell and the taste of him, half scrambling to understand what had scared him so much that he needed to pull over so suddenly.

His kiss slowed, then he pulled his lips off mine, my bottom lip popping out from between his lips with a groan on my tongue. My eyelashes fluttered open, a question on my face. "Clay?"

"Kiss buggie angel-hair red."

It took me only a moment to realise what he was talking about. A laugh escaped my mouth.

He grinned as he settled back in his seat and pulled back onto the road. "P.S. My version is *so* much better."

I couldn't argue with that.

* * *

The instant I stepped into my apartment the giddiness of the last few hours with Clay was slapped out of me. The TV was on, blaring away, but Salem wasn't to be seen. Had she gone to bed without turning the TV off? I pushed down the grit of annoyance as I grabbed the remote and switched it off. The room darkened and the silence took over.

I threw the remote on the side table before walking into our room, ready to snap at her.

But she wasn't in the bedroom.

"Salem?" I peered in the bathroom before realising that she wasn't home at all.

Where the hell did she go?

I reached into my bag for my mobile and paused. That's right, Salem didn't have a mobile. I had no way of reaching her. I searched the house but there was no note, to indication of where she had gone. *No note, no goodbyes, nothing.*

Later that night, the other side of my bed, Salem's side, felt emptier than it had been the last three years. I lay awake, staring at the ceiling, listening for the key in the lock, a low-level tension clinging to my body. Where did she go? When would she come back? What if she was in trouble? What if she never came back?

Relax. She'll come back. Salem and I are part of each other, like paper dolls…

A thirteen-year old-Salem lay on the bed, staring at the ceiling, her knees up and scuffed boots on the bed, a seething fury etched in every feature.

I sat on the edge of the mattress. "Do you…want to talk about it?"

"No."

"But you're hurting and−"

"What do you care?"

My heart cracked as my best friend and soulmate rolled away, turning her back on me. It was the first time she'd ever turned her back on me. But as last night showed…there was a first for everything. I could see her shoulders hunched up around her ears as she curled into a tight ball like she wanted to fold in on herself.

What should I do? What should I say?

I jumped off the bed and returned with a piece of paper and a pair of scissors from my desk. I began to fold the piece of paper in half in the middle of the longer side so that the two shorter edges were touching. Then I folded it again and again until it made a skinny rectangle. I grabbed the scissors in my lap and began to cut: one leg, one arm, half a head. When I was finished I slipped the scissors on the bedside table and unfolded the paper.

"Look." I held up the row of identical paper dolls to her.

She glanced at it for a second and turned back away. "I don't want to play any stupid games."

"This isn't a game. This is you and me, Salem," I said. "We're from the same piece of paper. Our souls are made of the same stuff. When someone cuts holes from you, they cut holes from me. When you're hurting, I'm hurting. When he…when he hurt you last night, he hurt me."

She turned suddenly, her eyes flashing like lightning in storm clouds. She launched at me, flinging her arms around my neck in a fierce hug, the paper dolls crushed between us. I put my arms around her skinny waist and hugged her back just as tightly, her body trembling with rage under my hands.

"The bastard," she hissed in my ear, and I flinched. She used the same bad word that Mama used to call him. At the time I hadn't really been sure what it had meant. Now I knew. "He won't ever hurt you. Never. I won't let him."

"You can't stop him," I said quietly, tears already rolling down my cheeks. She couldn't stop him from hurting her last night. How could she stop him from hurting me?

"Yes," she said quietly, her voice deadly like a snake's hiss, "I can."

She pulled back from me, her face as cold as marble and she carefully wiped the moisture from my cheeks. The way Mama used to do whenever I was hurt. God, I missed her. None of this would be happening if only she were still here.

There were no tears on Salem's face, only two fierce glass orbs glistening in her skull and a firmly pressed snarl that showed her white canines. She had always been the strong one.

"Did you hear me?" she said, her voice firm as I ever heard it. "I won't let him hurt you. If he tries, I'll kill him."

Chapter Seven

When I woke up the next morning my own face was staring back at me. Salem was standing at the open door to my bedroom, staring at me. "Salem." I sat up, clutching the sheets to my chest. "Thank God. I could barely sleep from worrying about you."

"You looked like you were sleeping fine."

I swallowed down my urge to retort back. "Where did you go last night?"

"Does it matter? You were off having all the fun in the world with loverboy." She threw herself onto the bed on her back, tucking her hands under her head and bending her knees up so her black Doc Marten's were on the bed. "Go on, spill it. I know you're dying to tell me."

"Tell you what?"

"All the dirty little details of your loverboy? Is he packing as much as those plastic versions you sell?"

I tasted a bitterness on my tongue. "Don't refer to my boyfriend's…thing in the same sentence as a dildo. Actually don't refer to it at all. Ever." Salem was not allowed to know or even *think* about Clay in that way.

"Come on, Aria. It's me. You can tell me. Is it huge? It's huge, isn't it? I promise not to stare when I finally get to meet him."

Jesus Christ. "I don't know. We haven't…you know."

"You guys haven't fucked?"

I made a face. "Do you have to call it that?"

"What's wrong with fuck?"

"It just sounds so…crass."

"Sex is crass. It's not like in the movies. Forget candles and violins and the tender press of two bodies. It's dirty and noisy and real. Slapping flesh, grunting, bumping uglies, rooting, doing it. Hard and fast and rough." Salem began to thrust her hips up at the air, making guttural noises in her throat while her face twisted into ugly expressions of pleasure and pain. Oh hell. I just got a look at how I might look when I…

I slapped her arm. "Stop it. Clay's not like that."

Thankfully she ceased her air-humping and rearranged herself on the pillow before giving me a look. "Clay's a guy. All *guys* are like that."

"He's not."

"Whatever. So, what are you waiting for?"

"Just…for the timing to be right."

"And for unicorns to fart rainbows and doves to shit fairy dust." She made a dramatic sigh. "They do call it '*hopeless* romantic' for a reason."

I pressed my lips together. "What's wrong with wanting romance?"

"It's the same as wanting a dragon as a pet. It's not real and you're just setting yourself up for disappointment."

I decided to ignore this. "I have to get ready for work." I threw off the sheets and climbed out of bed. I could feel Salem's eyes on me as I padded around my room, gathering my clothes. My annoyance loosened. She had reasons for being cynical. Perhaps if she could just see Clay and me together, she'd change her mind.

"So, I was thinking that maybe I could invite Clay over one night this week," I said casually.

I saw her stiffen. "So you want me out of here."

"What? No. I want you to meet him."

"Why do I need to meet him?"

"Because…you're the two most important people in my life."

"He's important to *you*. Not to me."

"Come on, Salem. I could cook us all dinner."

She scrunched up her face. "Have dinner with Mr and Mrs

Perfect? No, thanks."

"It'll be fun."

She let out a snort. "Fun is drinking a fifth of vodka and dancing until 5 a.m. Fun is not sitting around eating wholemeal pasta with you two lovebirds."

"Okay…you're obviously not in the best mood." I walked to the shower. "I'll ask you again later."

"The answer will still be no," she called out.

I was going to ask Clay about dinner with Salem as he walked me to work that morning. But he was a deathly silent and only managed one-syllable answers as we walked down the sidewalk. He held my hand in a death grip and practically dragged me down the street, his long legs pumping like pistons.

"Clay," I tugged back at his hand. "Slow down."

"Oh. Right. Sorry." He slowed down for me.

"What's up?"

He paused before saying, "Nothing."

And that's all he would say.

I felt instinctively that he just needed some silence. Salem would get like this sometimes. All quiet and intense. Any attempts to draw her out of that state would only seem to push her in further. But if I let her be, then she would come out herself when she was ready.

Clay remained silent and broody for the rest of the way. When we reached the Whip & Flick I wasn't sure if I'd even get a proper goodbye. But he grabbed me by my shoulders and spun me towards him, the look on his face stopping me in my tracks. He looked torn, as if something clawed at him from the inside, his eyes glassy and forehead furrowed as if it hurt. Something was wrong. My annoyance seeped right out of me. "Clay?"

He crashed his lips down onto mine. This kiss was unlike any kiss we had shared before. It felt like…goodbye, filled with desperate needing, as he clung to me like a little boy lost. I felt his heart flapping like a scared bird against my own chest, fear of some foreseen, inevitable pain. As if the earth might crack open between our feet and separate us.

...my mind misgives, some consequence yet hanging in the stars...

It scared me right down to my bones.

I pulled away, not being able to take any more. "Clay," I whispered, fear gripping my throat. "What's wrong?"

"I... It's nothing," he breathed against me "Just...work stuff."

Clay was lying. It was the first time that he had lied to me.

Before I could respond his phone dinged. He pulled it out of his pocket and stared at the text message, his brows drawing together. He turned, his eyes never reaching mine. "I gotta go."

"Who was that?"

"No one important," he called back over his shoulder. I watched his rapidly retreating back. What had gotten under his skin? Who had texted him? And what had that text said?

"Are we still on for tonight?" I yelled.

But he was already too far gone.

That afternoon when my shift ended I was surprised to see Clay waiting across the road, leaning against the door of his parked car. I let the door of the Whip & Flick swing shut behind me. Flick was still inside so I didn't have to lock up.

I approached him cautiously as if one sudden movement would cause him to take flight. "You're here."

"Of course I'm here." He laughed at me and tugged at my hair when I reached him. "Why are you looking at me as if I might suddenly grow an extra head?"

I peered at him. There was no sign of the Clay from this morning. Almost as if it had been a different person. "I'm just trying to make sure it's you."

"Who else would I be?"

"I don't know. The Clay from this morning was someone I'd never seen before."

His eyes dulled for a second, as if a storm cloud had passed before his mind. Then it disappeared, leaving just the brightness to his face that I knew. He chuckled. "Yeah, I'm sorry about this morning. Just work stuff. I've fixed it now."

He's lying to you. But why?

He interrupted my thoughts with a kiss, unhurried and tender and sending rushes of feeling through my body. But part of me felt like this kiss…was too perfect. Almost like he was trying to cover up the kiss from this morning. As if he was trying to show just how 'normal' everything was.

What about Salem? You haven't told him that she's back. Don't get mad that he's hiding things from you if you're still hiding things from him.

I'm not hiding. Just waiting for the right time.

Maybe he's just waiting for the right time too.

"I have something to tell you," I blurted out as he pulled his lips off mine.

"Do I get three guesses?"

"I don't want to make a game out of this."

"Come on. Let me guess. Hmm…you've decided to leave me to join a travelling Shakespeare troupe."

"No."

"You're going to start a band named the Udderly Irresistibles?"

"Come on, Clay, be serious."

"I am always serious about music and Shakespeare."

"Salem is back."

He froze, his whole body tensing against me. His lips pursed together. He let go of me and moved aside to open the passenger door to his car to let me in. I climbed in and he shut the door. Through the silent bubble I watched as he walked slowly around the car.

There was a moment when the sounds of the world tumbled in through his open driver's door before he climbed into the driver's seat and shut it behind him. The world became muffled again. His lips were still pressed together as he put his hands on the steering wheel.

"Aren't you going to say anything?"

His hands slipped from the wheel into his lap as he let out a breath. "What do you want me to say, Aria? Salem's back. Wow. That's great. You must be really happy."

I frowned at him. There was an edge to his voice… It reminded me of something. It reminded me of how Salem sounded when

I spoke about him. "I am," I said slowly.

"The prodigal sister returns, huh? It's you and Salem again. Like old times. Good old times. Call the *Daily Times*."

He was rambling. Why was he rambling?

Something flashed across his face. He was afraid. What was he so afraid of?

I grabbed his arm, stopping him so I could face him. "This doesn't change anything between us, Clay."

"Yeah, sure. Nothing changes and yet everything does."

He didn't believe me. And I even didn't believe me. He wasn't the main person in my life anymore. That position was now shared. Between Salem and Clay. My stomach started to grip with a looming warning.

"Do you want to have dinner with Salem and me?"

He looked at me as if I had struck him. "You're kidding, right?"

"Why would I kid about that? I can cook, something simple. I don't have a dining table but we could sit on the floor like the Japanese do. You could bring wine…"

He frowned and he looked as if he was choosing his next words carefully. "Is *she* okay with this dinner arrangement?"

No, but he didn't need to know that. I just needed one of them to say yes first, then I would get to work on convincing the other. "Why wouldn't she be?"

"I just don't see why Salem would agree to dinner with me when she's already made it perfectly clear that—"

"Clear that what?"

"Nothing. Forget I said anything." He started the car and pulled out into the road.

"No, finish your sentence. You said you didn't see why Salem would agree to have dinner with you when she's made it perfectly clear that…" Realisation stung me like nettles. "Oh my God. You met her already."

He sighed, resigned, and I knew I had guessed right. "I came by earlier this morning. She answered the door. I…I thought she was you."

My blood went cold as an image of Clay smiling at Salem as

if she were me came into my mind, his dark eyes sparkling like gems. *Hey angel, I missed you.* He leaned in to kiss her.

"What happened this morning?" I demanded.

"Nothing. She told me who she was before I could… She said you were busy getting ready."

I could see Salem flinching out of his grasp. *Don't touch me.*

Surprise broke apart the smile on his face. *Aria?*

I'm not Aria, freak.

Was this why Clay was so upset this morning? Of course it was. Stupid girl.

The remnants of the anger from this morning curled at his top lip. "Why didn't you tell me she was back?"

"I'm sorry. It only just happened. I was waiting for the right time…" My excuses sounded lame even to me. "Why didn't you tell me you met her this morning?"

"I don't know. I figured I'd let her tell you…or something." There was something in his voice that struck me. He was afraid of her. Afraid of Salem. Salem could be so unpredictable. And when she didn't like someone…

"What did she say to you? What did she do?"

He grimaced. "I…don't think she likes me."

"Why do you say that?"

He swallowed, his eyes were focused unblinking at the road. "I just don't want to cause anything… I don't want to get in between you."

Things were falling apart before they started. "Okay, so maybe dinner isn't a good idea. Not yet."

He let out a huge breath. "Aria, don't take this the wrong way, but I don't get the feeling that Salem is the kind that shares."

His words stabbed my skin and wriggled underneath me. *Just you and me, Rosey.* I feared he was right.

No, I refused to believe that I couldn't have Clay and Salem both happily in my life. I would fix this. They just needed to get used to the other. Over time they would warm up to each other, once they both saw that I wasn't going to ditch one for the other, that I wouldn't choose between them, they would be more understanding of each other. Then I could introduce them properly.

Then we could sit down for dinner. Me, Salem and Clay.

One happy family.

There was no cinema in Mirage Falls so Clay drove us to Noosa. At least movies were one thing we could agree on. There was enough darkness in my life that I didn't need to see it in films. Clay agreed. We watched an animated film, a light, funny flick.

After the movie was over we strolled along the low wooden boardwalk on Noosa beach. He bought me an ice cream cone from a small gelateria stand.

"You're not having one?" I asked him when he paid for mine without ordering another for himself.

He shook his head and grinned. "I'm sweet enough."

I rolled my eyes. As we walked side by side I took a large lick of my ice cream, then another one. It was only once it was almost totally gone that I noticed him starting at me, his top teeth biting into his bottom lip as if he was trying to hold down a smile.

"What?"

He shook his head and that bottom lip escaped into a full blown grin. "I just enjoy watching you eat that ice cream."

I blushed. I took another bite. A large one. One that made my head throb from the coldness. He was still looking at me. "You want a bite?"

"No, thanks."

"Quick before it's all gone."

"You enjoy it."

I frowned. "I don't have cooties or anything."

"I'm not scared of cooties. I kissed you, remember?"

"Don't you like ice cream?"

"I do, I just…" He shrugged. "I have to watch my diet."

I almost snorted chunky monkey nutter butter out my nose. "You? Diet?" I gave him a look over. No wonder he stayed in such great shape if he wouldn't even eat a single bite of ice cream. "Well, I feel like a fatty now."

He stopped us, right in the middle of the boardwalk, amidst grumbles of other beachside walkers. "You are perfect. And I'll challenge anyone who says otherwise. Even you." He leaned down to cover my mouth with his. I think I dropped the last of my cone. Ice cream, even chunky monkey nutter butter ice cream, had nothing on his kisses. I wrapped my arms around his neck, tangling my fingers in his hair and losing myself further and further in him. The mutterings and footsteps of people moving around us faded away. When had I stopped caring what strangers thought?

Finally he pulled his lips away. He kept his arm around my waist as he led me off the boardwalk. "You ready for me to take you home?"

I certainly was not. I felt so awake that I may never fall asleep again. In fact that kiss was still tingling through my arms and legs like a live wire.

I cleared my throat and tried to make my suggestion as casual as possible. "Why don't we go to yours? The night's still young and I don't have to work tomorrow…"

He tensed against me as we continued to walk to the car. "You don't want to come back to mine."

I frowned. "Why not?"

"It's a mess."

"I don't mind."

"Well, I do."

"I've never been to your apartment."

"It's not that exciting."

"But I've never even seen it before."

"Maybe another time, okay? I have something to do tomorrow morning. I'm pretty tired."

"What are you up to? Can I come?"

"No. It's just errand stuff. Really boring. You wouldn't want to come." But he wasn't looking at me as he said it.

* * *

"You're home early," Salem said from the couch as I walked in the door later that night. "It's not even midnight. Didn't the date with loverboy go well?"

"It was great." But even I could tell there was something flat in my voice.

She raised an eyebrow.

I didn't want to talk about it. I wasn't even sure I knew myself what it was that I didn't want to talk about. The date really was amazing like it always was with Clay. It was just the end bit…after I said I wanted to go over to his place.

"I asked Clay about the three of us having dinner." I said, changing the subject.

Clay had said goodbye to me on the sidewalk. He hadn't even wanted to come up to the front door.

Salem sat with her arms crossed on the couch. The top of her lip twitched. "What did he say?"

"Why didn't you tell me you met Clay?"

She scowled. "Did loverboy tell on me, did he?"

"No. I guessed it based on his reaction to−" I sighed. I had wanted to have been the one to introduce them, in a controlled environment. This morning would have been a shock for Clay, not knowing that Salem was even back, and a shock for Salem, not realising that Clay would be coming. Usually he waited for me on the sidewalk so I hadn't thought to warn her. "What happened between you two?"

Her eyes narrowed to slits. "What are you implying, dear sister?"

"I'm not implying anything. I'm just asking what happened this morning when you met."

"Nothing. He came to the door. I told him to come back later as you were otherwise occupied. End of story."

No, it wasn't. I knew there was something Salem wasn't telling me.

Add that to the list.

That night I couldn't sleep.

I listened to Salem's heavy breathing and stared up at the ceiling, thinking over everything that had happened today. Clay's strange behaviour this morning after he met Salem. The text. His refusal to take me back to his apartment.

Could they all be related? Why would he be so upset over meeting Salem? What had she said to him?

Then there was Salem…why didn't she tell me she'd already met Clay? Why did she get so defensive when I asked her about it? I turned my head and watched her chest rising and falling as she breathed, her long hair splayed across the pillow looking as dark as blood in the dim light.

I thought my life couldn't get better when Salem returned. Having Clay and Salem felt like my heart could barely contain the love I now had. So why did it feel like things were only just beginning to crack apart?

Why did it feel like both Clay and Salem were keeping things from me?

* * *

Salem was waiting for me in the bedroom when I got out of the bathroom.

"Hey," she said.

I tugged the knot on my bathrobe tighter around me. "Hey."

She broke eye contact. "Sorry I didn't tell you about meeting loverb– I mean, Clay."

"It's okay."

"Sorry, for…being weird lately. I know it must be hard for you to have me waltz back into your life like this, disrupting your plans…"

"Salem," I walked over to the bed and sat next to her. "You are not a disruption."

"Yes, I am."

"Yes, you are." Her mouth parted in a mild shock. "But," I continued, "I wouldn't have it any other way."

"Really?"

"Really."

She lunged at me, wrapping her arms around me. I hugged her, relishing the feel of her solid body under my arms. All those times in the last three years I thought I had seen her and it turned out it had just been a ghost in my mind. But now she was really here.

I sighed happily. These were just teething problems that Salem and Clay and I were going through. Soon the pieces would fall into place and we would all figure out how to live with each other.

"Let's go away," she said in my ear.

"What?" That was not what I had in mind. I pulled back to look at her.

"Yeah, let's you and me just go. Let's just pack up your car and drive away."

"Go where?" I pulled myself out of her grasp. "For how long?"

"Anywhere. Just away from here. And never come back. We can start over somewhere else."

"I can't just leave."

"You can. We can. Let's leave now. Right now." She stood, pulling at my arms, trying to drag me up to my feet.

I struggled against her. "No, I can't. I have a job here—"

She snorted. "You can't really tell me that selling dildos is a burgeoning *career* for you?"

"I can't just leave my job."

"You don't even have a job contract. You don't owe your boss anything."

"I won't let Flick down. She's my friend."

"Please. If she needed to get rid of staff don't you think you would be the first to go?"

"She wouldn't do that to me."

Salem growled. "That's beside the point. I'm your sister. I need you. You don't need anyone but me."

"I don't have enough money to just go."

"Don't lie to me. If I know you, you'll have plenty saved."

She did know me. When we were kids, I was the one who saved my shiny dollars to slip into my piggybank, a solemn red telephone box like the ones they had in England where Mama originally came from. Our grandmother had sent it, apparently. I hadn't known much about her.

"Come on, Rosey," Salem said, her eyes glassy, "come with me. I need you. I can't stay here. But I can't go without you."

"But I have a life here…" I trailed off as guilt wrapped its hands around my neck. This was the issue, wasn't it? What was more important to me: what she wanted or what I wanted?

"It's because of *him,* isn't it? You'd rather stay here with some guy than to be with your sister."

"No, that's not−"

"Don't lie to me. It's the truth. You're willing to throw me away for him." She paced my bedroom, her arms lashing out as she spoke.

I didn't answer. How could I honestly deny it? Out of everything that was keeping me here, it was Clay's face that shone the brightest.

"You barely know him, Aria. You don't even realise all the things he's hiding−" She pulled up short.

My scalp began to prickle. "What things? What are you talking about?"

"Things. Men are always hiding things."

"Clay's not hiding anything." But even as I said it, I felt like I knew I was lying.

Salem gripped my hands in hers, her eyes shining with fear. "Please Aria, he's here," she lowered her voice. "He's found us… me."

I glanced around us as if we were being watched. My stomach knotted. "Who's found you?"

Salem's eyes darted about her. "He's back. He's back. Bad bad bad. Back."

My father's face rose up from the inky darkness of the recesses of my mind, from the place I had shoved him and all the memories of him. His deep-set eyes like wells, smudged with purple shadows, his gruff unshaven jaw, the smell of whiskey and of body odour. I shuddered as a thunder of fear rocked through my body. I thought I had managed to…not forget, I'd never forget, but I thought that I'd managed to keep him away from my mind.

He won't leave us alone, Rosey. Not ever.

"But he's…dead. He can't hurt…" I trailed off, realising how much that was a lie. Can't hurt us anymore? Can't hurt her? Lies. He was still hurting her. His memories still affected her, permeating through her like smoke.

She shook her head. "He's not. He's alive and he's found us."

I tried to calm myself. Salem was being paranoid. She was

over-reacting. He was dead. I saw him die. No one had found us. "Salem, please calm down. You're scaring me."

"He could be watching right now."

I glanced over to the window. The curtains were open. Anyone could see us from the street. The hairs rose on the back of my neck.

Don't be stupid. No one was watching us. He was dead. But I'd feel better if I closed the curtains. I moved towards the window.

"No," Salem grabbed my arm, yanking me back. "You can't go near there. He's watching, outside."

"Oh, Salem…" I put my arms around my sister. Her cold, thin fingers curled around my back, chilling me to my core, but I didn't remove them. I would share my warmth with her. It was the least I could do.

I squeezed my eyes shut as I held onto the pieces of my other half as if I could hold her together. I had to find a way to help her, to save her. If I could have spared her… *You could have. But instead you were a coward and allowed* her *to do all the protecting.*

Her body was tense, tight like a coil wound up all the way. She shook with so much tension, but she didn't cry. She never cried. Not even when…

Salem, I sob-whispered. What do I do?

Don't watch.

I watched her lashes flutter as she squeezed her eyes tightly as if she were dreaming something horrible. What might she be remembering? I shuddered to imagine.

"You have to come with me," I heard in my ear, her voice hard as stone. "You *owe* me."

You owe me.

Three words that would haunt me for the rest of my life. Guilt stabbed me rapidly across my chest like a series of shotgun blasts, tearing holes in my soul.

She was right.

How could I put my life over Salem's? Not when she had put her life over mine. I owed her. She gave up *so* much for me. And now it was time for me to do the same.

But the thought of leaving Clay, of never seeing him again ripped through my heart, tearing it into shreds.

You owe me.

I had to say yes to Salem. I had to leave with her, even if it hurt me. I had to put her needs first for once, and if she needed to leave Mirage Falls, then I had to leave too. No matter the cost.

I felt my life crack apart; into the life I could have had and this new life I would soon depart from. My heart wailed silently for the loss of what would have been.

But I owed her. I had to leave with her.

I hung my head and accepted it with a nod. "Okay. We'll go."

Her face radiated with a wide smile. "You won't regret this. It'll be like it used to be. Just you and me." She hugged me again, so hard I almost couldn't breathe. Or perhaps I couldn't breathe because I was already mourning Clay. I knew that when I left with Salem, it would be Clay's ghost that would haunt me from then on. "I have to tell Clay."

She pulled back suddenly, her face all hard lines and marble. "You can't tell Clay."

"Why?"

"He'll try and stop you "

"I can't just leave without letting him know."

"You can call him to tell him that you've gone once we've stopped somewhere."

I couldn't leave without letting Clay know. It would kill him if I just disappeared. It almost killed me when Salem just left – no goodbyes, no note, nothing. But I didn't want to waste time arguing with Salem about this.

"Fine." I pulled myself out of her grasp and turned to walk out of the bedroom.

She followed me. "Where are you going?"

I ignored the guilt as I picked up my key from the kitchen counter. "I just have to run to the Whip & Flick to pick up a few things I left there and my final pay."

"I'll come with you."

"No," I said just a little too sharply. "Flick will think it's weird if you show up. I haven't told her that you're back," I lied. What was another lie between sisters, right? "I'll be back in thirty minutes, tops," I said and slipped out the front door before she could protest any further. As I closed the door, Salem was watching me from the living room, suspicion clouding her eyes.

* * *

I was waiting on a street several blocks from my apartment, my heart heavy as Clay pulled his familiar red Mustang up beside me. God, I would miss the sight of his showy red car. I would even miss the showy way the engine growled like a lion. Stiff as a wooden doll, I climbed into the passenger side. Tears pricked my eyes the second I smelled his familiar scent. When he pressed his soft, warm mouth to mine I couldn't even bring myself to kiss him back. I would miss his lips so much.

He pulled back, his beautiful features etching with concern. "What's wrong?"

Just say it. Get it over with.

"I…have to leave." I could barely get the words out, my heart hung so pained and swollen in my chest that it felt like it was crushing aside my lungs.

"Okay," Clay said. He was taking this well. Too well. "Where are you off to? Like a holiday? How long for?"

He didn't understand.

"No, Clay. I mean, I have to leave for good."

"What?"

"I'm sorry."

His jaw twitched. "When are you leaving?"

"Now."

Anger began to seep into his face, pinching his mouth, crinkling his brows. "Why? What's going on?"

"Salem needs me."

"Salem," he spat out like he hated the name. "How did *she* convince you to leave?"

"She told me that if I didn't go with her, I'd lose her."

"So you chose her."

"I'm sorry, Clay. I'm so sorry. I want to choose you both. But you don't understand. I can't let her down." Not again.

"What do you do when someone gives you an ultimatum?

114

Sticks a gun to your head and makes you choose?"

"What?"

"You refuse to bend. You push back. You find another way. You take that gun off him and put it back in his face. But you do not give in to demands."

"I'm sorry, Clay. I have to go."

"What does she have over you that you *have* to leave? Huh? I deserve to know, don't I?" He grabbed my shoulders. "Why are you leaving me?"

I cringed at the desperation in his voice. He did deserve to know. But it was her secret. I had to keep it inside.

It's your secret too. He deserves to know. He needs to know…

In my childhood bedroom the door handle turned. I froze. "Salem?" I hissed.

"Get back." She shoved me with her hands farther towards the wall that our double bed abutted against. "He's coming."

I was a coward. So I did what she said.

The door creaked opened. In the dim night, in the streaky moonlight filtering through the blinds of the room, there stood a dark figure, swaying.

I started to panic, my breathing going wild, my lungs constricting, air wheezing through the tightening space in my throat.

I need air. I can't breathe. Where's the surface?

I was shaking so hard that my vision began to shudder. Salem remained on the edge of the bed, a stoic solemn soldier, my soldier, my shield, from the monster who sometimes came to take his sacrifice.

He stumbled in through the door, spinning awkwardly to close it behind him. He always closed it behind him, as if he was afraid that there was someone else in the house who might see what he was here to do.

Here's the truth.

There was no one here.

Nobody was coming.

No one would save us.

Even from here I could smell the reek of alcohol, the stink of him as he fell into the bed against her.

"Go away," Salem cried as he grabbed one of her wrists. Her thin arms punched at him but they just bounced off his big hairy forearms.

In the silver moonlight I saw his wedding ring glint as he slipped his hand down between her skinny legs. "Catherine," he growled low in his throat. Our mother's name. "Sweetheart."

"Get off her. She's not Mama," I yelled from my safety on the other side of the bed, the side that Salem always made me take. He ignored me, like I wasn't even there.

He yanked her pyjama bottoms down, her bird-like hands powerless to stop him and she spat at him using sharp curse-words I had only ever heard adults use when they were mad. He ignored her, like he didn't even hear her.

He climbed on top of her, made a shoving motion with his hips and I heard a small sob come from Salem. It would be the only cry she made as he did what he did.

A low moan came from him. "You're so tight."

The whole room, the walls, the mattress, shook, like the world was falling apart. For Salem, it was.

"Salem," I sob-whispered over his grunting, tears squeezing out of my eyes. "What do I do?"

Her face was turned towards me as he crushed her from above. She reached out from under him, even as he moved and slobbered above her, and she found my hand on the mattress. I gripped onto it, as tightly as I could, the only thing I could do.

"Don't watch."

I shook my head and kept my eyes on her. "I won't leave you alone. Just look at me, Salem. Look at me." I wouldn't look away. She couldn't turn this ugliness off, she was under it, coated with it, being filled with it. I would not leave her alone with him. I was here. Even if the only thing I could do was watch, my witness being the only fragile support I could offer.

I squeezed her hand tighter and tighter, willing her to stay strong, but as they always did, her fingers became looser and looser until they were limp and dead in my palm.

"I'll be okay," she said. Even as the light began to fade in her eyes. Even as the ugliness skinned her raw and embedded her open wounds with dirt so that she would never be able to get it out. And when her skin would close over, it would become a part of her. "One day, it'll stop. One day soon."

That was a lie.

And we both knew it.

When I finished talking, the air in the car was thick with an invisible fog. I played with the fringe of my shirt until I could stand the silence no more. I looked up. "Say something."

Clay just stared at me, a wild anger burning out from his eyes. The next few words were spoken with venom and ice. "I'll kill him."

I shook my head, the last shards of that memory dropping like stones. "He's already dead."

"I hope he suffered before he died."

I swallowed, hard. "I don't know," I lied.

"Aria," he spoke my name with anguish, anger slipping from his features as they twisted into pain, "I'm so sorry." Over the console he pulled me into his arms. I didn't care that the gearstick was digging into my side; I pressed my nose into his shirt and breathed him in, letting the familiar feeling of his warmth and his body soothe me. It had been the first time I had ever told anyone else about what had happened to Salem when we were kids.

"It was a long time ago," I said woodenly.

Clay pulled back to look at me. "That is a horrible thing that happened to your sister. A fucking horrible, disgusting thing. But why does she have to leave? Why do you?"

"She needs me."

"You haven't answered my question. Why does *she* need to leave Mirage Falls?"

"Because…" The car filled with silence.

"Aria, you can't let her uproot your life based on nothing."

"It's not nothing."

"Please," he grabbed my hands in his, his voice and eyes now pleading. "Don't leave."

"I have to go," I said, limply. "I owe her."

Clay's lips pressed together, his face growing hard. "Is that what she told you?"

I said nothing. Somehow my silence felt like a betrayal to Salem.

"She's trying to manipulate you."

I felt as if he had slapped me, my mind whirring over my conversation earlier with Salem. "No…" Was Clay right? Had Salem manipulated me into saying yes to leaving? Had I just done what I had always done and followed her with whatever crazy plan she came up with?

You have to do this for me. You owe me.

I shook my head. I had to get out of this car before Clay convinced me to stay. God, how I wanted to stay.

But he grabbed onto me, his hold now desperate. I tried to push him away, but there was no fight in my hands. I was too busy fighting against my heart that was raging against me to stay, stay here in Clay's arms, to stay here where I belonged. "Clay, please, let me go."

"I love you. I'm not letting you go. I'm not letting her take you away from me."

"I can't let her leave me behind." Not again. Not again. I can't be left behind again.

"She won't leave if you don't. Salem needs help. You've even admitted it yourself. But you need help to help her. You need to be here, with Flick, with your job, with your life, with me… If you go with her, you'll lose yourself. Then you'll never be able to help her."

"I can't be so selfish. I can't just think of myself."

"You're not being selfish. You can't possibley help her if you don't have these things for yourself." He grabbed my hands. "You can't make someone better by loving them." He formed our hands into a cup. "You need to fill yourself up first, before you can let who you are spill out onto others. You can only help if *they* want help. I know…" he trailed off.

I stared at the cup of my hands, his hands around them. I saw water filling up into my palms, spilling over and over until it made a lake. *Watch me, watch me.* Suddenly I was a little girl again sitting on the banks crouched in a shivering ball waiting for Salem to emerge from the surface.

Don't spend your life watching from the edge, Aria. Life starts in the deep end. Then I was leaping into the water to join Clay, flying through the air like a bird.

And I realised…

With Salem I could never go in the water. With Salem I was stuck on the edge, just watching her. With Salem I became…less so she could always be…more.

But I had jumped in when I was with Clay. I chose that. He made me braver. He made me…more.

I didn't want to go back to the way things were. I liked who I was becoming. I liked who I was with Clay.

He threaded his fingers in between mine and the water of the lake faded away. "Salem won't leave if you don't. She's the one who needs you. She needs to stop running. You both need to stop and deal with it. We can deal with it together."

"I don't know how."

"I know a therapist. She can help you. She can help you help Salem. That's what you really want, don't you? To help her?"

"She'd never go to therapy."

"You have to make her. For her own good."

"I can't…you don't know Salem."

"You haven't even tried." His hands came up around my face. "Try…for me."

For him. I'd do anything for him. In the last few months Clay had become my best friend and my lifeline. I couldn't be without him. But I couldn't be without Salem. I could only hope that he was right and that Salem wouldn't leave without me. "She'll hate me."

"She'll never be able to hate you. She loves you more than anything. That's why she protected you. That's why she's still trying to protect you."

This was true. Whatever Salem did, it was to protect me. She hated Clay because she was protective of me. All this, he just seemed to understand.

"I love you. I'll never stop." Clay's hands gripped the sides of my face. "If you tell me you don't feel the same, I'll let you go."

"Clay−"

"Do you love me?" He peered at me. "I asked you once before but then I changed my mind and I told you I didn't want an answer. Today, I want that answer."

I licked my lips, which had gone dry. I loved him. Say it.

"Aria?"

Say it.

"Aria, I'm not letting you out of this car until−"

"I love you," tumbled out. I took a deep breath and I said it again, this time making sure that every word was clear.

A grin stretched across his lips, his dimple appearing on his cheek. He looked almost triumphant.

"What?" I asked.

"I told you I'd get you to admit how much you wanted me."

I rolled my eyes and tried to shove him away.

He pulled me in close and his face became serious again. "You tell Salem that if she ever takes you away from me, I'll come for you. I'll find you. No matter where you go, I'll find you."

Before I could say anything more he crushed his lips against mine and I let go of my jumble of thoughts. His lips were firm, his tongue possessive, claiming my mouth. My hands found his hair and his neck as I clawed at him to get closer, his hands shifting down my side and to my thigh. Then I was moving, being lifted, up and over and across the gearstick and God knows how he managed it but he pulled me across his lap so my knees were on either side, my skirt pushing partway up my thighs, our mouths still locked. My ass hit the steering wheel, causing a sharp beep to sound.

One part of my brain screamed at me that we were in public, that people would see, that the loud beep would cause all the street residents to push aside the curtains or venetian blinds and check out the source of the noise. But the larger part of me − the part that had lain dormant for far too long − just didn't give a damn. There was fire coursing through my veins from his lips, from his tongue, from his thick hardness pressed up against the very sensitive part of me, separated only by my underwear and his jeans. All I wanted was to press as much of my body against his naked skin.

I reached down for the hem of his shirt and grabbed it, my

knuckles dragging against his hard abdominals. He groaned underneath me and a feeling of power seared through my body. I felt larger, more powerful, and sexier than I had ever felt in my life. This feeling was addicting. I wanted more. I wanted him. All of him. Now.

Before I could pull his shirt all the way up his hands came down on mine. He broke his mouth away from mine. "Wait," his breath heaved in and around my mouth.

I searched his eyes. What was wrong? "What is it?"

"We're in a car in the middle of the street, and it's still daylight."

"So?" I lunged for him, desperate for the taste of his lips again.

He laughed as he turned his head, keeping his mouth from mine. "What happened to the Aria who didn't even want to dance in public?"

I sat back on his thighs and considered this. What happened to that Aria? She got sick of being invisible. Because of you, she wants to be more, to have more. "You corrupted her. This is your fault. Accept the responsibility and deal with the consequences." I leaned down to him again. Before I could catch his lips, he slipped his fingers in between us so our mouths were stuck on either side of these fleshy bars.

He chuckled. "You're adorable. Come on. Let me take you home."

Home? My jaw stung. Didn't he want to take things further? Shouldn't he be trying? I mean all men wanted...*more*, didn't they?

"Why don't you take me to yours instead?"

"It's not a good time right now."

I pulled back and stared at him. His eyes found mine but they looked away, then looked down. There was a crease between his eyebrows, just enough to know that there was something he was worried about. What could he be worried about?

"Do you have webbed feet?" I blurted out.

He flinched, then stared at me before laughing. "No. Why would you ask that?"

I frowned. No webbed feet. "Are you one of those guys who

likes to…beat their girlfriend during sex?"

Now he just looked horrified. "God no. Aria, what the hell are these questions?"

"I'm just trying to figure out why you stopped. I mean, we were kissing and you," I made a motion down to the bulge in his pants, "and I…" my hand flailed at myself and I flushed. "I'm… you know."

He raised an eyebrow, a smirk beginning to pull at his handsome features. "No, Aria. I *don't* know."

"Don't make me say it."

"Why, Aria, I don't know what you're talking about."

I almost rolled my eyes. He was going to make me say it.

"I'm…" I leaned in and whispered something.

"I can't hear you." I could hear the amusement in his voice.

For goodness sakes. "I'm wet, dammit."

Before I could move I felt Clay's hand travelling up my skirt to the top of my thigh. His fingers traced the edge of my panties before his thumb took a long slow brush right across the centre of me. All breath left my lungs. Stars twinkled before my eyes like I'd been hit in the head. Hard.

He hummed in my ear. I realised, sometime in the last few seconds, I'd fallen against him. "Appears that you are…wet." He pulled his hand out from my skirt and it settled on my hip.

I let out a whimper. "Why would you stop?"

He didn't answer.

A startling cold realisation settled in my belly, dousing the fire inside me. "It's me."

"It's not you," he said quickly. A little too quickly.

"It *is* me," I whispered, feeling like he had cut out a hole in my chest.

"It's not you…"

"Is it because I'm a virgin?"

"No…well, yes, a little."

"You don't think I'll be any good?"

His mouth dropped open. "Jesus, no. Aria, being with you that way would be the most amazing thing in the world."

"But you don't want to do it?" I squeaked out.

"Of course I do." He grabbed my hand and pressed it to his erection, tugging me towards him with his other arm so that my hand was trapped between us. At my touch he grew even harder. "Do I need to explain what that is?"

"I know what that is. I want you. You want me. Why won't you want to take me to yours?"

"It's better if we wait."

"Wait for what?"

"I want to do this right for once. I want to take it slow. I want to make every moment for you perfect."

"It already is."

He kissed my forehead and pulled my hand off him. "Come on, let me take you home. Salem will be waiting for you. And you need to tell her that you're not leaving."

I sighed. He was right. Salem was at home waiting for me. I said I would only be thirty minutes. How long had it been now? Probably longer than that. "Fine. But this," I motioned between our bodies, "isn't over, Clay Jagger."

The lascivious look that he gave me almost had me changing my mind about going home. "Not by a long shot."

Chapter Eight

I walked from Clay's car like I was being led to a firing range. When I entered the apartment, Salem was waiting for me in the living room, her arms crossed over her chest. "I know where you've been," she said before I could say anything. She scowled at me, her eyes hardened steel. "I saw you."

"You followed me?"

"You lied to me. You said you were just going to Flick's."

I inhaled and exhaled. This conversation wasn't going well already. I needed to focus on what was important for me to say. "I wasn't going to leave without saying goodbye to Clay. I know how it feels when someone you love just disappears without a word. He deserved more than that."

Her eyes narrowed. "So that's it then, huh? You're siding with him?"

I licked my lips. "It's not about sides."

"It is about sides. It's about him or me, and you chose him. What happened to choosing me? Choosing us?"

"It's not about choosing sides," I said firmly, and I shifted my feet a little wider on the carpet as if it might anchor me to the ground.

I heard Clay's voice. *You refuse to bend. You push back. You find another way. You take that gun off him and put it back in his face. But you do not give in to demands.*

"He is hiding things from you."

"Jesus Christ, Salem. Stop saying that. You have no proof of–"

"Did he tell you he's seeing a shrink?"

"I know a therapist. She can help you. She can help you help Salem." Clay didn't tell me he was *seeing* this shrink. What for? "How do you know that?"

"I saw him going into his appointment. I just happened to be driving past."

"You have a car?"

"I was in your car."

"You took my car without asking?"

She made a face. "Since when do I have to ask to borrow your things? Anyway, I saw him when I drove past. I parked. Waited for him to come out, then I went to see for myself. He's been visiting someone called Dr Bing."

"So?" I thought about the darkness that sometimes seemed to drape around Clay's shoulders. "Lots of people see therapists these days."

"Only psychopaths need shrinks. He's dangerous."

I swallowed, shoving away her implications. "Salem, you're being ridiculous. Clay isn't a psychopath. And he isn't dangerous."

"How do you know?"

"You're just making wild accusations about him to try and get me to leave with you."

She began to pace, her movements twitchy and agitated, her voice trembling. "How could you do this to me?"

"I'm not doing anything *to* you. I'm giving you a choice. You can leave. Or you can stay here with me. I hope you stay. I want you to stay."

She halted, glaring at me. "You selfish little bitch. You know I can't leave without you."

Her words stung but I tried to ignore them. "Salem, please, stay here with me. Let's make a life for ourselves here."

"You might have a life here. But I don't."

"And what do you hope to gain if we left? I'm tired of running, Salem. I'm so tired of running. We can't outrun this."

"You promised me. You *owe* me."

Guilt lashed my insides. I did owe her. But giving her exactly what she wanted was not the way to help her. I owed it to her to try and get help for her. "Salem, I want to help you. I can help you if you let me. *We* can get you help. Clay knows someone who can help you. I'll go with you. We can face this together."

"You don't know what you're doing. You don't know *anything*." The hurt in her voice as she screamed at me was enough to shatter my heart for her.

But I had to stay strong. I had to stay strong for us. This was the best thing for *us*.

Her shaking finger came up to point at me. "You'll regret this. You'll regret all if it." She rammed my shoulder as she shoved past me.

"Salem!"

The front door slammed behind me and she was gone.

I fought the urge to run after her. She just needed some time to calm down. She wouldn't leave. All of her stuff was here. She'd have to come back. She'd always come back to me. Right?

* * *

It was a few days later when I opened the door to my apartment that I saw her sitting on the couch. My body flooded with relief. And yet my muscles were all tense, ready for the next round of our fight. We had never fought like this before. Only because I always used to give in to her.

I knew instinctively this would be a long battle, both of us tearing pieces off each other before one of us gave in. I would not give in this time.

I forced myself to step inside the apartment even though a large part of me wanted to run.

She sat up straighter when she saw me. "Hey."

"Hey," I replied, cautiously.

"You look like shit."

"I've barely slept."

"How was work?"

I stared at Salem from my doorway for a second. I kicked the door closed behind me and dropped my bag and keys on the kitchen counter. My arms cross over my chest like a shield. "Really?"

"What?" she asked, her eyes going wide with feigned innocence.

"You're going to just pretend that nothing happened? You're going to act like you didn't just blow out of here days ago leaving me to worry sick about where the hell you went."

She stood up and her arms crossed over her chest as she mirrored me. "Thought you wouldn't care where I went. You were perfectly happy to give me up for some *guy*."

I squeezed my eyes shut and rubbed my eyes. Every night I had slept alone in that cold bed, staying up, willing to hear her key in the lock, signalling that she was home. Now that she was here…

A vein throbbed in my temple. I needed an aspirin.

I heard her walk towards me. When I opened my eyes she stopped, metres from me.

"Shit," she muttered. For once in her life, Salem actually looked…uncertain. "I didn't come back to start another fight."

"Well done. You managed it anyway."

"I came back to say sorry. You were right. I…I shouldn't have run out without telling you where I've been."

Well, I'll be damned. I think this might be the first time Salem actually admitted that she was wrong. "Don't do it again."

"I won't."

"FYI, you suck at apologies."

"I know. I'm not used to giving them. Just like…just like I'm just not used to sharing you. That's something I guess I'm going to have to learn now that loverb–, I mean, Clay is here to stay."

My stomach panged with sympathy. This wouldn't be easy on Salem. I don't know how I would have reacted if I had found her and she had someone else as important to her in her life. I stepped across the divide between us and pulled her into a hug, squeezing her to me. "I'm glad you're home," I whispered in her ear.

She squeezed me back.

When we pulled apart she shot me a hopeful smile. "Have you got plans this afternoon?"

"No. Clay has a deadline so he's busy working."

Salem nodded her head, slowly. "So we can do something, you and I?"

Maybe things would start to get better for Salem and Clay and me? Maybe the three of us could finally learn to coexist? "Sure. What do you want to do?"

A slow smile began to creep across Salem's face. "Let's go for a drive."

"Where are we going?" I asked Salem as she directed me off the highway and into the nearby town of Noosa Heads.

She lounged in the passenger seat, her black Doc Martens on the dashboard. "You'll see."

She gave me more directions. We drove farther into the town until we ended up driving through a leafy residential suburb, built up of modern-looking townhouses and low-level apartments, all with large balconies and decks to take advantage of the great weather and sea air.

"Pull up over here."

I did so, put the car into park and turned off the engine. Salem pulled her legs off the dashboard and sat up. But she didn't get out.

Her fingers drummed on the console as she stared out my window and across the street. I turned my head but couldn't tell what she was looking for. "What are we doing here?"

"It's a nice area," she replied, still looking out beyond my shoulder. "Don't you like this area?"

I frowned. "Sure. It's a nice area. Do you want to go for a walk here?"

"No."

"Then what—"

"Just wait."

Salem was being weird.

Before I could respond again she straightened up and pointed over my shoulder. "There."

I turned in my seat. I had to blink several times to be sure my vision wasn't betraying me. Across the street Clay had stepped out from inside one of the townhouses. What was he doing here? I thought he had a deadline.

He moved aside and I could see that a slim blonde woman was holding back the red front door he had just come out of. She beamed at him as he turned back to speak to her.

"I thought you should know," Salem's voice came from behind me, a smugness to her tone, "Clay comes here when he tells you he's working on a deadline. That gorgeous blonde always answers the door and he always stays in there with her for several hours."

I watched, my vision shaking, my hand to my throat, as Clay leaned in to embrace her.

Her voice was so close it sounded like it was coming from inside my head. "He's cheating on you."

Chapter Nine

I kicked the car door open and climbed out. Salem didn't try to stop me.

I was angry. I was numb. I just couldn't believe that Clay could cheat on me. I knew the way he looked at me, the way he touched me. But there he was across the street pulling away from the arms of another woman, a woman who now disappeared behind a blood-red door. Seeing is believing.

I slammed the door behind me, barely looking both ways before darting across the street.

Clay was halfway down the stairs when he saw me, the surprise evident in his widening eyes. "Aria? What are you doing here?" We met on the sidewalk. He didn't try to touch me, in fact he just stared at me. More evidence of his guilt.

"You bastard." I gripped my hands into fists so tightly that my fingernails dug into my palms. "You said you were working."

The only sign that he was uncomfortable was a throat swallow. "I was. What are you doing here?"

"Salem brought me here."

His mouth twisted into a snarl. "Salem," he said her name with venom. "I should have known."

My eyes darted to the townhouse door, the number 29 on the front in brass numbers.

"It's not what you think."

"Really? That blonde woman at the door isn't your other

girlfriend?"

"No."

"Then who is she?"

"She's an employee."

I laughed. Was he really trying to pull that on me? "You really expect me to believe that?"

"It's true."

"What does she do for you then? As an employee?"

"Quite frankly, that's none of your business. All you need to know is that I'm not, nor have I ever, or will I ever sleep with her."

My mouth dropped open. I had never heard such a frosty tone coming from Clay. He had never ever spoken to me that way. If I even believed that he wasn't sleeping with her, I knew he was still hiding something. *Can you live with any more secrets?*

"If you won't tell me the truth," I swallowed, "we have nothing more to say to each other." I turned to leave, tears already pooling in my eyes.

Clay grabbed my arm and spun me back. His tone was softer now. "Stop, Aria. My relationship with Tenielle is strictly professional. I swear, it has nothing to do with you and me."

Tenielle. The stupid bitch. I'll kill her. "That's where you're wrong, Clay. If it has something to do with you then it has everything to do with me. This won't work if we won't share all of who we are, good and bad."

I felt a stab in my gut. You hypocrite. If you demand his secrets, then you have to give him all of yours.

They're not just *my* secrets. They're Salem's too.

Clay stared at me for a long moment, his brows furrowed with resigned anger. "You want to know all of it? Fine." He grabbed my arm and pulled me up the stairs behind him.

"What are you doing?"

He didn't answer. When we reached the door he stabbed the doorbell with his finger, the buzzing echoing through the inside of the townhouse.

Salem. I almost forgot about Salem. I turned my head towards the car still parked across the road. But Salem was nowhere to be seen.

I turned back when I heard the sound of heels clacking on the ground from behind the door.

"Aria," Clay spoke in a low menacing tone, "I was going to bring you here when I was ready. But once again you seem keen to push me into doing things I'm not ready to do."

My stomach tightened. What had I done?

The door flew open. There stood the most beautiful blonde woman I had ever seen, sapphire blue eyes and hair of golden threads, pulled back in a chignon, her long elegant neck on display. Her pouty lips flew into a smile when she saw Clay and my heart stabbed. "Clay, did you forget something?" She spotted me behind Clay, one step down. Her thick, dark lashes fluttered as she took me in. "Who's this?"

"This is Aria."

Her mouth widened to an O. Her large blue eyes opened to saucers as they went from me to Clay then back to me. "Oh, wow. Aria. This is Aria. I didn't know she was coming."

"Neither did I," Clay said coldly. "Can we come in?"

The woman nodded and stepped aside. As she pulled open the door I saw a flash of something on her hand. A ring. An engagement ring.

Were they engaged? Did that make *me* the other woman?

My head spun. But I refused to entertain any more thoughts about that damn ring. No assumptions, Aria. Assumptions are what got you into this mess. Just keep your head about you until you know everything.

Clay walked in first without looking back at me. Before I could follow, the woman stopped me with a hand on my arm. "I'm Tenielle, by the way."

"Aria. But then *you* already knew that."

She winced, before sending me what I guessed to be an apologetic look. "You guys should talk. Go on." She pointed to where Clay was walking down the hallway.

Yes, it was certainly time to speak to Clay.

Tenielle disappeared and I was left to face Clay alone. He stood at a doorway, his hand on the handle. He glanced at me as I approached through this thin corridor. So far the other doors were shut and the bright ceiling light bounced off the white hallway walls, making this place feel so sterile and empty. There were no pictures on the walls, no paintings, nothing to show any character of the people who lived here. Did Tenielle live here? Who was she?

I stopped in front of Clay. He looked so torn. So sad and conflicted. I wanted to touch him but I wasn't sure I should.

"I lied to you." He swallowed, pausing long enough for my heart to jam up into my throat. "A harmless lie in my opinion. I just…wasn't ready to talk about her yet."

Her.

Her.

The woman. The woman he lost? The woman he loved?

Why would Clay be hiding her? Why would he still be visiting her? My heart began a steady increase in pace.

"Before I take you inside to meet her," he said quietly but firmly, "you need to know a few things about her."

He wanted me to *meet* her?

"She suffers from schizophrenia. Do you know what that means?"

Flashes of *Jane Eyre* came into my mind. The crazy woman in the attic. Clay was hiding a wife. He was already married and there's something wrong with her.

This was why he was so hesitant to sleep with me. This was why it always felt like he was holding something back. He had already made a vow to another woman.

I shook my head even as images of wild-haired and spitting patients in white jackets came to mind. I stared at the closed door beyond him. I didn't want to meet her. I wanted to turn and run. Why did Salem have to bring me here?

"Schizophrenia is a brain disease," Clay explained. "It can cause delusions, hallucinations and paranoia as well as a host of other symptoms, but those are the most well known. Medication and therapy can help but there's no cure."

"Do you still love her?" I needed to know.

I didn't want to.

But I had to.

He glared at me, like he was angry that I would even think to ask him that. "Of course I love her. I'll never stop, not even because of what she has. You can't put conditions on love. That's not real love."

I suddenly felt like the floor was swaying under my feet, so I grabbed the wall to hang on to the earth. He loved another woman who was mad. So what was I? Just someone to pass the time? Someone to fill the hole in his life?

"Every person who suffers from schizophrenia is different," Clay continued, oblivious to my struggle to breathe. "She hears voices, mostly. She would hear them and talk back to them. She was depressed most of the time. Sometimes she became paranoid that everyone was laughing at her behind her back. At her worst, she attacked me once because she was convinced that I wasn't her son." He fingered his chest where I knew his scar was.

"Her son?"

He frowned. "Yes. My mother thought I wasn't her son."

She was his mother. She was the woman? Not a wife? My heart felt like it pulled back into my chest.

I'm an idiot. Stupid stupid stupid. "I'm so sorry." I moved closer and placed a hand on his arm. "When did you realise…?"

"In women, symptoms usually develop in their twenties and thirties. She began to show signs of it when I was thirteen, when she was thirty-two. She attacked me when I was eighteen. That's when I knew I had to get her help, professional help. Up until then I had thought that maybe if I loved her enough…she'd get better."

My heart clenched as his face filled with pain. *"You can't make someone better by loving them. I know…"*

"Schizophrenic sufferers get a bad rep in movies and books. Most sufferers can get better with medication, living relatively normal lives. Unfortunately she was one of the unlucky ones who couldn't. She needs twenty-four-hour care to make sure she doesn't harm herself."

"Tenielle is her carer," I realised.

He nodded. "She takes the day shift. Usually she'll call or text me if Mum is having a good day and I'll come out here to spend some time with her while she's coherent."

That explained the random calls or texts that he sometimes got. And why he was so eager to drop me off the other morning.

"She was having a good day, but...I can't guarantee how she'll react to you." Clay turned and he pushed at the handle. Then paused. "You don't have to meet her."

"I want to."

He stared at me for a long time before saying, "Okay, then." He pushed open the door, took my hand and pulled me into the living room behind him.

It was a bright, airy room encased in windows letting in lots of light. The carpet was dark and several armchairs were placed around. The radio was on low.

It was only when we moved around one of the armchairs that I even realised there was another person in here. A woman sat sunken into the armchair, so skinny and weathered that her skin sagged around her. If I calculated right, Clay's mother would be in her mid-forties but she looked much older.

"Tony," her voice warbled and she lifted up her face to squint at Clay as if he were too bright, as bright as the sun, "is that you?"

"Tony is my father," he mouthed to me. "No, Mum, it's me, Clay." He kneeled beside her and took one of her leathered hands in his.

Clay's mother frowned as she stared at him. But the flash of recognition never came across her face. His mother didn't recognise him. I couldn't imagine how that must feel. My heart ached for him. I squeezed Clay's shoulder, just to remind him that I was there and that I was here for him.

"Mum, I'd like you to meet a friend of mine."

Her eyes swung at me. Then widened. "Olivia." The name dropped from her lips with a shudder.

Who was Olivia?

"No. This is Aria. Not Olivia. You haven't met Aria before."

I lifted up my hand to her. "Pleased to meet you, Mrs Jagger."

She stared at my hand as if it were a foreign thing. She frowned, then looked back up to stare into my eyes. She had Clay's eyes and they sparkled with a brewing anger. "How dare you come back here after what you've done."

Clay pushed my outstretched hand down as if he were afraid of his mother. "Mum, it's okay. This is Aria, my girlfriend."

"Get away from my son." Her gaze remained fixed on me even as her hands started to flutter around her face as if she was trying to bat away invisible flies. "Do you know how much he's suffered because of you?"

"I think I should go," I whispered to Clay, my chest hurting from where her words had stabbed me. Clay stared at his mother, a hollowness to his eyes. I slipped my hand into his and tugged him. "Let's go, Clay. Please."

"Get out!" she screamed, her voice going hoarse. "Get out. Get out!"

Tenielle raced into the room to Mrs Jagger's side, murmuring calming things. She was holding a syringe. She shot an apologetic look to Clay and me.

"Sorry, Tenielle." Clay finally snapped out of it and began to turn. "We'll leave."

Clay stormed out of the front door and down the steps with me trailing after him.

"Can you slow down, please? Clay?" I grabbed his arm just as he reached the sidewalk. "Clay—"

"Don't touch me." He yanked his arm from me. "Crazy is contagious, don't you know?" he said, bitterness dripping from his lips.

"Don't talk about yourself that way."

His shoulders dropped and he pressed one hand to his face. "That's why I didn't want you to know about her. That's why…"

At that moment I hated myself for ever getting out of the car and confronting him. "I'm sorry."

"No, I'm sorry." He sighed and finally lifted his eyes towards me. "I'm sorry she reacted that way to you."

"Who's Olivia?"

He flinched and closed his eyes. "Olivia," he breathed around her name. Then he opened them and shrugged. "She's no one."

He was lying. Why was he lying? "She can't be no one."

He shrugged. "She's just an ex of mine."

"Did you—?"

"Let's not talk about her right now, okay? One day, but not today. I don't know why my mother brought her up. It doesn't mean anything. You saw how she is. Sometimes she thinks that I'm my father." He turned his face away, a flush creeping up his neck. He was embarrassed.

I stepped to stand in front of him. "It's okay, Clay."

He winced and I knew he didn't believe me. I tried again to hold his arm but he pulled away.

I grabbed onto his shirt, forcing him to look at me. "Do you hear me? It's okay."

The strong façade that he wore cracked, his eyes misting over. He grabbed me, his arms going around me, crushing me until I almost couldn't breathe, and he pushed his face into my neck like he wanted to disappear. In that moment I knew I was the only thing holding him up.

* * *

"So did you dump him?" Salem stood in my living room that evening as if she had been waiting for me.

I paused for a second in the doorway before I shut it and locked it behind me. I turned to study her. She was wearing the same clothes from earlier but her shoes were off, kicked across the living room carpet. "How did you get home? You left the car with me."

"Who cares how I got home. Did you end things with Clay?"

"No."

"What?" Her voice rang out, shrill in my ears. "But he's—"

"He's not cheating one me."

"He is. I saw that woman—"

"You don't know what you saw." I strode through the living room towards the bathroom. I had to get away from her before I said something I'd regret.

Salem leapt up from the couch and grabbed my arm. "Don't walk away from me."

I yanked my arm from her grasp and turned to glare at her. "I met her. Her name is Tenielle. She's not his other girlfriend."

"And you believed him."

"She's his mother's carer."

That made Salem flinch. "Carer?"

"His mother's not well. She needs twenty-four-hour care. Tenielle is her carer."

She shrank back, her face paling. "I didn't know."

"No, you didn't. And I would appreciate if you kept your nose out from where it doesn't belong." I shoved past her towards the bathroom so I could lock her out.

* * *

"Okay, Aria. That's it. What the hell is up with you today?"

I jolted. I had been so lost in my own world I hadn't noticed Flick sidling up to me as I stood by the back counter. It was the after-lunch lull on my next day of work. No one had come in for a few minutes, giving me too much room to get lost in my thoughts.

"Nothing."

She raised a stern eyebrow. "Don't give me that. Firstly, you came in late and totally flustered. You haven't been late ever since you started here."

"Sorry."

She waved off my apology. "I don't care that you were late. Secondly, you've been somewhere else all day."

"No, I haven't."

"Puh-lease, you put the anal beads back with the vibrating eggs. I know you're inexperienced but I know you know which hole is which."

Oops. "Sorry, I'll fix it up now."

She grabbed my arm to stop me from running off. "I've already fixed it up. What I need you to do now is to spill it. Now."

I glanced around. For the moment there were no customers in the store. Where did I even start with what was bothering me? I wasn't ready to talk to Flick about Salem yet so... "It's Clay."

Flick frowned. She grabbed a huge rubber dildo from the nearest shelf and slapped it against her open palm like she was holding a bat. "Do you need me to break his legs?"

I couldn't help but laugh. "Firstly, I doubt *that* would be enough to break anyone's legs."

"You don't know how deadly I can be with a dick."

"Flick…I don't wanna know. Besides, no leg breaking required." *Not yet*, a cynical voice inside me said. It sounded too much like Salem.

Flick placed the rubber appendage back on the shelf. "So, what's the man doing?"

"It's more what *we're* doing…or not doing…yet. But that I want to…and he wants to…I think."

"Could you possibly repeat that, in English?"

I took a deep breath and recapped the last few times that Clay and I spent together. Every time things got hot and heavy, he pulled away. And he refused to take me back to his place. "I don't think…" God, this was embarrassing.

Flick just waited patiently for me to garner the courage to spit it out.

"I don't think he wants to have sex with me."

"That's ridiculous," she said, flinging her arms into the air. "How could he *not* want to have sex with you? You're hot. Like super-hot. *I* want to have sex with you and I'm not even gay."

I smiled, despite my worry. "Thanks, Flick."

She frowned. "Talk to me, babe."

"I think he's worried because I'm a virgin. Like he might break me if he…"

"Fucks you."

I made a face. "I hate that word."

"And your disdain for cursing might not be helping."

"What's wrong with not liking to curse?"

"Honey, you can't even say the word, how are you expected to ask him to do it to you?"

I gulped. The woman had a point. "What do I do?"

"You need to make him look at you *that* way. You need to make it so he forgets all his hesitation."

"How?"

"I have a plan. But you have to trust me. When I'm done with you, you'll be so freaking seducible, Lord help me, I'll sell this store if he isn't eating out of your lap by the end of the night. Literally."

At the image of Clay kissing me down between my legs, my body burst into flames.

Flick pointed a finger at me. "But first, you have homework."

"Homework?"

"Don't look so terrified. I want you to practice saying 'fuck me' until you can say it without blushing."

I had to *what*?

She raised an eyebrow at me. "Don't argue with me. You can't even think the f-word without your cheeks going red."

"Okay, fine," I muttered.

"There'll be a test next week."

Dear God, I was almost afraid to ask. "And the other part of your great plan?"

"With that one…I'm going to need a little help from my friend, Victoria."

"Victoria?"

"Oh yes, honey." She grinned. "Victoria's Secret."

* * *

"Fuck," I muttered. Hmmm…it didn't seem that bad this time. "Fuck, fuck, fuck."

I had managed to get to a point where my cheeks didn't feel like I'd swallowed too much hot coffee when I said the f-word.

Okay, step one of homework done. Now for the hard bit.

I cleared my throat. "Fuck mmmm."

Dammit.

I tried again. "Fuck mmmm." I couldn't do it. How could I get Clay to do it to me if I couldn't even say it?

"What the hell are you doing?"

I jumped.

Salem was standing at the doorway to my…*our* bedroom. I hadn't heard her come home.

"Nothing." I hid my face as I turned back to my bed and continued folding a few clothes into a bag.

"Sounded like you were practicing how to say 'fuck me'." Her voice sounded amused.

I gritted my teeth. I would never hear the end of this. "So what if I was?"

"Aww, my little girl is finally growing up."

I grabbed a pillow from the bed and threw it at her. She ducked to the side and it went flying into the corridor. "Some things change but you still throw like a girl."

I stuck my tongue out at her.

She laughed. "Real mature, Rosey. So tonight I thought you and me could stay in and watch cartoons, you know, like old times."

Crap. I forgot to tell her about my plans tonight. "Oh, um. I'm actually going out."

There was a flash of disappointment in her eyes but she hid it with a bright, forced smile. "Where you going?" She spotted my bag. "You're going over to Clay's?"

"No. To Flick's place."

She slumped against the frame. "For a sleepover or something? I didn't realise you and your boss were that close."

"I'm just going over there to get ready. Flick and I are heading out to a Latino social at a club in Noosa with Clay and Jed, a guy Flick is seeing."

I saw her eyes darken. "You, loverboy and another couple, having fun out in a club. Well, don't let me stop you."

"You can come if you like," I said without thinking, then chastised myself. I didn't want it to sound like a last minute concession invitation. But that's exactly what it sounded like.

Salem snorted and crossed her arms over her chest. "And be the fifth wheel. No thanks, I'd rather poke my eyes out with bamboo sticks. I'll just sit here, home alone on a Saturday night."

Guilt stabbed me in the gut. "Come out with us. Come on, Salem. It'll be fun." I tried to inject some cheer into my voice, but even to me it sounded flat. Truth was, I wasn't a fan of nightclubs and if it weren't for Flick's ambushing Clay that day when he came to pick me up and Clay saying yes, I wouldn't have gone anyway.

"You don't really want me there."

"I do."

"No, you're just asking because you feel sorry for poor little Salem. No man who loves her and no one to keep her company at night. Boo hoo." Her voice rose. She was taking this harder than I expected.

I cringed as I zipped up my bag. "Salem, you know that's not true. I can spend the whole of Sunday afternoon with you. We can watch as many Disney movies as we possibly can and I'll make popcorn. Or we can even have cereal buffet for dinner, remember how you used to love doing those?"

"I'm not twelve anymore," she snapped, causing me to turn towards her. "And you can't just throw a pathetic cereal buffet at me as a consolation prize." Her eyes flared with a bitterness that I couldn't fix. Not without crumbling my world down to fit with hers.

This was the problem. We used to be the same, Salem and I. We used to share everything. Now, I had everything. And she… she still had nothing except for me. And now she had to share me.

"It's not a consolation–"

"Sorry I don't fit into your perfect little world anymore." She turned and fled, her footsteps heavy across my carpet, leaving me stunned. How did this happen? One second we were just talking, the next, she was going ballistic. I heard the front door open and slam, the wood shuddering in its frame.

"Salem!" I yelled out after her. Shit. "Stop." I chased after her, leaving my front door wide open as I tumbled through.

But by the time I had reached the sidewalk, Salem had gone.

Salem hadn't come back by the time I was due to leave for Flick's. I cursed the fact that she didn't have a mobile. Seriously, who doesn't have a mobile these days? I left a note for her asking her to call me on my cell when she got home.

Flick lived a ten-minute walk from my apartment so I didn't bother driving. I was still musing over where I went wrong with Salem when I arrived at her place.

"Welcome to the party!" Flick swung open the door, a

welcome glass of champagne already in her hand.

She was wearing a very short, very tight, black bandage dress that hugged her ample curves like she was a screen goddess, her shapely legs like a fitness magazine model in those towering fuchsia and gold satin pumps. Her thick, wavy hair had been curled into luscious waves that framed her face, highlighting her lightly bronzed cheekbones, not that she needed it. A plum-red lipstick and dark Cleopatra eyes perfected the look.

"Wow," I breathed, my problems momentarily forgotten, "you look like a movie star."

"Really?"

"So hot I'd jump you right now if I were gay and you were gay."

"Puh-lease, you wouldn't jump a puddle if it were in front of you."

I could barely muster a laugh.

Her face dropped. "Girl, you better do something with that frown. That's not something makeup can fix."

"Sorry, Flick." I forced a smile so wide it hurt. "Better?"

She pursed her lips before moving aside to let me in.

Flick lived in a two-story townhouse. It was modern and clean, two bedrooms upstairs. One for her, one for her clothes, she liked to joke. Downstairs were the kitchen, dining and living rooms, which now looked like a bombsite, clothes and shoes littering the floor like shrapnel.

"Flick!" I exclaimed. "I think someone broke into your house and ransacked the place."

"Very funny, wise guy." She shoved a glass of champagne in my hand. "Drink that. Then tell me what's wrong."

"Nothing."

She gave me *the look*. The *I'm going to hound you until you tell me so you better just tell me* look.

I sighed. You couldn't win with Flick when she pulled out *the look*. I've seen silly men try to and it never ended prettily for them.

I pretended to take a tiny sip of champagne just so I didn't look rude and winced as the bubbles tickled my lip. "I had a fight with Salem."

"What about?"

"You. Tonight. Clay."

She nodded, a knowing look coming over her face. I had told her bits and pieces about Salem after the day Clay had accidentally met her. I felt I had to let Flick know my sister was staying at my place, just in case Flick dropped by the apartment – it was her apartment – and Salem happened to be there. I didn't want what happened with Clay and Salem to happen with Flick.

"So Salem's feeling a bit left out. Why didn't you invite her? I'm sure I could have gotten Jed to rustle up a friend for her."

I shook my head. "I did invite her. She went ballistic, calling it a consolation prize, saying that she didn't fit into my life anymore. Then she stormed out and I haven't seen her since."

"She'll get over it."

"I hope so." But something told me that this crack in our relationship was only just starting to widen.

"Well, you can't do anything about it right this minute so just let it go. Time to get you sexified!"

I slid my untouched champagne on the counter before handing over my bag.

Apparently nothing I had brought was sexy enough, so Flick led me upstairs.

"Wow," I breathed as I stared at her spare room, clothes bursting from clothing racks crammed all around the space.

"Yeah," she said, "I ran out of space in my closet so I turned this room into a walk-in."

"What will you do when you get a live-in boyfriend?"

"Easy. He won't need clothes." She winked at me. "Alright, start with this one. And this one. Ooo, and definitely this one." She began to shove a pile of material into my hands. And so the night began.

An hour and a half later, I had been waxed, plucked, moisturised, cleansed, toned, rouged, blushed, filled in, and had been made to try on a hundred different dresses.

Just in time, too, because as I was slipping into a pair of Flick's silver strappy heels (thank God we were the same size) and testing out my first steps in them, a car horn beeped from outside.

Flick and I grabbed our purses and headed out to meet Jed.

Jed was an Italian-Australian whose parents had migrated to Melbourne first then went north in search of warmer weather. He was hot, as I would expect from Flick. With his thickly gelled black hair and a dimple in his chin, he had a John Travolta circa *Grease* vibe going on about him.

He leaned out the window of his dark blue Mercedes. Apparently he was a real estate realtor along the coast selling holiday homes to wealthy folk, hence, the flashy car. "Ladies, you both look beautiful. Every man in that club is going to die of envy when I walk in with the two of you on my arms."

I managed a weak smile.

Flick snorted. "Can I get a pizza to go with all that cheese?"

I introduced myself to him and he eyed me over the rim of his sunglasses, although why he needed sunglasses at night I didn't know.

"Jed, honey, stop checking out my friend."

"You're feisty tonight, babe. I was just saying hello."

I hopped in the backseat as Flick and Jed made out in the front seat and I looked everywhere except at them. I was beginning to understand a little more now why Salem didn't want to come.

Flick and Jed finally broke apart. "And we're off," Flick exclaimed.

* * *

Apparently this club, called Malibu, had valet parking, and apparently our friend Jed knew the bouncer so we strode right up to the front, past the grumbling guys with polished shoes and girls balancing on skyscraper heels. Clay said he'd meet us there.

My phone buzzed just as I was tripping past the burly guards at the front into the small alcove reception area where Jed was paying our entry fee, a red velvet curtain separating us from the club. I wasn't used to this damn tiny clutch purse thing. I dropped my lipstick and keys before I managed to get out my phone. I missed the call. It had been Clay.

Crap. And there were already three previous messages and

three missed calls I somehow missed.

Already inside. This was sent at 7:55 p.m.

You did say 8 p.m. at Malibu's, right? Sent at 8:17 p.m.

Then his latest one, his worry clear. *Aria? Where are you? Are you okay?*

We were almost twenty-five minutes late. Before I could call him back, Flick grabbed my shoulder. Over the rhythmic drumming of the music coming from just past a set of velvet red curtains, I heard her yell, "You ready to rock his world?"

I nodded as I put my phone away. He'd know very soon I was there and I was okay.

Jed and Flick went through the curtains first, leaving me to make my entry all by myself. To one side of the reception there was a thin full-length mirror, which I stopped in front of.

I smoothed down my dress, a pure white body-hugging designer piece to mid-thigh with a sash that went across the front of my breasts, draped over one shoulder and hung down the back to about mid-calf. I fluffed the roots of my hair, which Flick had teased and curled into a wavy flame that swooped across one eye and hung down to the small of my back. The ensemble was topped off by a pair of crystal drop earrings, a matching necklace and a silver clutch and silver strappy heels.

I flushed at the thought of the underwear I was wearing, one of Victoria's, *wink wink*. Flick had made me try on a bazillion sets before sending me home with these 'on the house'. I had tried to pay her but she refused. She had probably already found the cash I had folded and slipped into her purse without her seeing. I already knew I would probably get 'accidentally' overpaid in my next pay.

The set I chose was white Brazilian-cut knickers in a delicate lace with a matching balcony bra, a line of five diamantes dripping elegantly from between the breasts and from the top centre of the panties. I had never owned a pair like it, all of my previous undergarment purchases were designed for comfort and *not* to be seen.

I had never in my life ever been dressed up like this before. I had never had any reason to. My mother wasn't around to teach me how to do makeup or to do my hair. Apart from a little mascara,

I never wore any makeup. Tonight, Flick had painted my eyes dark and sultry and I looked almost sinister with silver highlighting my brow bones and the inner corners of my eyes, making the grey of my eyes pop like gun metal. We didn't have the same complexion, Flick and I, so she didn't have foundation for me. But in all honesty my skin didn't need it. She had dusted my cheeks lightly with pale blush to give me a glow and along my cheekbones 'to make them pop'.

I took a deep breath. My heart began to beat like a small drumroll as if waiting to announce me to the man who was waiting for me on the other side. I felt my phone buzz again. I had to hurry. Clay was already worried.

I slipped my hands in the slit of the velvet curtains, pushed them aside, and stepped through.

The warm air hit me first. I almost choked on the clash of expensive perfumes, musky spice and soft sweet vanillas, and dancing bodies exuding sweat. The music blared a catchy salsa melody of guitars and drums.

I didn't really know what to expect for this Latino social. I had never been to one before but Flick said she went to them all the time. Nightclubs hosting the social would open earlier, at 7 p.m., and play solely Latino music, the focus more on dancing rather than drinking. It was the only reason that Clay agreed to come.

The inside of Malibu was overwhelming. I didn't know where to look. It was an irregularly shaped nightclub dressed in silver and dark fabrics, large flat aquariums were installed as partitions, the shimmering dancing figures moving between the jewel-like fish and swaying coral.

I eyed the crowd, searching, seeking, not really seeing anyone, until my gaze slid onto his familiar figure. Clay Jagger stood some metres away at the bar, running his hands through his hair, messing it up and glaring at his phone. My breath shook in and out between my teeth. My God, he was beautiful. Would there ever be a time when I wouldn't be struck by seeing him? He was clean shaven, his dark hair curling against the collar of the black button-up shirt hugging his thick torso, dark, fitted denim showcasing his powerful thighs. Aggression rolled off him, making him seem almost dangerous.

The other patrons in the bar sensed this too. They left a respectful space around him and yet their heads tilted towards him, their bodies leaning in closer, their eyes stealing glances. All drawn towards him. But he didn't seem to notice.

I strode over to him, trying my damndest to strut with my hips as I'd seen Salem do before. I prayed that I wouldn't fall over in these spindly heels, which seemed to have grown even more precarious in the last five seconds.

I felt my phone buzz but I ignored it. He would see me soon.

He looked up and our eyes locked. He straightened, his elbow slipping off the bar top and his mouth parted. My periphery faded into a blurry smudge of shadows as he became the only object in focus. I found myself moving towards him but I could barely feel my legs.

I stopped right before him. "Hey, hot stuff," I said in my sexiest voice, my hands on my hips. Flick was right. Dressing up like this made me feel powerful and sexy and I loved the way he was looking at me…like he could devour me.

His eyebrows came down over his eyes as a look of anger stole away every lustful sign from his face. His hands gripped my upper arms and he pulled me to him, to hiss in my ear, "What the fuck are *you* doing here?"

What? I tugged against him but it felt like I was fighting against steel chains, his hands were clamped so tight. When I pulled back from his face, his dark eyes were hard as stone.

"Get the hell out of here before–"

"Clay? You're hurting me." I blinked back tears.

Confusion began to creep into his features.

"Please, Clay," I tried again, my voice cracking. "You're scaring me."

"Aria?" His face broke out into a mask of horror. His grip sprang open from my arms. Air drew sharply into my lungs and tears pricked at my eyes as I rubbed the band of red heat where his hand had been. "Oh my God," he breathed. "I didn't realise it was you."

I inhaled sharply. "You thought I was Salem?"

He nodded, his top teeth cutting into his bottom lip as he stared at me.

Salem. He'd thought I was Salem. "Why did you think I was her?"

"You weren't answering your cell. The way you're dressed… This isn't you."

Because only wild, crazy Salem would wear something as daring as this. Quiet, timid little Aria wouldn't. Why couldn't I wear this? Why couldn't I be wild and sexy for once? "And you thought you had a right to speak to Salem that way?"

His mouth pressed together. "I won't apologise for speaking to *her* that way."

"How dare you."

"If you only knew…" he muttered.

"Knew what?" I demanded. He shook his head. I grabbed his upper arm and tried again. "Don't keep things from me. The secrets you keep will just grow and fester between us. *They* will be the things to end us, not Salem."

His eyes softened and he opened his mouth to speak.

"There you guys are." I recognised Flick's voice. I turned to face her and saw the moment when she realised that we were in the middle of something. Her eyes flicked back and forth between Clay and me. "I, er…Jed's found us a booth. But you can join us later if you want."

"No," Clay said, his voice returning to its usual smooth, deep cadence, as if nothing was wrong. "Lead the way."

Flick hesitated for just a second, her eyes pinned me in a question, before she spun. "Follow me."

Clay placed his hand on my lower back. Our eyes locked for a second and a silent conversation happened through our looks.

This isn't over, Clay Jagger.

I know. Not by a long shot.

I gave him one more meaningful look before I followed Flick through the club.

The booth was a clamshell of dark brown leather curled around a pearly coloured marble table. Ornamented bars twisting from the top of the seating up to the ceiling looked like black seaweed.

I slipped in next to Flick and Clay slid in beside me.

Introductions were made between Clay and Jed, and they stretched their hands to shake across the table.

"What do you think, Clay?" said Jed as he leaned back into the couch and stretched out his arm across the back of the booth around Flick. "You and I have scored ourselves the two most beautiful women in here."

Clay stared at Jed for a moment, his eyes giving away nothing, before his gaze shifted to me. "Indeed."

"You guys want a drink?" Jed called over the music.

"Just a soda." Clay didn't break eye contact with me, a low flame seeming to roll off him, heating me. His eyebrow lifted up. "Do *you* want something?"

Me. Right. What was his problem anyway? I turned my head, my cheeks flaming, and smiled at Jed. "Just a tonic water with lime, please?"

"Neither of you want anything to drink?"

"No. Thanks." We both said together. I could still feel Clay's eyes on me.

Jed shrugged. "Alright."

"Why don't you drink?" Clay asked.

I snapped my head around to look at him. "Why don't you drink?"

"I asked first."

I shook my head. "See, it sucks when people keep answers from you, doesn't it?"

I matched his glare, the rest of the club disappearing into a grainy fuzz.

"I, um," I heard Flick's voice through the muffle, "I think I'll go and help Jed."

Neither Clay nor I moved an inch while she scooted out of the booth, her legs sliding against the leather and making it vibrate.

"Aria, this is not the time or the place for the explanation you need."

"When is?"

He sighed as if everything had just gotten too heavy to hold. "Soon. When we're alone. When we don't have the Gypsy Kings blaring over the loudspeakers and those damn lights shining in my face every two seconds. Now, why don't you drink?"

"Will you answer if I answer?"

He nodded.

"I don't drink…" I swallowed, my throat suddenly closing up and surprising me. I didn't think after all these years it would affect me like this. "My father started to drink. After my mother died. He wasn't a nice person when he drank. I don't like it. I don't like the smell of it. I don't like the taste of it. I don't like what it does…to men."

Clay's eyes widened a little, then his jaw softened. He took one of my hands in his large hands. "That's understandable," he said simply.

I swallowed away a knot. "Why don't you drink?"

Something passed over his eyes but it was gone before I could figure out what it was. "I just don't."

He was lying.

"I told you why I don't drink."

"I just don't like the taste."

"Bullshit."

He flinched. Before I could say anything more, Jed and Flick returned with the first round of drinks.

"Yay," said Flick, as she sipped her pink cocktail. "Isn't this fun?"

Yeah. Fun. I gripped the cold glass, pushed forward a smile and bit at the straw with my teeth.

Clay leaned back against the booth, fisting his glass. He had shifted away so he wasn't touching me anymore and my body felt lost. He ignored me as he gulped down half of his soda in one go, staring out to the crowded dance floor.

Flick caught my eye and gave me a look like, *are you okay?*

I shrugged.

Jed hooked his arm around Flick's neck and began to whisper things in her ear that made her eyes widen and throaty giggles escape from her pouty lips. Jed wanted Flick. I could tell.

Their hands were all over each other. He would probably make their excuses and head home soon. Why wasn't Clay doing that to me? Wasn't I sexy? Didn't he want me?

But Clay was tearing a cardboard coaster into pieces instead of tearing clothes off me. And I was sitting there staring with jealousy at the dance floor, at the gyrating, wriggling sweaty bodies that I wanted desperately to join. I wanted to press against Clay, his hips against mine, making me moan with every sway until we wished we were alone somewhere else.

Screw this. I wasn't going to sit around and pout all night. I looked hot, dammit, and we were supposed to be having fun. I leaned into Clay and gave him my best throaty voice. "You want to dance?"

His fingers froze. His eyes slid up to the dance floor, then to me. "Not really."

I bit back annoyance. "Flick will dance with me. Won't you, Flick?" I turned to her with pleading eyes. *Please get me out of this booth.* I couldn't stand to be this close to Clay when he was refusing to touch me or tell me what was wrong.

Flick glanced at Clay then at me. "Uh, sure."

Jed moved so that Flick and I could slide out, and I stormed onto the dance floor with Flick in tow. I pulled us to a spot on the opposite side of the dance floor so I couldn't see the booth where I could *feel* Clay glaring darkly at me.

"What is going on with you two?" Flick asked over the music as we began to sway.

I made an exasperated sound. "I don't friggin' know. All I know is your plan backfired. Instead of getting turned on at the sight of me, it has just pissed him off." I didn't want to tell her that he'd mistaken me for Salem.

Flick glanced in the direction of our table. "Oh, I think he's turned on, alright."

I shook my head and spun so my back was to that side of the club. The *bad* side. "Let's just dance and have a good time, okay?"

"Okay."

I closed my eyes and swayed, trying to lose myself in the music. I tried not to think about why Clay was acting so weird tonight. I tried not to think about what had happened between Clay and Salem on the day they met that would make them act so hatefully towards each other.

I felt hands closing around me from behind. I flinched, my eyes snapping open. Flick was gone. I pushed at the arms until I recognised his deep voice, rumbling in my ear. "You are going to get into trouble moving like that." The light-hearted tone to his voice brought a smile to my face even as I tried not to. Moody Clay was gone. The Real Clay was back.

"Really? What kind of trouble?" I pressed back at him, rolling my ass against him. I felt him tense and heard him groan.

I kept rolling my body against him. The fingers of one of his hands bit into my hips. "You're playing with fire, angel."

"Don't you know that's how redheads came to exist?" I teased. "We were baptised in flames. Fire doesn't burn us. We're born in it."

He chuckled in my ear. "I didn't know that."

"It's true."

The music changed to a slow, sensual beat, guitar strings and a set of drums. He spun me to face him, his right hand grabbing my left and his left arm cradling around my back to pull me in flush. I couldn't help the gasp that dropped from my lips as our bodies connected. My liquid against his rock.

His eyes turned to dark orbs. "This is a lambada. You know they call this the forbidden dance."

I blinked rapidly. "You know how to dance?"

He smiled as if he were sharing an inside joke with someone, but I didn't understand it. "Someone I used to know made me take lessons. Have you ever danced a lambada?"

I shook my head. He began to rock his hips side to side in a one-two-three-pause motion, his hand on my back shifting in time. "Feel how I'm moving? Starting with your left, you step one-two-three, one-two-three…" I made tiny steps as he instructed as we remained on the spot. "That's it. Ready?"

"No."

"I'm going to move us."

"Wait."

I felt him step out and his arm tugged at me. I hesitated and stepped forward all too late. He winced as my heel came down on his toe. "Crap. Sorry."

"Just let go, Aria. Let me lead."

"I don't know how. Let's just go sit down."

"Yes, you do. Just don't think." He pulled back to look at me. "Do you trust me?"

I bit my lip. *Life starts in the deep end, Aria. Jump in.* I nodded.

He held me and we swayed to the music again, remaining on the spot. Just small movements at first, then larger ones so that our knees were bending into the space between the other person's legs. His thigh kept pressing right against the sensitive spot between my legs. My body felt light and my head felt dizzy. I shut my eyes against the flashes of light glancing off the mirrors and off the sequins on the other dancers' dresses. Then suddenly we were moving across the floor, we were swaying like palm trees in a tropical wind, one-two-three, one-two-three. We were the music, ebbing and flowing, swaying and rocking, against each other, with each other.

My body ignited as we moved. My feet felt as if they were stepping on clouds, my hips rolling like they belonged to someone else. Clay spun me out and I felt myself unfurl. He turned around me, my hand passing around his back and to his other hand, then he rolled me back in, his eyes only briefly leaving mine. Somehow I didn't lose the rhythm. My legs and my hips kept that one-two-three just like a clock knew how to keep its own time.

We moved and we swayed and we rocked until I was breathless and my body was on fire and his thigh against my core built this wanting into a throbbing ache. He let go of my hand and dipped me back, his arm around my back secure and I let go, my arms stretching out over my head almost to the floor, trusting him completely. My legs were notched over his thigh keeping me from moving, and it felt so good to be pressed up against him in his arms like this. Just as I thought it couldn't get any hotter, he ran his right palm up my stomach, between my breasts and across my exposed neck like a fan. I imagined him naked against me like this, me secure around him and my body completely under his control. A jolt of heat shuddered through me.

I heard clapping and some whistles. I wasn't even sure if they were for us but I didn't care. Trumpets blared from the speakers and faded as Clay pulled me back up to him. Our mouths were inches away, our hair tangled and sweaty in our faces, panting into each other's open mouths. I was less than a minute away from embarrassing myself by losing my mind right here against his leg. And by the telltale stiffness against my thigh, so was he.

"Clay." I gripped his lapels. "Take me back to yours."

"Fuck." He growled into my mouth. "Aria, no."

"Why?"

"I have…things to do tomorrow morning."

"I'm not talking about tomorrow. I'm talking about tonight."

"I can't."

He let go of me and stepped back, the cold air rushing in between us only fanning my anger. Frustration raged through me. "Why don't you want to screw me?" I hissed.

"I do."

"Then why are you so scared to take me back to your place?"

"I just want to wait."

"Wait for what?"

"Come on, Aria. Let's not ruin a perfectly good moment. Flick and Jed are waiting."

"No." I shoved him before he could pull me towards the booth. Rejection for all the times we had kissed and he had stopped it flowed through me. "Why won't you fuck me?"

He flinched at my words.

"Yes, Clay. I learned how to say the word fuck. Why won't you fuck me?"

A few heads turned towards us but I ignored them. Right now, I was beyond giving a crap about what anyone thought of me.

"I can't believe this," he growled low. "If I were the woman and you were the man, it would be too much pressure. Flick would tell you to dump my ass."

"I'm not pressuring you for sex."

"Really? Then what was that? 'Take me back to your place, Clay. Fuck me. Fuck me, Clay.' I'm not a piece of meat."

"I know you're not. That's not what I meant."

"Then what did you mean?"

I made a roaring noise out of frustration. "What's wrong? Why won't you sleep with me?"

"I will. Just not tonight."

"Not tonight. Not tomorrow. Not ever," I snapped.

"Aria, we just haven't slept together yet. There's nothing wrong. Why is this such a big deal?"

"Most men would be chomping at the bit to be used for sex. But not you. Don't you want me?" Tears pricked at my eyes.

"Of course I want you. Jesus Christ, sometimes all I have to do is look at you and I get hard."

"I just feel like you're hiding something from me."

His left eye twitched. He was hiding something.

I shoved him away. "Good night, Clay. Call me if you ever decide to tell me the truth." I pushed my way through the other dancers.

At the booth Flick and Jed were making out something fierce. I snatched my bag from the table, startling them both apart. "I'm going home," my voice cracked, my vision blurry from the tears that had already started falling, "Thanks for tonight."

"Wait, Aria." Flick began to scramble out of the booth.

I wasn't in the mood to explain things to her. Nor did I want to wait around for Clay to catch up to me, so I just bolted towards the first green exit sign I saw.

I ran out into the balmy night, a tall, wide bouncer holding open the red rope for me. A line had begun to form along the dirty wall down the side of the club. I felt rather than saw eyes on me, appraising me. I didn't care. I just needed to get out of there. A cab. Where was a cab?

I spotted one up across the road with his lights on. He was free. Perfect. I stepped off the sidewalk just as I heard my name called from behind me.

I ignored Clay, clenching my jaw together so I wouldn't be tempted to yell back, and kept walking. I got to the cab and reached out for the door handle.

Clay slammed his body against the door so I couldn't open it. "Aria, wait."

"Leave me alone, Clay. I'm going home."

"I can take you home."

"I'm not getting in a car with you."

"I didn't have a single drink."

"That's not the point."

"Is this guy bothering you, ma'am?" The cabbie had gotten out of the car, a gruff-looking man in his fifties with salt-and-pepper stubble.

"He's fine. He's just my boyfriend." I glared at Clay. "Maybe."

Clay's face visibly paled. "Aria—"

"The point is," I cut him off, "I'm so mad at you I think I might say something I regret. I don't want to be around you right now. I'm catching a cab home. End of story."

His lips tightened to a pinch. I thought that he might try to argue with me again. But he didn't. He turned and strode down the street and disappeared.

He just left. This realisation hit me in the base of my stomach. I had wanted him to leave me alone and now that he had, I realised that's not what I really wanted. How ridiculous was that?

I slipped into the cab and mumbled my address to the driver. I still couldn't believe that Clay had just…left. No goodbyes…

As we pulled away from the curb a familiar red Mustang pulled up behind us with a growl. Clay hadn't left. He had just gone to get his car. He was following me home.

He followed the cab all the way to my apartment and pulled up behind us at the curb. The driver glanced in the rear-view mirror, his thick grey eyebrows pressed down together.

"It's okay," I said to him as I paid him. "He won't hurt me. He probably just wants to continue arguing."

I got out of the cab and slammed the door, glaring at Clay's figure through the front windscreen as if daring him to get out. But he didn't. He just sat in the car, watching me from the shadows. As I walked up my driveway my anger began to flake off my body.

In my apartment, I locked the door behind me. Leaving the lights off, I walked over to the living room curtains and peered out. His car was still there and I could feel his eyes on the window. Even though I knew he couldn't see me, I felt him watching. He remained there for another few minutes before the car started and he slowly pulled away.

He just wanted to make sure I got home safely.

My stomach panged. I had secretly hoped that he would follow me, knock on my door and we could just forget about this argument and his secrets. And mine.

I shook my head. I couldn't move forward without knowing what he was hiding when it was clearly affecting us. When it had clearly wedged a wall between us, preventing us from getting any closer.

What if Clay wouldn't tell me? What if he refused or continued to put me off? I couldn't accept that. I couldn't keep living around secrets like they were things to be tripped over. It would drive us apart. Look at what was happening between Salem and me.

I had to prepare myself that I might have to walk away from him. My heart cracked at the thought. Would I be strong enough? I had to be. I had to be strong like Salem, to walk away from someone she loved if it was for the best.

What if he told you? Then you'd have to tell him your secrets…

My blood drained. Could he still love me if he knew what I'd done? If he knew…what I let happen?

Chapter Ten

Can we talk?

I stared at Clay's text on my phone, sent the morning after the club incident.

Now it was two days since then and I had been moping around in my apartment alone. I hadn't seen Salem since she last ran out. I alternated between worrying about her whereabouts and worrying over what would happen between Clay and me. Damn them both for tearing me apart.

I stared at the text again. I was going to have to deal with Clay eventually. I couldn't take this not knowing anymore.

I wrote back and hit send. *You have five minutes.*

A knock came on my door. Finally Salem was back. Thank God. She had left her house keys behind again. I found them on her bedside table.

I padded from my bedroom and through the silent living room and opened my front door. But it wasn't Salem on my threshold.

It was Clay.

And damn him if he didn't look good wearing stonewashed denim jeans and a light black t-shirt that fit snuggly around his chest and biceps.

"Hi," he said. His gravelly voice immediately brought prickles to the back of my jaw. I would miss his voice so much if I never saw him again after this. His eyes were shadowed and his hair was a mess. At least he hadn't slept well either.

"I thought you were going to call."

"I was in the neighbourhood. Thought I'd drop by instead. Talk to you face to face. I missed looking at you."

I crossed my arms over my chest. "You're going to have to start telling the *truth* if you want me to listen to anything more that you have to say."

"Okay, okay. I've been sitting in my car down the road since I sent my text."

I blinked at him. "You've been sitting in your car for almost two days?"

He shoved his hands into his pockets. "Something like that."

The air whooshed out of my lungs. That explained why he hadn't been sleeping well. Had he eaten? Where had he gone to the bathroom? All things that weren't important right now.

Clay's Adam's apple bobbed as he peered past me into the living room. "Are you…alone?"

"Salem's not here, if that's what you're asking."

He face softened with relief. "Can I come in?"

I held open the door and he stepped inside.

I closed the front door behind me and leaned against it. He looked so damn good standing there, his wide back to me, filling up my apartment with his strong presence.

Clay Jagger was here. With me. In my apartment. Alone.

I could feel my resolve wavering, my body clamouring to run over to him and wrap my arms around him and find his stomach under his shirt. Maybe I should have insisted that we go for a walk?

"Nice place," he said as he stood in the middle of my living room, looking around.

"I didn't think you were here to talk about my apartment."

"I'm not." He spun and gazed at me, his eyes roaming over me. "God, I've missed you."

"Clay—"

"I'm sorry about the other night."

Maybe he was ready to talk? "Why did you get so mad when you thought I was Salem? Start there."

He sighed and rubbed his face. "I thought maybe she had

162

come there to…gloat. To tell me that she'd won."

"Won what?"

"She's trying to take you away from me. She promised me she wouldn't stop until I was out of the picture. You tell me whether you think that's reason enough to…be wary of her."

I inhaled sharply. "She wouldn't." Salem said those things to him? I couldn't really believe that. Right?

Unfortunately I could. That sounded just like Salem.

Clay winced. "I didn't want to say anything to you before. It felt petty to tell on her. Like I was trying to make you pick sides. I'm not trying to do that," he added quickly.

I nodded. I believed him. "And why…" my throat suddenly felt very thick, "why won't you sleep with me?"

For a long while he just stared at me, his dark eyes mournful, hesitant. What was he so scared of? "You know my mother is… sick."

I nodded.

"Do you know what the chance is of a child developing schizophrenia if they have a parent who suffers from it?"

The blood drained from my face. "No."

"Ten percent chance. Only ten percent, so you'd have to be really unlucky… In men, the symptoms begin to develop in their teens or twenties. When I was eighteen, the same year as my mother was diagnosed, I started…seeing things. Faces. People who weren't really there. It wasn't long before I was diagnosed too."

Oh my God. The memory of his mother's behaviour flashed before my eyes. Would this be what Clay turned into? Would he one day stop recognising me? Accuse me of being someone else? I swallowed hard.

His face twisted in pain. He seemed to know what I was thinking. He lifted his palms as if to placate me. "I'm not dangerous, I swear. Please don't make me leave before I explain everything to you."

I don't know how I managed to speak, but I did. "Okay."

"Most sufferers can actually lead normal lives on the right medication and therapy. I'm one of the lucky ones who can still function relatively normally. That's why I don't drink, I keep a strict diet and I work out every day, it helps keep me…okay."

"That's why you're seeing a therapist," I blurted out.

"You know I'm in therapy?"

"Salem…" I trailed off.

A darkness came over his face. "Salem told you. Of course. I've caught her following me before."

Jesus. Salem had been stalking him?

Of course. How else had she found out about the therapist? And Tenielle? Did you really believe that she had just been driving past Clay both times out of sheer coincidence?

And Clay had caught her. He'd probably known all this time that she'd been following him. What must he think? I felt my cheeks burn with embarrassment. "I'm sorry. She's just trying to protect me. I know that's no excuse but…"

"I know." He didn't sound angry. "Sometimes I think maybe you do need protecting from me."

Suddenly I wasn't sure whether I should be here with Clay Jagger in my apartment alone. "Do you…do you get violent?"

"Most schizophrenics aren't violent or aggressive, in fact we're more likely to be the victims of violence." He licked his lips. "I'm not going to lie. It's possible that we can get aggressive if we're not taking meds and are stuck in a bad delusion. Stress can cause us to relapse, too. When I get stressed, there's a greater chance for me to relapse. Right now, I'm so terrified of losing you that everything is becoming overwhelming again. I'm getting confused. Sometimes I start mistaking people for someone they're not. Sometimes I get paranoid that…people are trying to harm me or the people I love."

Which was why he kept thinking that Salem was trying to take me away from him.

But she is. Deep down, you know she is.

"It's why I've wanted to keep things slow between us," he said. "It's why I've prevented taking things to the next level, not because I don't want to. God knows how much I want to. I just needed you to know what you're in for if you stay with me before we…"

That explained why he was always the one to pull away.

I'm an idiot. I thought he was worried that I was a virgin or it was something petty about how I looked or acted or what I wore.

"I think I've been putting off telling you because there's always a chance that you can't live with this…with me." He inhaled deeply and let it out audibly. "I just hope that you can."

I felt him studying me, trying to garner a reaction. Truth was, I wasn't sure what to think yet. I was still trying to let it sink in.

I squeezed my eyes shut as I clung to the door behind me to keep myself steady.

"Aria?"

"I need a minute."

Schizophrenia. He had schizophrenia. There was no cure. He would have to live with it forever. But could I?

Or had he changed to me forever?

I forced my eyes open and looked over at him. He was just as beautiful as I've thought him to be. No, he was more beautiful because I knew how strong he was to stand and fight this disease every day.

I knew right then that I loved him anyway. We would find a way to live with this, together.

I realised then what it meant to truly love. Unconditionally.

This was what Salem was talking about. This was what she and I had. She still loved me, despite all the ways I'd failed her. I loved her, despite what she was doing. A part of me filled with a hope. Perhaps Clay could love me despite everything too?

I walked up to him, stopping only when we were toe to toe. I brushed strands of his hair from his forehead and he turned his face so he could muzzle my palm. He breathed my name against my skin, his voice raw and desperate.

I turned his face so he was looking at me. "It doesn't matter to me if you have an illness. I love you. I'm so happy that you had the courage to tell me. That you trusted me enough to tell me."

He inhaled sharply and pulled me into him, his mouth consuming mine. This kiss was everything: thank you, I missed you, dear God, I love you all in one. It would have brought me to my knees if he wasn't holding me up.

When he pulled away we were both shaking, my chest filled with so much emotion that I could barely breathe around my swollen heart. He leaned his forehead down on mine. "You are incredible, Aria. Most women would have run away screaming."

I grinned. "Was that supposed to be a compliment?"

He smiled. Then his face became serious. "This is something I will have to live with every day for the rest of my life, Aria. I'm... broken."

So am I. "The cracks are how the light inside of you shines out."

He smiled. "My angel said something like that to me. That day that I told you I had gone to the bridge. I went there just after my diagnosis. I thought it was only a matter of time before I became..."

"Before you became your mother," I realised.

He nodded. "I couldn't stand the thought of going crazy. I saw what the disease did to her. It ate her from the inside until she wasn't my mother anymore, she was just a wild, pained animal wearing her skin and smelling like she used to smell. I went to Mirage Gorge to...to end it."

Thank God for this hallucination, this angel, otherwise he wouldn't be here and I wouldn't be standing in his arms. I could see even now the affection that shone from his face as he spoke about her.

"This angel you saw... Do you still see her?" Silly girl, jealous of a hallucination.

"No. She's gone." His faced clouded with something. "But it's okay that she's gone. She led me to you. You're my angel now. My real life angel." His nose traced my cheekbone.

"That's the real reason you call me angel, isn't it?"

He nodded. "Do you remember the day we first saw each other?"

I did. He had been coming out of the Mirage Falls convenience store with a map in his hands and he'd stopped dead when he saw me. I had never seen him before so I just ignored him even as he continued to stare.

"You shone to me. Just like my angel did. But I could also see

166

you had your own demons to fight. I knew that you were someone who understood darkness. I knew that if anyone could accept me for everything that I am, you could. You could love me despite my illness." He gripped me. "You are my Northern Star. If I lost you, I'd lose myself."

"You won't lose me."

"Don't make promises you can't keep."

"You won't lose me," I repeated, more firmly.

He leaned his forehead against mine. "I love you so much. I'm terrified of losing you. Like I lost…everyone else." I flinched at the pain in his voice. His fingers came up to brush my cheeks. "I'm afraid that you'll leave me. Like…like you almost left with Salem."

My stomach stabbed with guilt. Would I ever not feel guilty about the other when I was with either Salem or Clay? "I'm not leaving."

"If you left…I don't know whether I would have the strength to keep myself together. I would rather just go off the meds and believe that you were still here with me. I'd rather live with that delusion than without you at all."

"Clay, I said I'm not leaving you."

He pulled back. "Promise me you'll never leave me. Promise me."

"I promise."

He stared at me, his eyes fixed intensely on mine. "Remember this promise, Aria Adams. One day, you may be forced to keep it."

* * *

"I'm still not sure why I have to come with you to therapy."

"Aria." Clay paused right outside the office of Dr Bing PhD, PsyD, EdD. MD. Any more letters and she'd have an alphabet behind her name. "Don't take this the wrong way."

"Okay," I said slowly. Whatever he was about to say I knew I wouldn't like.

"Sometimes the ones we love are the ones that can stop us from healing the most. Because the ones we love, love us for who we are, exactly who we are. We don't need to change to keep their love, even if we need to change to become better. Does this make any sense?"

"You're telling me that I'm bad for you."

"No. But you could be. But if you come with me to see Dr Bing, she can make sure that we remain good for each other." He squeezed my hand. "Sometimes we can't face things alone. We need help, professional help, and this doesn't make us weak. It makes us strong to admit it, okay?"

I let go of the breath I was holding. I was being silly. Clay was the one who had to struggle with this disease every day.

I hated doctors. I hated waiting rooms. I hated the stupid fluorescent lights they all seemed to insist on using. I hated it all. But I would go to see this Dr Bing if it would help Clay.

We didn't have to wait long in the waiting room. A woman walked out and introduced herself as Dr Bing. She was gorgeous in an exotic way, perfectly straight ebony hair, smooth olive skin kissed by the sun, and a tiny, petite figure.

For a second, I felt like someone had chopped their hand to the front of my throat. She was gorgeous. Had Clay ever slept with her? Had he ever wanted to? Did she want to sleep with him?

Don't be ridiculous, Aria.

"Please come in." Dr Bing's voice broke through my thoughts. She directed us to sit on a couch in her room, while she sat in an armchair. Her office didn't look like what I expected it to. There was no desk with cold chairs in front of it. It was like someone's living room with a shelf of well-used books and green plants amongst the warm cherry wood furniture.

"Do you know why Clay has asked you to join us here?"

I realised she was speaking to me. "So I can help him?"

She nodded. "It's important that the people close to him understand his illness and know the best ways to help him manage it."

"I want to help. I'd do anything to help him."

She smiled. "You care about him."

"Very much."

"Good. It can be a challenging thing to love with someone

who has a mental illness. It can test the strength of your bond, of your commitment to them."

"I'm here. I'm committed."

Clay slipped his hand over mine and squeezed.

"Okay, let's talk about schizophrenia, what it is, what it isn't, and how you can help Clay if he starts to relapse..."

At the end of the session my head was spinning. Dr Bing had spent most of the session talking to me, Clay just sitting silently beside me, holding my hand. I tried to push away the small nagging worry that I might not be able to handle it if Clay were to relapse.

"How are you feeling?" Dr Bing asked me as she showed us to the door.

"I'm okay."

"It's a lot to take in." She slipped a card in my hand. "If you have any questions you can always call me."

I felt weird taking her card but I slipped it in my bag anyway.

"I'll see you next time, Aria." Dr Bing closed the door behind her before I could say anything.

"Next time?" I turned to Clay. "Why would I have to come back next time?"

He grabbed my hand. "I'd like you to come, at least for a few sessions. Is that okay?"

"Yeah...I guess so."

* * *

I arrived home that evening to find Salem on our bed lying on her stomach and reading a magazine. Clay's admissions echoed in my mind and my blood began to shimmer. *I've caught her following me before. She promised me that she wouldn't stop until she took you away from me.* I stormed into the bedroom.

"Oh hey, sis."

"Where the hell have you been?"

"Nice to see you too, Rosey." Salem rolled her eyes like a truant teenager would. "I've been out."

Everything began to bubble over. My vision began to shake

and my hands clenched into fists by my side. "Damn you. I'm your sister and you live here with me in my apartment. The very least you could do is to have the common decency to let me know where you're going and when you'll be back so I don't kill myself worrying."

She snorted. "You and loverboy didn't seem to be worrying much earlier."

I blinked, my mind stuttering. She couldn't have… "Were you following us?"

"No."

"You liar. I know you've been following him. That's stalking, Salem."

Salem shoved the magazine away and rolled out of the bed so she was standing toe to toe with me. I stood my ground. "You don't know where he goes when he's not with you."

"I trust him."

"You're naïve and stupid. Like always. I'm just trying to save your ass. Again."

"Jesus Christ." I rubbed my face with my hands. She couldn't see how ridiculous, how insane she was being. "I know that you threatened him."

"I'm protecting you. He's lying to you. He's bad for you."

"Stop it, Salem. Just stop it."

"You don't know. You don't know what he's hiding."

"I know. He told me everything."

Her mouth flew open in horror and she stumbled back. "No. He can't have… How are you still…?" Then her eyes narrowed. "What did he tell you, exactly?"

"That's none of your business."

"You don't know anything about him. I'm your sister, your blood, and you'd take sides with some guy over me?"

"Don't try and guilt me."

"It's true, isn't it?"

"Truth? You want to talk truth? You're just jealous. You hate that I'm not your poor pathetic little Rosey who needs big brave Salem to look after her anymore. You hate that I have a life that doesn't revolve around *you*. And you hate that I don't *need* you anymore."

Salem's mouth pinched into a pale line. "I'm just trying to protect you. To do what's right for you."

I roared and my hands flew up, making a strangling motion. If I reached out just a little bit more I could have my hands around her stupid neck.

Salem's eyes narrowed at me. "You going to try and kill me too?" She lifted her chin so her neck was exposed to me. "Go on, then."

I stumbling back, gasping for air. I couldn't be here another second longer. I wrenched my hands away, spun and ran out of the apartment, the front door slamming behind me.

* * *

I stood on the sidewalk a few blocks from my apartment staring into space. I barely noticed as Clay's Mustang pulled up. I hadn't taken my car keys when I'd run out of the house. Luckily I still had my purse slung over my shoulder with my mobile in it so I could call Clay. The summer storm was going full throttle, the large drops of cool rain running down my arms and soaking through my hair and clothes. I didn't have the energy to move yet. It was like everything in my brain was going in slow motion.

"Aria?" Clay called over the crack of thunder. The following flash of lightning lit him up, separating his face into light and shadows of concern as he ran to me. His arms wrapped around me and I fell against him. I closed my eyes and let his presence wash over me, calming me, bringing me back to life. I felt his lips on my forehead.

"I'm sorry to drag you out here."

He shushed into my hair. "I'm glad you called me. Come on. Let's get you somewhere dry."

Clay drove me to his apartment. He kept his arm around me as he led me from the parking garage and into the elevator. He had thought to bring a towel, which he wrapped around my shoulders.

My curiosity over being at his place for the very first time overruled most of the turbulent emotions left over from my fight with Salem and at least for now, made me forget about my problems. He lived on the top floor of a five-level block of new apartments, a small gym on the ground floor. The marble flooring and stylish mirrors along the white walls oozed modern comfort.

He unlocked his front door, number 501, and pushed it open.

Clay flicked on the light and let me step in. It was stunning. An open plan apartment with floor-to-ceiling glass encasing it, a large wrap-around balcony going around the spacious living area, white and black leather furniture, and a view over the lights of Mirage Falls partly hidden by the steady drops of rain from the passing storm. A large moon shone in through the glass. "Wow," I breathed. "This place is incredible. How do you…?" I stopped myself mid-sentence. It was none of my business.

"How do I afford it?"

I nodded feebly. He'd caught me out. "You don't have to answer. It wasn't right for me to ask."

"It's fine. My parents had money. When my mother was hospitalised my father just left everything and disappeared. I was made trustee over everything."

My heart panged. I couldn't imagine being made to look after his mother at the age of eighteen. I'd only just started feeling like I could look after myself. "I can't believe he just left."

"He just couldn't take having to look after her, I guess. At least he left us with most of the money. Out of guilt, I suppose."

"Where is he now?"

Clay shrugged. "I don't know. I don't even know if he's alive."

"I'm sorry."

He let out a gentle laugh. "You don't have to be sorry for everything bad that's ever happened to me. My situation could have been worse, much worse. Money doesn't solve your problems but it makes dealing with them easier. Because of the money I can afford twenty-four-hour care for her. She can remain at home instead of in a facility."

"That's so incredible that you can look at it that way."

He frowned. "I didn't always feel so lucky, trust me. I had my own fair share of feeling sorry for myself. Happiness can't shape you, only the things that leave scars do."

I nodded, understanding exactly what he was saying.

"Besides, if I wasn't in such a dark place, I wouldn't have met you." His eyes darted to me as if my reaction to his words was important.

"What do you mean?"

"I mean," he said slowly, "if I hadn't been going through a dark moment, I wouldn't have gone for a drive, a long drive, I wouldn't have stopped in Mirage Falls and I never would have seen you, walking down the main street at dawn looking like an angel with the sun in your hair."

I smiled at his words, recalling that day.

His face softened. "Look at me. I'm talking your ear off while you're standing there soaked and freezing to death."

He took me by the hand and led me through a door off the living room into the bathroom, all white and chrome with a large shower in the corner.

He slipped his fingers under the edges of the towel and pulled it off my shoulders. That one small movement sent a riot of tingles through my body and I felt frozen to the ground.

His hungry gaze roamed over me. Only then did I realise what I must have looked like to him, my white summer dress soaked and see-through, clinging to my body. I wanted to lift my arms across my chest but I kept them at my side instead. I wanted him to see me.

"You can," his voice came out croaky. He cleared his throat and tried again. "You can have a shower if you like. Use the new towel over the hanger. This one's soaked."

"Thanks," I said, my voice a mere whisper. The rain had made my skin cool and clammy but under his gaze, I felt like I was standing near a fire.

He shook himself. "Right. I'll go now. Give you some privacy."

"You can stay…if you want." I don't know where this boldness came from.

He flinched and his lids fluttered shut. "I…" He inhaled deeply and let it all out before opening his eyes. He wouldn't meet my gaze. "I'll find something for you to wear."

I tried not to feel rejected as he closed the bathroom door, leaving me standing there alone. But I knew his reasons. I could be patient.

I stood under the hot water for longer than I needed to, my mind ticking over what would happen next, nervous because I was at Clay's place for the first time. Was there protocol for this kind of thing? A list of dos and don'ts? A manual? Maybe I should have looked this up. But I hadn't planned on having a fight with Salem. I hadn't planned on staying here.

When I got out of the shower my wet clothes were gone. I noticed them in the washing machine tucked in one corner. He had touched my clothes, my bra, my underwear…

I flushed. Thank God I had worn one of the lacy boy shorts sets that Flick had sent me home with.

There was a pile of folded clothes on the toilet seat. I picked up the shorts folded on the top. Pyjama bottoms. Woman's pyjamas, a cream singlet and boxer shorts with cherry patterns.

Whose clothes were these?

I pulled the shorts on and pulled the shirt down over my head. They fit.

And they smelled faintly of lavender. I looked down at them, tugging out the hem with my hands and looking at the patterns. He didn't have a sister… Did he actually have the nerve to hand me an ex's clothes? I was mulling this over as I dried my hair with the hairdryer he had left out for me.

When I turned the hairdryer off, I heard a knock on the door. "Come in."

Clay opened the door and stepped in, smiling when he saw me in the clothes he'd laid out.

"Whose clothes are these?" I demanded, more harshly than I had intended. "Are they your ex's?" *Did they belong to Olivia?*

He chuckled and tapped me on my nose. "Do you really think I would give you another woman's clothes to wear? They're new. I saw them a while ago and thought of you. I know cherries are your favourite fruit."

I couldn't remember when I had told him that, but I must have. That was really sweet that he remembered. "Thank you."

But the smell. "They smell…worn."

"I washed them. I don't like wearing clothes straight from the store. You never know who's tried them on before you."

"Oh. Right."

"We can keep them here for when you want to stay over. Or you can take them with you if you're really attached to them."

…for when you want to stay over. That's what he said. Which meant that I would be staying over again. I felt a flutter of happiness in my chest.

He handed me a new toothbrush in a shade of pale blue and pressed a dollop of toothpaste on the bristles. We brushed our teeth side by side in the sink. My elbow kept grazing his side, sending flares through my body. He had changed into a pair of navy boxers that highlighted his sprinter's legs and a black sleeveless shirt that showed off his round, tanned shoulders. I tried not to stare in the mirror but my eyes kept being drawn back to him, his arm flexing as he worked his brush over his teeth was a mesmerising sight. A sight that made me squirm. I pressed my thighs together. Good God, would everything be erotic to me about Clay?

When we finished he pushed his fingers through mine and led me into his bedroom. Just inside the door he paused. He looked like such a boy, his teeth fussing along his bottom lip, an unsure look in his eyes. If I wasn't so caught up in my own nerves I may have laughed.

His bedroom was cleaner than I expected for a man. Everything was put away and his bed was made up with cream and brown sheets. He had carried my handbag up from the car and had placed it on one of the bedside tables. That must be my side. He had given me the side farthest from the door. Like Salem always did.

Salem. She would be sleeping alone tonight. I swallowed as a knot began to lodge in my throat. I hated that we had fought. I hated it so much.

I quickly looked over to his side of the bed, trying to push all this sadness away. I noticed the photo frame, the only thing on his table. I walked over to it and picked it up. There was an older couple in it. He was handsome with dark hair and dark eyes, and I recognised Clay's hair and jawline, his top-heavy mouth, and his tanned skin. She was stunning too, brilliant blue eyes and thick golden hair and a smile that radiated. It took me a second to realise that this must be Clay's mother, the same woman I had met earlier.

Oh God. The poor woman. It was clear to see how much she had deteriorated from when this photo was taken. Her eyes no longer shone with intelligence, her cheeks were no longer rosy, merely shallow pits. My heart filled with sadness. What if this happened to Clay? What if he got worse just like she did? Could I stand to watch him disappear into a shell of himself?

I felt his presence at my shoulder and when I turned to look at him he was staring at the photo as well.

"You look like your father." I traced his face with my fingertip.

"But I got everything else from my mother," he said quietly. He picked up the frame and placed it back down. "I have something for you."

"Something else? Clay, you're spoiling me."

He grinned. "I haven't even started."

He tugged me over to the other bedside table, his movements jerky like an excited child. He gripped the handle of the top drawer and grinned at me. There must be something in the drawer. With a flourish he pulled it open.

It was empty.

"Er, thank you?"

"This is your drawer. You can keep things here for when you stay over. That way you won't have to pack so much." He frowned. "Is it okay? I can give you a bigger drawer."

A drawer. He was giving me a drawer. At his apartment. He was making room in his life for me in a serious way.

"No, this is perfect." I stretched up to kiss him. When our lips melded the ache in my core picked up straight where it left off in the bathroom. My hands roamed across his neck and down to his chest, so hard under my palms and so warm.

He broke the kiss off. "It's late. We should…" his eyes flicked to the bed.

I nodded, my throat too closed to speak.

I slid under the cool sheets and he climbed in next to me. Our limbs clashed as we moved in to hold each other, obviously both trying to get into a position that conflicted with the other.

I was so nervous I burst out laughing. "I don't actually know how to do this."

He smiled as he used his hands to move me into position in the crook of his arm and against his chest. "Here. You fit right here."

I leaned my head on his chest and let a breath out, the air cascading around my thudding heart, and my body relaxed against his, melding against his hard lines like water finding its level around a rock. For the first time in my life I fully appreciated how beautiful the differences were between a man and a woman and how these differences seemed to let us fit.

With more courage than I thought I had, I lifted my hand to his chest and began to trace his hard lines with my fingertips, from the stray dark hairs peeking out of the top of his singlet down to his abdomen.

I felt him tense. I paused and glanced up to him. "Is that too much?"

He let go of a breath. "No. It's perfect."

I kept exploring, feeling a thrill running through my body as my fingers travelled over the hard ridges of his six-pack. His fingers dug into my back and he let out a small moan. The sound was deep and rumbling and it travelled through my body like a tremor, lighting sparks inside me. I flattened my hand against him and touched him again from his stomach to his neck, this time with my palm. His breath began to shake and he clenched me tighter and an ache grew in me. I shifted my leg further over him and the pressure in my touch grew.

I ran my finger over one of his nipples, hard underneath his cotton shirt. This time he didn't try to hide his moan as he pulled me tighter against him, my core pressing against his thigh and the sparks turning into a low flame. He caught my hand and he lifted the tips of my fingers up to his mouth, brushing them against his soft lips. "Dear God, I've missed you."

I couldn't help my smile. "Missed me? You only saw me earlier today."

"I know. But I still missed you. You haunt me, Aria.

When you're not with me I'm just a shadow in the dark, waiting for you to return so you can breathe life into me."

My heart stuttered. I not sure which one of us moved first, or perhaps we moved together, realising that to be of two bodies suddenly wasn't enough. He tugged me up his body, crushing my lips against his and holding me tight. My legs fell on either side of his thigh so that my core was pressed up against him. God that felt good, pleasure radiating through my body out from that tender spot.

Our kisses were desperate, needy, as if we had spent a lifetime apart and were only just returned to each other. And I understood what he meant when he said that he missed me. I missed him too. My body flared in a sweet relief at the feeling of him hard against me, mere cotton layers between us. Like I had been holding my breath waiting for this moment for a long time.

My hands were all over him, grabbing, tangling in his hair, no hesitance in my touch. I pressed my hips against him and his hips pushed up into me, slowly at first, then again and then again. It was the sweetest, most Earth-shaking movement in the world. It was like we were dancing a lambada to a melody only we could hear. And I knew on a greater level why they called it the forbidden dance.

My shirt rode up, cool air pebbling my skin, as his hand found my breast and thumbed across my hard nipple. I gasped as pleasure shot through my body, making constellations inside of me.

I rocked my hips harder against him, a feeling of uncontrollable motion tumbling and building inside of me.

"Wait," he groaned, "stop."

But I didn't want to. I moved against him again, small noises falling from my mouth and into his.

His hands dug into my hips trying to hold me still. "Stop!"

But I couldn't. I was already cresting this wave. At that moment not even God could have stopped the inevitable. A pleasure unlike anything I have ever felt lashed through my body, making my back arch and my eyes roll back and my fingers grab at Clay's shirt. A cry tore from the very depths of me and I saw stars. No. I *became* stars.

"Aria? Aria?" Clay's voice broke through my fog. He was on top of me, his hands on my shoulders shaking me. He must have rolled me at one point.

"Yeah," I hummed, my body still tingling from the aftershocks.

"You're okay?" He sighed, sounding relieved.

"Why wouldn't I be okay?"

Clay bit his lip. "You were screaming. I thought something was wrong."

A laugh escaped me. "No…I just…" I felt my cheeks warm. "I think I just…you know."

A slow smile stretched across his face. "What do you mean, Aria?"

"You know…"

The grin on his face widened. "No, Aria, I don't know."

Bastard. He was going to try and make me say it. "Yes, you do," I muttered.

He laughed. "The word won't bite you. Although I might."

That promise sent a small shiver through me. "Come," I blurted out.

"Oh, was that what you were trying to say." He grinned.

I poked my tongue out at him. Then frowned. "You looked so shocked when I... Isn't that what usually happens when a woman…comes?"

"Not quite like that. And not usually so easily."

It felt like the most natural thing in the world.

I wanted to make *him* do that.

I reached for him but he rolled off me and lay along my side, his hand broad across my hip to keep me from rolling with him. "We're not going any further than this tonight."

"But you're…" I waved at his erection, so obviously pressing against his boxers.

He gave me a smile. "I know. And the guys downstairs are going to murder me for saying this, but you've already had a first tonight and I still want to take it slow."

I made a hmmpfting noise. But I let him roll me to my side, tucking me up against him with my back along his front.

179

Even after I fell asleep, I kept rising up to wakefulness, just to remind myself he was there, just to revel in his warmth, just to feel the shudder of giddiness through my body at his touch before I dove back into sleep.

Sometime during the night I heard his voice, calling me back to wakefulness. It wasn't his words, because whatever he said I didn't hear them, but it was the tone in which he said them that tugged at me. Anguish. Pain. Something scraping him raw.

I opened my eyes. But before I could move I heard him speak.

"Please," he whispered, his voice shaking with anguish. "I can't fuck this up." He thought I was asleep. He was talking to himself. "Please…don't let me screw up this time."

This time?

What did that mean?

Olivia. Her name floated up into my mind. He must have been talking about Olivia. Then I knew. She had meant more to Clay than he had let on.

A stab of jealousy went through me as an image of some other woman's hands over his naked body flashed into my mind. I had to fight to keep my breathing even.

Don't be ridiculous. Clay said it was over. And I believed him. It was over between him and this…Olivia. Right?

* * *

"Time to wake up, Aria."

I huddled under the covers, moaning, preparing myself for someone loud and annoying and way too perky before midday to jump on me. It was like I was thirteen again.

The presence moved to the end of the bed. The covers shifted and I prepared for an onslaught of tickling, tucking my feet up as much as I could. Something grabbed my foot and I let out a squeal.

There was no tickling. Instead I felt warm kisses and soft hands unfolding my legs. Clay kissed his way over my knees and up my thighs, his tongue occasionally coming out to taste me, his stubble lightly scraping my skin, a glorious contrast.

Damn. I wasn't used to being woken up like *this*. But it was something I could definitely get used to.

I tensed, holding my breath as his mouth moved up the top of one thigh and up my hip. I was disappointed he didn't linger there. Until his mouth moved to my breasts then closed over one nipple through my shirt. Dear God. A wanton noise tore out of my mouth.

"God, you look so good in my bed."

"Please," I panted, "do that again." My back arched up into him, begging him.

But he didn't. He pressed his face in between my breasts and groaned, the sound vibrating through me.

"Clay?"

He lifted his head with a renewed energy. "Come on. Get up before I do something I regret."

That stung. Before I could turn away Clay covered me with his body and put his face in mine, forcing me to look at him. "Hey. I didn't mean it like that. You know I didn't."

I knew that. He was sensitive to not going so fast physically because of his illness. But it was still frustrating. So very frustrating.

I buried my nose into his neck and sighed. He smelled so good. And felt so warm. "Can't we stay right here and never leave?"

"You're going to be the death of me," he whispered. "I want to. But I have work to do. And you have a sister to go make up with."

I pouted. "She can wait a day or two."

"Aria…"

I sighed. He was right. I had to face her soon.

I opened the door to my apartment with trepidation. The only sound I heard was the slight creaking of the old hinges as I stuck my head into an empty living room. "Salem?"

No one called back.

My body flooded with relief. She wasn't home. I didn't have to face her and deal with all this crap that was piling up between us. At least not yet, anyway.

Guilt flooded in over the relief like a wave cancelling out a footprint in the sand. What kind of sister was I that I was *glad* that she wasn't home? What if something had happened to her?

What if she needed my help and I had no idea where to look for her? Where did she disappear to all the time?

She's with Clay. Watching him. Following him.

She wouldn't dare. Would she? She couldn't still be doing that, even after I told her to leave him alone. Right?

Chapter Eleven

A siren clanged though my mind. I startled, instinctively grabbing my phone and shutting off the offending alarm before slumping back, blinking, still trying to get my bearings as my memories flicked into place.

I was on my couch, in my apartment.

I hadn't been sleeping well lately so I must have dozed off.

Salem? Was she home? I called out her name but heard nothing in response. She still hadn't returned. It was the next day and Salem still hadn't returned. Where the hell was she?

Something else was nagging at my subconscious. My alarm. I knew I set my alarm for some reason…

What time was it? Crap, what time was it?

I stared at the clock on my phone. It was 6 p.m. Why had I set my alarm, again?

The therapy session. Clay would be here soon to pick me up for the next therapy session. I groaned. And I wasn't even ready yet.

I ran around my bathroom and bedroom, brushing my teeth, washing my face, putting on deodorant, and slipping on ballet flats. All the while my eyes kept darting over to Salem's corner of the room. Her bag was still on the chair on her side, clothes thrown all over it. She had never gotten round to unpacking properly and I had tired of asking her to. Did her side look different from earlier? Had she been home and I slept through it?

No time to analyse it now. I grabbed my bag and glanced at the clock at my bedside. It was already quarter past six.

Clay was late. He was never late. I checked my phone. There were no messages from him or missed calls. If he was going to be late then he would have let me know. Right? My stomach tensed. Something was wrong.

I called Clay's number, chewing my lip as the ring tone sounded in my ear. *Come on, pick up. Pick up.*

The phone clicked and I heard his voice. For a second relief flooded through me until I realised it was his pre-recorded message. I'd gone through to voicemail. Confusion gripped me as I hung up. Where was he?

Maybe he's driving right now. He'd never pick up the phone while he was driving. I walked over to the curtains, peering out onto the street. The familiar red Mustang wasn't there. Just my old Ford parked out front. Maybe I got it wrong. Maybe I was meant to meet Clay at Dr Bing's office.

Yes, that's it. God, Aria, get it together.

If I drove to Dr Bing's office, then I'd only be five or so minutes late. But I didn't know where my damn car keys were. I swear Salem had hidden them from me. It was something she used to do when we were kids; hide things like keys and books and homework.

Looks like I'd have to jog to her office. Then I'd be more like twenty minutes late. I'd leave a message on Clay's phone letting him know I'd be there soon.

I walked back into the living room and stopped dead.

My car keys were right there in the middle of the kitchen bench. I swear they weren't there before. Was Salem here?

Suddenly my neck prickled as if I was being watched. I glanced around me, expecting someone to be standing behind me. But there was no one there. I hurried over to the window and tugged the curtains closed. The feeling still wouldn't go away.

I grabbed my car keys off the bench. "Salem?" I called out. But there was no answer.

Stupid, Aria. You just hadn't noticed the keys before, that's all. Salem must have come home sometime when you weren't here. Stop freaking yourself out. Besides, you're late.

"I'm so sorry I'm late," I said as I tumbled into Dr Bing's office six minutes late.

Dr Bing stood up and held out her hand. "Aria, good to see you again."

I shook her hand and glanced round her office. "Clay's not here yet?"

"No. But he often comes from his mother's and at this time of day the traffic can be unpredictable on the M1. Please, take a seat."

I glanced back at the door again, willing Clay to come through the door now. But he didn't. I felt uneasy being here alone with his shrink but it would be rude to leave.

I walked over to the couch and sat. I checked my phone again – no missed calls or messages – before slipping it on the side table.

"Do you want a drink of water? Coffee?"

"No, thanks."

I thought Dr Bing may take the armchair as she did last time. Instead she strode over to the couch and seated herself right next to me. I gave her a tense smile as she arranged herself comfortably with one leg crossed over the other and her arm out along the back of the couch, facing towards me. "Clay tells me you have a twin sister."

Clay had been talking about Salem? What had he told Dr Bing? I studied her but her face gave away nothing. "Yes."

"Tell me about Salem."

I flinched. *I* didn't tell her Salem's name. "What has Clay told you?"

"I'm more interested in hearing what *you* have to say about her."

What was that supposed to mean? "I don't see how this has anything to do with Clay."

"I understand that she doesn't like Clay. How does that make you feel?"

I felt my defences automatically coming up. Even though we had been fighting lately she was still my blood and I would defend her to the death. "She's just trying to protect me. She's just doing what she thinks is right. It can't be easy for her coming back into my life and finding she's been replaced."

"Has she been replaced?"

"No one could ever replace Salem."

"But you have Clay now."

"What I have with Clay is…different." But Salem didn't know that. My heart began to soften. What a horrible sister I've been. I hadn't even thought about what she may have been feeling to react so badly towards Clay. Everything she had been doing was a cry for my attention. The least I could do was to be more understanding. I had to find her. I had to make things right. "Oh, God…I've been so selfish."

"Why do you say that?"

"I keep putting myself first when I should be putting her…" I trailed off. Oh, Dr Bing was good. She had me spilling my guts before I realised what I was saying. Well, I wasn't saying any more. I crossed my arms over my chest.

"So you think that you should be putting her first?"

I remained silent, my eyes on the door. Come on, Clay. Where the hell are you?

"What if that's not the choice you have to make?"

My gaze snapped back to Dr Bing. She was just sitting there watching me with an unreadable look on her face. Okay, Dr Bing, I'll bite. "What do you mean?"

"What if you don't have to choose between Clay and Salem?"

"Then what would I choose?"

"Choose you."

This was why I didn't like therapists. All this confusing Confucius babble. I narrowed my eyes at her. "I thought this session was for Clay?"

"It is."

"Then why does it feel like I'm the one being analysed?"

She tilted her head, her almond-shaped eyes trained on me like lasers. "What are you afraid I might find?"

My skin broke out in goosebumps. What was I afraid of?

The shrill ring of my mobile made me jump. Thank God. Clay. Finally. "Excuse me," I said as I grabbed the phone, clattering across the table as it vibrated.

It wasn't Clay.

It was a private number.

I paused for a second for I answered it. "Hello?"

"Ms Aria Adams?" An unfamiliar voice came on the line.

"Yes," I swallowed hard, a creeping feeling coming over me. "Who is this?"

"This is Nurse O'Shea from the Sunshine Coast Hospital. I'm sorry to tell you this. There's been an accident."

Chapter Twelve

Please, God. Please. Let everything be okay.

I drove like a madwoman all the way to the hospital, speeding, which I never do. But at that moment, I didn't care.

At the hospital I flung the car into the first parking spot I could find and raced inside, slamming into the front desk in my haste. The receptionist, a bespectacled woman with a pinched mouth, continued to type, the only other thing moving were her pupils, to focus on me. "I'm Aria Adams. Someone called me. My boyfriend Clay Jagger was admitted in here a few hours ago."

Her eyes flicked to her computer and she continued typing. Did she even hear me? Did she even care? I was about to snap at her when she said, "Clay Jagger. Room 408."

"Is he okay?"

"He was in a minor car accident but he'll be fine. Room 408. Fourth floor."

I almost leaned over the desk and hugged her. But I doubted very much that she would appreciate it so I just thanked her and sped to the elevators.

Room 408. Fourth floor.

I found his room easily enough. When I pushed through the door, Clay was sitting up in a hospital bed in a flimsy hospital gown. He had a bandage wrapped around his head and a few raw gashes and bruises on his arms, but other than that, he looked okay.

He frowned when he saw me. "Aria?"

"Oh my God. Clay." I rushed to his side and gave him the most ginger hug I could, even though I wanted to squeeze the damn life out of him.

I heard him laugh. "Come on, angel. I'm not going to break."

I held on to him tighter. He nestled his face in my neck and inhaled. "God, you smell good."

I pulled back and he made some room for me on the edge of the bed. I traced his forehead alongside the bandage.

"I'm okay, angel."

"They said you were in a car accident. What the hell happened?"

His mouth pinched for a mere second. Or was I imaging it? "I'm not too sure. Something went wrong with Sally and I just... lost control. Ended up in a ditch."

"Jesus," I breathed.

"I'm okay. Just some scrapes and bruises. And a concussion." He indicated the bandage on his head.

My eyes almost bugged out of my head. "Oh my God."

"They want to keep me in here for observation overnight. But I should be free to go tomorrow."

"I'll stay here with you. As long as they let me."

"Actually, I was hoping you'd do something for me?"

"Anything."

"Could you stop by my apartment and grab a toothbrush and a few things?"

"Of course."

I stepped inside Clay's apartment and locked the door behind me with the spare key he had given me off his key ring. His dining table, which he said doubled as a work space, had papers and pens and pencils about the place. I knew I probably should just grab what he needed and get out but curiosity took hold of me. I walked over to the table, glancing around as I did in case I was being watched.

Silly, I know. I was there alone. But I still felt a little guilty thrill as I surveyed his papers. It looked like he was starting some sketches. One caught my eye, a half-finished drawing of a woman, thin and pale with long red hair and a blue mask across the upper part of her face showing just her grey eyes. Her features were pulled into grim determination, her palms out and some kind of blue magic was pouring from her hands. I guessed she was supposed to be some kind of superhero.

Maybe I was reading into it too much, but this cartoon looked…like me.

I read the title scrawled in the top right-hand corner. *Adventures of Aria: The Temple of Yesterdays.*

This *was* me. Clay had made a character from me? He had made a comic from me?

I couldn't help the grin that formed on my face. Clay was drawing a character based on *me*. I traced my image sake, my heart fluttering. He really cared about me, didn't he? He even found a way to weave me into his work.

When was he going to tell me? Maybe this was supposed to be a surprise. Well, I wouldn't say anything to him.

What if he actually got this comic published? I would be immortalised in ink. How fun. His love for me there on printed paper for the world to see. My smile slid off my face. What if someone recognised me? What if they came looking for me to find Salem?

I shook my head as I turned my back on the table. Don't be silly, Aria. That was three years ago. And it's just a cartoon, not a mugshot.

I tried the door to his bathroom but it was locked from this side. I'd have to go through his bedroom.

His bed was unmade. There were a few clothes about the place. I stopped in his bedroom, chewing my lip. The place was messier than the last time. Dr Bing said that keeping things tidy was an indicator of how 'okay' he was. If things began to slip in his head then so would his environment.

I began to feel a little uneasy. Clay had said that his accident was an accident, but…what if he was beginning to relapse? What if he saw something on the road that wasn't there? What if he heard something that wasn't real that caused him to run off the road?

Should I bring this up with Clay?

I was still pondering this as I stepped into his bathroom. I grabbed his toothbrush, toothpaste and a comb. He also wanted deodorant but I wasn't sure where he kept it. Maybe under the sink? I froze when I opened the cabinet. A box of condoms sat in the middle of the top shelf blaring at me in bright red packaging.

An open box of condoms.

Condoms that he *wasn't* using with me. Who the hell was he using them with?

Calm down, Aria. This doesn't mean anything. You know he had sex before you. This was probably just a box left over from before. Right?

Slapping flesh, grunting, bumping uglies, rooting, doing it. Hard and fast and rough.

Stop it. Clay's not like that.

Clay's a guy. All guys are like that.

I didn't really believe that. That was something Salem said, not me.

I spotted Clay's deodorant and snatched it, slamming the cupboard shut.

I couldn't get my mind off that box of condoms in his bathroom. Then to the mess in his room. It was almost as messy as Salem's side of the room.

Clay had said once that when he relapsed he would sometimes hallucinate that a person in the room with him was someone else. Could he ever cheat on me without realising it? Would Salem…?

God, I was being stupid. So stupid. I was letting Salem's paranoia cloud my own judgement. Clay loved me.

"Are you okay?"

An unfamiliar voice broke through my thoughts.

I glanced around. I was in the elevator at the hospital and the nurse, who just stepped in, was looking at me strangely. I had left Clay's apartment and had driven all the way over to the hospital with these stupid thoughts jumbling about in my head.

"I'm fine," I lied.

She pointed at the panel where none of the buttons were lit. "You didn't press any buttons. What floor did you want?"

My floor.

I glanced up to the floor number. I was already on the fourth floor. I stuck my hand out to stop the lift doors from closing. "This is my floor. Thanks."

She frowned at me as I shot her a thankful smile over my shoulder. I must have looked weird just standing there, staring into space.

In between doctors and patients my eyes caught a flash of red at Clay's door. Someone with long red hair was walking away down the corridor. Was that...Salem? Coming out of Clay's room?

I frowned. It couldn't be.

I began to stalk down the hall towards her, my footsteps clipped and hurried. She didn't glance back so I didn't see her face but she was the same height and build. I wanted to call out to her but the corridor was too crowded and I just wasn't sure. I dodged several people and a wheelchair.

The redhead pushed through a door and disappeared. I walked faster, almost jogging now. I reached the door, *Stairs* marked across it. I shoved it open and fell into a fluorescent-lit double-wide stairwell. I gripped the railing and stared up and down the swirling stairs. But it was empty.

She'd gone.

She must have gotten off at one of the other floors.

I walked back to Clay's room, my mind a whir. Could that really have been Salem? Why would Salem be visiting Clay?

My blood ran cold. Could she have come here to...hurt him while he was weakened?

I barrelled into Clay's room and found him awake. Thank God, he was fine. I was just being silly.

His face lit up when he saw me, then soured to concern. "What's wrong?"

"Who was just here?"

He frowned. "No one."

But I saw her coming out of Clay's room.

Did you, Aria? "Are you sure?"

"Of course I'm sure."

"No one came to visit you while I was away?"

"Who would come visit me?"

"I don't know." Could Clay be lying? Why would he be lying? Unless he didn't want me to know that Salem had been here. Why wouldn't he want me to know that?

"Aria, what's the matter? Come here. You're freaking me out."

As I walked over to him I discreetly sniffed the air. I could be mistaken but was that the faint scent of a woman's perfume? I sat on the side of his bed and settled the bag of Clay's things on his lap and he began to paw through it as if it was Christmas. "I can't wait to put on my own underwear. These hospital ones are itchy. Oh, and my toothbrush and toothpaste. Come here, you." He pulled me closer and planted a kiss on my mouth.

I pulled back. "Maybe you'd been asleep or something and didn't see her."

"What?" His brows drew together. "See who?"

"The person who was here. I saw someone come out of your room."

He narrowed his eyes at me. "I've been awake this whole time you were away. Are you feeling okay, Aria?"

"Never mind." I took a deep breath in and let it out, releasing my thoughts about Salem. "No one. I must have been mistaken."

I stayed with Clay until the nurses kicked me out that night at the end of visiting hours. I didn't realise how exhausted I was until I stepped out from the fluorescent lights and stumbled into the parking lot.

My car was one of the few left in the section of parking I was in, the lights flooding pools of white about the gravelled area. I wondered if Salem was home yet.

As I approached my car I noticed something that made me frown. Something I hadn't noticed before. There was some kind of mark on the front passenger's side. I stepped closer and bent over to inspect it further. Salem must have been in some kind of minor accident when she took my car because I didn't do this. It was a dent and a scrape, chips of paint embedded in it. Red chips of paint.

Dark red.

Mustang red.

The hairs on the back of my neck stood on end.

I straightened, stumbling back from my car, my eyes still on that dent. Could she have…?

I was just jumping to conclusions. Stupid conclusions. She was my sister. She would never hurt Clay. Salem wasn't capable of hurting another person. Right?

He won't leave us alone, Rosey. Not ever.

I shook my head. Not now. Go away. But this time the memories would not stay at bay.

"Please," my fifteen-year-old sister begged me. "You have to make him go away."

"We can run away. Just you and me, Salem. I've been saving money from my part-time job."

"It's not enough. He'll come after us. He'll find us."

"What else can we do?"

"You need to make sure he can never hurt us again."

"I don't know what you're asking me to−"

"You have to kill him. Kill him for me."

My body felt drained of blood, seeping down, out through my toes onto the cold tiled floor and lapping around my ankles like warm sticky puddles. The way that his blood would drip if I did what she asked of me.

Kill him for me. Her voice echoed in my head.

I trembled at the thought of what she was asking me to do. I couldn't. "Salem, please. Don't ask me to do that."

She just stood there blinking at me as if she couldn't believe that I had refused her, like I had turned down her request for me to help her with her homework. She shook her head, her lip beginning to tremble. She began to cry, fat tears dribbling down her smooth cheeks like tracks in snow.

At first I was so shocked I couldn't move. She had never cried. She had never ever cried before now, not even when he…

She fell into my arms. I clung onto her, holding her trembling bird-like body in my arms. I felt how gaunt she had become, how worn thin she now was and it shocked me. When did this happen? When had she started to disappear and I hadn't noticed?

You were too busy hiding in the corner letting her protect you, all the time letting her protect you. Guilt slammed into me like someone had punched out a hole into my gut.

"Please," she whispered. "You have to do this for me, Rosey. I can't take it anymore. I can't. I'll go crazy."

I shushed into her hair. "It's okay. We'll figure something out." I was responsible for this. I was responsible for what happened to her. I couldn't keep being selfish and letting her take it all. I couldn't keep hiding. I had to face him.

"Friday," she said. "Friday is the perfect night."

Friday night he was drunk again, passed out on the couch, having not been able to make it up to his bedroom. He wouldn't be missed by his workers until at least Monday and maybe not even then as he had a reputation for sometimes not showing up on Mondays. It was only because he had colleagues who pitied him, who felt so sorry for him after his wife died that they covered for him.

He had a gun.

It was supposed to be locked up in his safe in his study. But Salem stole the key to the drawer and he hadn't realised his key was gone yet.

It was heavier than I thought it would be, the gun I now held in my shaking hand. We weren't even in the living room yet and my shoulder and fingers were aching from holding it. Perhaps I shouldn't grip it so hard, but all my muscles just seemed so tightly coiled.

His figure lay sprawled across the couch, one arm fallen down so his knuckles brushed the carpet, the air filled with his heavy breathing and reek of cheap rum. We stood a metre away from him, looking down at him, his open mouth, his jowls scrunched under his chin.

"Just do it," Salem hissed at me from over my shoulder.

I shifted my weight from foot to foot, trying to get my balance. I just felt so off. So off.

"Just like when you rip off a Band-Aid. Just do it…"

I could do this. I had to do this. For Salem. I conjured up the images of her, trapped under him, the light dying in her eyes that looked exactly like mine, and resolve heated my blood. He deserved it. He deserved worse.

I pointed the gun at his chest, his chest rising and falling. Rising and falling. Once I pulled the trigger it would rise and fall no more. I gripped the shaking gun and…

I dropped my arm, the metal slapping against my thigh.

"What the fuck?" Salem hissed.

I turned around to face her. I could see the disappointment in her eyes even in the dark. "I can't."

"What'sssss goin' on?" A voice slurred out from behind me.

I jumped, almost dropping the weapon. Oh God. He was awake, his bleary eyes were open and on me. Then on the gun at my side. "Whatta you doin' with that?" He suddenly seemed so awake and alert as he pushed himself up on the couch, the devil flashing in his eyes even as his voice was low and gentle. "Come here, sweetheart."

I shuddered. I hated when he called me sweetheart.

He rose up to his full height. I stumbled back, hissing as the back of my leg banged against the corner of the table.

"Shoot," Salem cried. "Shoot him."

His eyes fell upon the gun in my hand. "Give it to me."

I tripped on the edge of the carpet and fell to the ground, my palms opening to try and break my fall. Pain jarred up my arms. The gun made a clattering noise. My vision shuddered as I hit the base of my skull against the ground.

I dropped the gun. Where was it?

Salem fell to my side, her eyes were firm and fierce. I saw the flash of metal in her hand. "I won't let him hurt us anymore," she hissed.

I watched her turn to him, her arms coming out straight in front of her, the barrel pointed up towards his chest. Her hands weren't even shaking. Not like mine had been.

"Sweetheart…"

"Go to hell." She fired. And again.

Bang bang bang the noise exploded through the room and through my head, making my vision clatter like dice in a box.

My father's eyes bugged open as blood spread across his torso from the six holes that Salem had plugged into him. All six bullets we had loaded. Now in his body. He made a strangling noise.

"You will *never* hurt me again."

He fell, dropping like a sack of potatoes across my legs.

I screamed and kicked back along the carpet until I was free of his dead weight, his wet, heavy body, his lifeless arms. I clambered to my feet and cowered next to Salem, who was already upright, standing there, staring at the carpet, a cold, dead look on her face, blood spray across her cheeks and fingers.

"Salem," my voice shook, "what have you done?"

She turned her muted eyes at me, matte and cold, and a slight smile touched the corners of her lips, making me shiver. "I did what you couldn't." She shoved something cold into my hands. It was the gun. "Get rid of it."

My eyes snapped back up to her as she stood contemplating our unmoving father, the smile on her face growing wider.

"What?"

She made an exasperated noise. "He's dead. That gun killed him. Think. We can't let the police get a hold of that gun. It's evidence of what we did."

"*We*? But you shot him."

Salem's eyes narrowed on me. "Whose fingerprints are on the gun?"

She was right. Both our prints would be on it. Both of us. Even me. Even though I didn't pull the trigger. "How do I...?"

"Throw it in the river or the sewers."

"Then what?"

She flinched. I heard it too; the distant sound of police sirens. She leaned in close and stared right into my eyes so her face was all that I saw. "Run, you idiot."

Chapter Thirteen

I drove to the hospital the next day to pick up Clay when he was released. Salem hadn't returned to the apartment yet. I hadn't been able to confront her about the dent in my car.

The dent. The Mustang red paint chips. It played in my mind over and over again.

If she had run Clay off the road, would she even come back? Or would she be too afraid that Clay would turn her in?

It would explain why she would leave the car. She was too smart to drive off in a car that she'd committed a crime in. Once again she was leaving evidence of her actions in my hands.

She could be anywhere by now. Or…my skin prickled as I stared around the parking lot…she could be here, watching.

"Earth to Aria. Are you okay?" Clay was staring at me with a concerned look on his face as we walked from the hospital hand in hand.

I shook off my dark thoughts. "I should be asking you that. How's your head?"

"It's fine."

We continued to walk in silence, the air heavy with all the things we weren't saying. As we neared the car I made a decision that I would not hide my suspicions from Clay. "Actually, I'm not okay. I need to show you something."

"What is it?"

I walked to the passenger side of the car and pointed, watching

Clay's face for his reaction. "Salem's been taking my car without asking. This dent wasn't there before your accident."

I thought I saw a flash of panic on Clay's face before he smothered it with a shrug. "She must have scraped against a parked car or something."

"That doesn't look like a parking scrape. That looks like she rammed into something beside her."

"Did you talk to her about it?"

"I haven't seen her in days. I know you told the police that you just lost control of your car. But I want to know the truth." I took a deep breath. "Did Salem try to run you off the road?"

Clay's brows pressed together, anger lining the corner of his eyes. "No."

"'Cause if you're protecting her for me...because of what you know about her past...?"

"Why are you so determined to prove she did something to me?"

"Why are you protecting her?"

"I'm not. Aria, I swear to you, my car just ran off the road."

"I want to see it."

"What?"

"Your car. Where's your car? I want to see it."

"It's being fixed. The damage wasn't that bad." Clay narrowed his eyes. "You don't trust me. Aria, you're being paranoid. Salem had nothing to do with my accident."

Hard to trust you when you're lying. I knew he was. I just had this feeling deep down inside but I couldn't tell you where it came from or why. Clay was hiding something.

Flick stared at me when she opened the door. "What's wrong?"

"I'm sorry for just showing up like this. I need to talk to someone." *Someone who isn't lying to me.*

She stepped aside to let me in.

I stayed at Clay's last night. But the tension was there underneath everything. Clay had tried to pretend that everything was fine but I knew he was covering. I knew it. I wasn't just being paranoid. Too many things were suspicious to me.

This morning I left early instead of spending the day. I made an excuse and drove around, my mind wandering, my arms turning the wheel automatically, not wanting to go home in case Salem was there. That's how I finally found myself at Flick's place.

Flick made us both a coffee and sat me down on her couch and waited.

This would be the first time I ever confided in anyone who wasn't Salem or Clay. But I couldn't seem to talk to either of them about this. Shouldn't I be able to talk to my sister and my boyfriend about anything? How did I get here? How did we get here?

"It's about Salem…and Clay."

Flick's eyes widened. She motioned for me to continue.

I began to tell her bits and pieces of the last few weeks: Salem's growing resistance against Clay, her refusal to have dinner with him, them meeting accidentally, her advice to break up with him, her anger that I wouldn't leave Mirage Falls with her, and that she'd been stalking Clay. Finally, I told her about Clay's accident and about the scrape suddenly appearing on my car that looked like Mustang red paint.

"Jesus, is Clay okay?"

"He's fine. He was released yesterday."

"What does Clay say about this? I mean, he was there. Did he see Salem driving the car that ran him off the road?"

"He says he just lost control of the car. He refuses to admit that there was another vehicle present."

Flick frowned. "So you think he's lying? Why would he lie about Salem trying to hurt him? Why would he protect her?"

"I don't know," I whispered. "Maybe he thinks he's protecting me by protecting her. I mean, if he turned her in then there'd be grounds to arrest Salem and…if she was arrested…" They'd figure out who she was. They'd tie her to our father's murder. And then she'd go away for life. This made sense. This was why Clay was protecting Salem. He was protecting her for me.

Except…I never told Clay about my father's murder.

I rubbed my face with my fingers. "Salem's had a rough life. She's still trying to deal with things that…" I shook my head, "if those things had happened to me, I don't think I would be able

201

to cope the way she has. I'm not sure I'd still be alive. I'm so worried about her. I think she needs help that I can't give her." Not anymore. Or maybe I was never able to help her. I only thought I was helping.

"Honey, if she needs help, you need to talk to someone. A professional."

That's exactly what Clay said. I sighed. I wanted to but, "I can't."

"Why not?"

"I know her. She won't go."

"Maybe you just have to make that decision for her."

I froze. "What...what do you mean?"

"Hang on a sec." Flick disappeared into her room. I sat sipping my coffee, which I could barely taste, and I heard the sound of drawers being opened and shut.

She returned and held out a white business card.

I didn't move to take it. "What is it?"

She cleared her throat. "I had an uncle who needed...help. We called them and they...took care of him."

I frowned and took the card.

Hellingly Country Hospital - Psychiatric Facility
Peregian Beach, Queensland

There was an address and a phone number underneath.

"You had him committed."

"Cruel to be kind, honey. Cruel to be kind."

"I can't do that to Salem."

"You'd rather she gets worse?"

"No, but..."

"Just take it. You don't have to use it. But just take it, just in case."

I stared at the card, the letters blurring together.

I could call them. I could confess everything I knew about Salem. Perhaps I had been crazy for thinking I could help her on my own.

Then she'd hate you. She'd see this as a betrayal.

I could already see Salem's face, round, disbelieving eyes as they dragged her away. *How could you do this to me?*

I couldn't just send her away. I had to talk to her first.

Salem was my twin, my best friend. My soulmate. I'd get her side of the story. Then I'd make her see that Clay wasn't a threat. She would never hurt me. Right?

I slipped the card into my bag. I wasn't going to use it. So why did it feel like I was already betraying her?

It was late afternoon when I left Flick's and finally headed home.

"Salem?" I called as I pushed open the door. My living room was empty like it had been for days now. *Salem, where are you?* I wanted to scream. *I'm not mad, just please come home. Let me know you're okay.*

I shut the front door behind me and dumped my bag on the kitchen counter. I walked into our bedroom and stared at her corner. Did it look like her stuff had moved? Had she been home when I wasn't here? Why would her duffel still be there? Wouldn't she take it with her if she was leaving for good?

She wouldn't leave without you.

So where was she?

Maybe something amongst her things would tell me where she'd gone? Maybe she'd return to somewhere she'd been before? I grabbed her pile of clothes and threw them on the bed so I could go through them properly, turning out pockets as I went.

Wait…was that *my* dress? I frowned. It was. My white peasant dress with the cute buttons up the front. I'd wondered where that had gone. When had I even last worn it?

When we were kids we used to share clothes. But as adults it had seemed that our tastes had peeled apart. Why would she borrow my dress?

Unless she wanted to look like me.

Unless she wanted *Clay* to think she was me.

I shook my head. Ridiculous. That was ridiculous. Why would she want that? But I couldn't shake this uneasiness that had settled in the pit of my stomach.

I found nothing in her pockets or amongst her clothes. They all needed laundering. Had she even bothered to wash anything since she got here?

I picked up her duffel bag and threw that on the bed. There were wads of cash stuffed in the pockets. This made me sink a little with relief. Salem wouldn't leave for good without her money. She would be back for sure.

But where was she now?

There was nothing else in here. No ID. No receipts or books or scraps of paper. No semblance of identity at all. I put her duffel back in the corner and threw all the clothes from the bed back on it. Something white, blending in with her pillow, caught my eye. It was a small book left open, the pages flapping lightly from the breeze coming in through the window. I hadn't noticed it sitting there before I had thrown the clothes on top of it.

The pages flicked across to one that had writing on it. I recognised Salem's messy scrawl that only I seemed to be able to read; it hadn't changed from when she was younger.

This looked like her journal.

I picked it up, then paused. I shouldn't be reading her journal.

But it might tell you where she's gone.

She left her money here. She'll be back. You can't invade her privacy like that.

I went to close it but I spotted Clay's name on the page. I frowned, scanning the page. She'd been writing about him.

I shouldn't. I should leave her to her privacy. But…she had been so *off* I just needed to look inside her head and see what was going on with her.

I glanced over my shoulder. I was still alone in my apartment. I closed the bedroom door, sat on the bed and began to read.

Wednesday, 4 November

Clay fucking Jagger. I heard your knock. It sounded through the living room like a gunshot boom boom. I should have known better than to have answered it.

I saw you standing there, eyes like forget-me-nots, and I almost stopped breathing. I'd almost forgotten how fucking hot you were. Almost. You brushed your fingers through your hair and that single movement, that deliberate movement, so adorably boyish adding a youthful innocence to your sharp masculine jaw and bottomless dark eyes.

You're far from innocent. I know it more than most.

The smile you gave me almost stopped my heart. Hah, there, I'm dead. No one *ever* looked at me the way you looked at me. No one ever smiled the way you smiled at me.

"Hey, angel," you breathed, and your voice rumbled into my body. A stark realisation unlatched the bottom to my stomach. You weren't looking at *me*. You were looking at *her*. You thought I was her.

"I missed you." Your voice, your fucking *voice*. Vibrant and rumbling and barbed, digging into my skin and making it pebble. I couldn't take my damn eyes off you. They roamed all over you, your strong jaw, your rounded shoulders, your wide torso, your strong legs and the thick package I knew lay underneath those jeans.

I snatched my eyes away from your crotch. Just as you lifted up your arms to pull me into a hug. Those devilish arms. It would have been so easy to just let you. It would have been so damn easy for me to close my eyes for just one second and pretend. For a moment I almost let you.

"Come here."

I saw an image of you covering your mouth over mine. I could almost feel what they felt like – soft yet firm and your greedy tongue prying open my mouth, demanding entrance to me, your fingers twisting into my hair so hard, my back arched into you and my scalp and core tingling.

I shoved those thoughts away. Bad thoughts. Bad bad thoughts. Thoughts I should not be having. My brain was made wrong. Bad brain. Always thinking bad bad things. Always.

"Get the fuck away from me." I stuck out my arm to keep you back. Your chest bumped into my palm, hard and warm like volcanic rock even through your t-shirt.

You laughed a devil's laugh. "What kind of game is this, Aria?"

"I'm. Not. Aria."

You jolted. "You're not−"

"I'm Salem." I crossed my arms over my chest.

"Salem." My name on your siren's lips was a curse, your face falling into a mask of horror. "You're back."

"I'm back."

I watched your Adam's apple dip and bob in your tanned neck as you tried to swallow.

Why are you here with her? I wanted to ask. But I sensed her coming. I couldn't let her see you and me together. It would be a bad *bad* thing. She would know.

She would *know.*

And it would fuck everything up.

"We never met. Come back in ten minutes like you only just arrived." I slammed the door in your face.

Thursday, 19 November

You were so easy to follow. You made it so easy. Or perhaps you meant it to be that way.

Your wide back disappeared around the dirty brick wall. I felt a strange anxiousness, a sense of loss at the thought of losing you, so I hurried.

I shouldn't have been worried. You were there waiting for me around the corner.

You shoved me up against the wall in a sweet crush, pieces of rough brick marking my back. You leaned into me, so close I could barely breathe, so close I could see the flecks of lighter blue in your sapphire irises. My body broke out into tingles and burned as you breathed onto me. "Nice to see you again, Salem."

"Wish I could say the same for you."

Your eyes narrowed. "Why are you following me?"

"I wasn't. I was just around."

"Don't lie to me. You've been trailing me since I left my apartment."

You knew I'd been following you. I should have known. You're smart. Too smart. So I have to be smarter.

"Whatever you're trying to do, stop it."

"I don't know what you're talking about," I lied through gritted teeth as I tried not to inhale your familiar scent, that scent that made my stupid knees wobble.

Your fingers dug into my shoulder and side like pins into a butterfly. I had to escape you but I couldn't move. "You told her I was cheating on her. You tried to get her to leave with you just so we'd be forced to break up."

"Isn't it still cheating if you're with someone and you really want to be with someone else?"

You flinched. I could see all those memories flash across your face, all those sharp, sticky memories. "I love–"

"You love a ghost. You're going to hurt her when she finds out."

Your face screwed up and you pressed against me as if to

emphasise your words. "I'd never hurt her. *Never*."

"You really think you'll be able to stop yourself?"

"I will. I am."

"That's a lie and you know it." Just to prove it to you I pressed my hips into yours and I felt you stiffen. I leaned in real close.

Your whole body tensed, your face screwing up as if it was an effort to keep from moving, or perhaps it was an effort to remain still. "What are you doing?"

"Do you remember?" I whispered. "Do you remember how this feels, Clay?" I licked a soft line with my tongue against the seam of your lips until they opened with a groan, a low rumbling noise which I sucked into my body with glee.

"Stop it." But that's not what your body was saying. Your fingers clawed into me and your body grew harder as I rolled my hips against you with more urgency. The memory came back with ease now. My hips and yours. Your lips on mine.

I shoved it away.

"You're bad," I spat out, gritting my teeth so hard I could feel the tension shooting into my brain like tendrils. "You're going to hurt her just like you hurt–"

"That was an accident." He cringed. "I didn't mean for it to happen. I didn't know…"

"Now you do. Leave us alone."

"I can fix things. Give me a chance to fix it."

"You can't."

"I can. I have a therapist who's–"

"You really think some clueless shrink with all her cold academic credentials is going to help?" I shoved you back and you let me. I almost smiled at the relief the cold air between us gave me, and yet I wanted to cry at how my body missed yours. "Leave us alone or I will find a way to end you."

"Is that a threat?"

"It's more than a threat. It's a promise."

Monday, 23 November

You won't let it go. You won't leave. It's only a matter of time before you fuck up and hurt her.

It will destroy her.

I can't let that happen.

Adrenaline flooded my body as my fingers gripped the steering wheel, my eyes fixed on the tail of your Mustang up ahead on this stretch of long, lonely road.

I pressed my foot down and the car sped up until I was almost at your bumper. I pulled out around you as if I was going to overtake. For a moment I kept pace, glancing over, taking my eyes off the road ahead, until you looked over and our eyes met. I could see when you recognised me. I could see when the recognition turned to fear, when you realised what I was about to do.

Did you underestimate me, Clay Jagger? Did you underestimate the lengths that I would go to for her?

That was your mistake. It would be your last.

I yanked the wheel over, just as you hit the brakes. In that fateful moment everything slowed so that the micro-increments between the seconds, that pause between heartbeats, became the steady tick tick tick.

To my surprise, a cold dread flooded my body. What was I doing? Destroying my heart and hers? I tried to pull back.

But it was too late.

My car clipped the side of yours, the sick crumple of metal crackling through my ears like static. I was thrown aside in my seat, the belt catching around my ribs. You swerved off the lane and into the overgrown gutter.

I kept driving and my heart dropped into the bottomless pit that had become my stomach.

Tuesday, 24 November

You recognised me the instant I stepped into your hospital room and closed the door behind me. "Salem." Your eyes narrowed and your hands clenched into fists in the sheets.

"You look like shit." I stepped cautiously towards your bed, eyeing you over, trying to ignore the bothersome feelings of guilt threading their way through my body.

"Thanks to you." You swung your legs over the edge of the hospital bed and stood, your gaze and your posture never wavering. "If you came here expecting an invalid to manipulate, I'm afraid I have to disappoint you."

Through your thin hospital gown I could see the outline of your thick, muscled body, that body you worked on every day to keep your demons at bay. Damn you and your flimsy gown. Damn you. I could almost see you as you stood naked before me for the first time. I shoved that thought away. Now was not the time to get sentimental.

"Stay away from us." I tried to keep the shake out of my voice. "I'm warning you."

"Warning me?" You took a step towards me and the walls began to feel like they were closing in. "Like running me off the road was a warning?"

"I didn't want to warn you. I wanted to *kill* you." If I made you afraid of me then maybe I would stop shaking in my shoes like a pathetic little girl. "Don't fuck with me, Clay."

"I don't believe you."

"What?"

"I don't believe that you wanted to kill me."

I did.

"You could have slammed straight into me, sending me out into a tree, instead you only clipped my car. You pulled back at the last minute, didn't you?"

"Screw you."

"If you wanted me to die then you wouldn't have called emergency after you ran me off the road."

I flinched. "I didn't."

"I called emergency as well, as soon as I was able to get a hold of my mobile. They told me my accident had already been called in. An anonymous caller. There was no one else on that road except us. I don't care how hard you protest. I know you care about me."

"Shut up. I do not."

"You do. Maybe you even love me, too."

You took another step closer and my head began to swim. "Stay back. Keep away from me."

You wouldn't take your eyes off me, those intense blue orbs framed by those dark lashes, boring into my very soul. You lunged for me and caught my arm before I could back away, pulling me in close so that your hot breath swirled around my forehead, reminding me of things I'd rather forget. "Let go of me."

"Why are you fighting me?"

"Because of what happened *that night*. You remember what happened that night, don't you?"

The pain and guilt etched into every one of your beautiful, hateful features. "How could I forget?"

"What you did…it was unforgivable."

"I haven't slept with her. I promise you, I won't." You raised a hand to my face and you brushed your thumb across my cheek. It was gentle. The gentlest touch I have ever felt in my life. And yet, it scared me more than any tight fist and scarred knuckles I have ever encountered, because the touch reared something in me I wasn't sure I could control. I wanted to give in. I wanted to give up my promise to Aria, my promise to protect her, to always put her first.

"We shouldn't fight," you said. "Let's find a way through this. Together."

My skin broke out, my mouth parted, the air sucking right out of me. I felt lightheaded. Before I knew what I was doing I turned my head to brush my lips against your palm. "Clay," I breathed.

Shit. What was I doing?

"I…I can't stay away." Your voice was equally as pained. "I've tried. Don't you think I know it would be better for her…

for you…if I stayed away?" Your arm wrapped around me to pull me closer and I *let* you. My stomach twisted with my betrayal. But my body flooded with pleasure as your fingers threaded through my hair. "Please," your lips brushed against my earlobe, "come back to me, Olivia."

Olivia.

That name shattered everything, sending the flutters of pleasure scattering like dried leaves. "Don't call me that. Don't you *ever* call me that." I shoved you away and stumbled back, clawing desperately for the door. "I'm warning you. Stay away. Or you'll ruin *everything*."

Chapter Fourteen

I dropped the journal. It clattered to the ground as pieces of this puzzle began to slam into place.

Salem was Olivia.

Salem was Clay's ex-girlfriend.

That's why she hated Clay. That's why she was trying to get rid of him. To protect me.

His mother saw me and called me Olivia. She mistook me for Salem.

Why would they not tell me? Why would Salem keep this from me? Because she thought she was protecting me?

Why would Clay want to be with *me*?

Oh my God. The realisation seized me like a thick, calloused hand around my throat.

"I haven't slept with her. I promise you, I won't."

This was why Clay refused to sleep with me. He was saving himself for Salem. For Olivia. *"Come back to me, Olivia."*

Clay was using me to get to her, to make her jealous. I was a replacement for *her*. It was all for her. All of this was for her.

My body lashed with pain like I was being whipped, and I rocked back and forth as my legs trembled and I threatened to topple over. Why would he do this to me?

Why did they ever break up?

"What you did...it was unforgivable."

Something happened. Something happened *that night,*

something terrible…because of Clay's schizophrenia? Did he relapse? Freak out? What happened? Did he hurt someone? Did he hurt…her? Did he hurt Salem? Is that why she left him?

What do you really know about him?

She tried to warn me. My throat burned as I choked on my first sob.

No, I couldn't believe it. I couldn't believe it. I could see the way that Clay looked at me, the way he touched me.

Every time he looked at you, he was seeing Olivia. Every time he touched you, he was touching her.

Calm down, Aria, calm down. They're just words. False words on lying pieces of paper. Salem said he was cheating on you but that was a lie. You already know she's trying to get you away from him. What if this is just another one of her schemes? You think it's a coincidence that she left her diary out for you to find? You *know* Clay. He wouldn't cheat on you. Salem wrote these lies and left it out here for you to find. She's growing unstable. She *wants* to break you and Clay up.

Because Clay's no good for you. He's hiding things, you know he is. He even told you himself. He lied about his car accident. He lied about Salem being in the hospital. What else is he lying about?

Shut up. Shut up stop talking crazy you sound like Salem. It's not true. It's not true.

Maybe.

Maybe. Can you put your faith in maybes?

No. I need to know the truth. The truth. Even if it kills me.

My phone. Where's my phone?

In my bag. Where's my bag?

In the kitchen.

My hands trembled as I rummaged through my bag on my kitchen counter, my trembling fingers feeling clumsy and thick. Fuck it. I turned my bag upside down and the contents bounced across the smooth countertop. I snatched up my phone. I hit the call symbol and it came up with the last number I dialled.

Clay.

My heart cracked.

Just be calm. Don't accuse him, just ask him. This could just be another one of Salem's stunts to try and break you two up. I swallowed down a thick knot and forced myself to keep calm as the ring tone sounded in my ear.

It clicked over to his voice message. "Clay," I said, trying to keep the shake out of my voice. "You need to call me. As soon as you get this. Call me." And I hung up.

Where was he?

There were only two places he could be. His apartment or his mother's.

I'd start at his apartment. This was a conversation we needed to have face to face anyway. I needed to look into his eyes when he answered all the questions I had for him.

I grabbed my bag to throw everything back in there when I heard something clinking in the bottom. Something was caught in the small hole I had in the lining. I frowned as my fingers closed over it and pulled it out.

It was Salem's house keys. Identical to mine. I must have picked up her keys by mistake. When did I do that?

Or Salem put them in your bag. But why would she do that? Unless this was her way of telling you she was watching you.

I know where you've been. I saw you. I shuddered as the hairs on my neck rose.

My car keys just appearing.

Salem's keys suddenly in my bag.

Her journal suddenly on her pillow.

But no sign of her. Except a flash of the back of her hair between hospital patients.

If she was trying to scare me, she was doing a damn fine job.

Chapter Fifteen

My fingers were shaking when I pressed the buzzer to Clay's apartment, anger making me hold the buzzer down longer than I probably needed to. I yanked my finger off the button and took a deep calming breath as I stared at the speaker, willing it to come to life.

Nothing. He wasn't at home.

Through your thin hospital gown I could see the outline of your thick, muscled body, that body you worked on every day to keep your demons at bay. Damn you. I could see you as you stood naked before me for the first time.

What if he was with Salem? What if he was with her right now? Upstairs.

Together.

What if that open box of condoms was for her?

"I haven't slept with her. I promise you, I won't."

My breath came out in short bursts as my lungs clamped together. What if Salem was trying to get me to break up with Clay so *she* could have him back? What if I was just some pawn caught up in their lovers' tiff?

I lifted up my eyes to where I knew his balcony was. Nobody was on it. I needed to get up there.

Clay's key. I still had Clay's spare key from when I brought him his toiletries at the hospital. I rummaged through my bag and found them before letting myself into the lobby.

My heart pounded at an increasing pace as I neared Clay's apartment door. Was I really doing this?

I couldn't hear anything through the door. No laughter, no moans, no talking.

That didn't mean they weren't in there.

As quietly as I could I slipped the key into the lock, bit by bit before turning it. The lock opened with a loud click, making me flinch. I twisted the handle, pushed open the door and stuck my head in. The kitchen and living room were both empty. The TV was off. So was the radio.

I slipped inside and shut the door behind me before any of the neighbours could spot me. The state of the place hit me. There were unwashed dishes in his sink, dishes on the counter, papers scattered across his dining room table and some fallen on the floor.

I crept as quietly as I could to his bedroom but it, too, was empty, just clothes strewn about the room. My eye fell upon the drawer he had given me.

My drawer. How ridiculous was I being? Of course Clay loved me. He had given me a drawer and clothes…

The cherry print pyjamas. They weren't brand new. They had been *Olivia's*. Of course they fit me. Salem and I were the same size.

I shook my head, fighting back an angry sob, as I stormed over to his side of the bed. There must be something here in his things that would prove his lies. Or exonerate him. I yanked open the top drawer a little too hard, causing the drawers to shake. Inside were cords, coins, receipts…

But there was a piece of paper underneath everything. I moved everything aside and picked it up. It was a familiar drawing. A comic.

It was the Aria comic, exactly like the partly drawn one I spotted on his table the other day, *Adventures of Aria* written across the top in bright yellow font.

My eyes found the date in the corner.

21 July.

Five months ago.

But Clay hadn't met me until early August. How could he

have drawn this comic based on me in July?

What the fuck?

"Hello, sister dear." A voice came from behind me.

I leapt to my feet, my heart cramming into my throat. Salem stood at the door to Clay's bedroom, leaning against the doorframe. Was she following me? Or…had she been watching Clay's place?

"How did you get in?"

She gave me an amused look that managed to look not amused at all. "Through the front door."

"But…I locked it." Didn't I? I thought I did. I mustn't have. Or maybe Clay gave her a key.

"When were you going to tell me about this?" Salem held up a small rectangular piece of card.

Shit. It was the card that Flick gave me. "I don't know what that is."

"Don't lie to me. I found it in your bag."

"You went through my things." When had she done that?

"And you're telling me you didn't go through *my* things?"

I opened my mouth, then shut it again. How did she know that I read her journal?

She shook her head, flicking the card to the floor. "You were going to have me locked up."

"No."

"After everything I've done for you."

"I was just worried about you. I was just thinking about whether it'd be good for you. I hadn't decided to use it."

"I'm not crazy."

"You tried to run Clay off the goddamn road. You could have killed him."

"I'm not fucking crazy," she screamed as she pushed off the doorframe and walked into the room. That's when I saw the flash of metal in her hand that had been hidden behind her back until now. She was holding a gun, a glinting metal contraption of death.

"Salem, what are you doing with a gun?"

"Did you ever stop to think that perhaps it's *you* who is crazy?" She strode farther into the room, her gun punching the air to punctuate her sentences. "That you're the one who needs help?"

I stumbled back towards the head of the bed.

She's dangerous.

She's not dangerous, she's your sister.

Doesn't mean she's stable. She's holding a fucking gun.

I glanced over to the ensuite door, slightly ajar. It was my only other way out. But there was no way I was getting past her. Not when she had a gun in her hand.

She'd never shoot me.

Would you bet your life on that?

"Hellingly Country Hospital – Psychiatric Facility. Who put this into your head?" She pointed the gun at me as if it were her finger. My throat closed up at sight of the winking black eye of the barrel now being turned on me. "Clay? Or that nosy boss of yours, Flick? What kind of name is Flick anyway?"

If I told her, would she try and hurt Flick too? "No one put it in my head."

"Liar."

"*I'm* the liar?" Anger trickled out through the fear. "You lied to *me*. I found your journal. You and Clay had a relationship before me. I know *you're* Olivia."

"Olivia," she spat out. "That name is cursed."

"What happened that night? What happened to break you two up?"

"There are some things that should stay buried. Some secrets that should never come out in the open. They can't." Her face softened. "Let's just forget about it. We can just leave. You and me, Aria."

"I won't forget about it. I need to know the truth."

"The truth… You don't want the truth."

"I do."

"You don't know what you're fucking talking about."

But I did.

I wanted the truth.

The truth.

Even if it killed me.

Did I? *Did* I?

I gripped at my hair, shaking my head, trying to dislodge all these jumbled thoughts, trying to let these puzzle pieces settle in where they belonged. But they just rattled away.

Salem snarled. "Goddamn it, I knew I should have gotten rid of him sooner." She scratched her head with the barrel of her gun. "Think, Salem, think."

She wanted Clay.

She wanted Clay dead.

What the hell was the truth?

I jumped when my phone rang in my bag, buzzing against my leg through the leather. There was only one person who could be calling.

Salem's eyes snapped to the bag. "Give me your phone."

"What?"

"Your phone. Give it to me."

"W-Why?"

"I'm the one with the gun. Give me your phone."

I slowly pulled it from my bag and handed her the phone, praying that he'd just hang up. She snatched it from my hand and answered it, her eyes boring into mine.

"Clay Jagger," she said into my phone. My heart almost stopped. "No, it's not Aria. Yes, that's right." I flinched towards her, desperate to grab the phone off her but I could barely move. The gun she thrust at me, keeping me back, kept me feeling like I was a mere ghost with no power to affect anything.

"Meet me at the place we first met. You do remember where we first met, don't you, Clay, darling?" An unnerving smile lifted the corner of her mouth. "You took Aria there when you first told her you loved her. Good. Twenty minutes. Tick tock."

Salem hung up the phone.

Her words remained ringing in my ears. *You took Aria there when you first told her you loved her.* "How did you know? I never told you about that." The realisation dawned on me. "You...you were following me. No...you were following *him*."

She didn't answer as she approached. She grabbed me by the arm and spun me towards the door, shoving the gun into my back. "Move."

She forced me out of Clay's apartment and down the hallway

to the stairs. I prayed with every shaking step that someone would appear so I could alert them to get help. My sister needed help, serious help. She was unstable. Delusional. But nobody was around. Why was nobody around?

When we got to the lobby she led me to my car, shoving me into the driver's seat before she got into the passenger's side.

"Drive," she said, the black eye of the barrel still pointed straight at me.

"What are you doing?" My voice trembled as it escaped out between my teeth. For the first time in my life I was terrified of her. It was like I didn't know her.

"We're going to end this. Once and for all."

Chapter Sixteen

We were the first ones to arrive at Mirage Gorge.

Salem walked behind me as I trudged a solemn march from the car to the bridge. Clogging my nose was the smell of wet earth and rotting leaves, and the moisture from the waterfall felt like cobwebs on my skin. All sunlight was hidden behind thick sooty clouds, making the misty bridge across the gorge seem like a walkway across to some kind of mystical hell.

"That's far enough."

I stopped in the centre of the bridge and turned slowly around to face Salem. Her features were firm with determination and finality. She looked so normal for someone so insane. She eyed the side of the bridge and ran a finger tenderly across the railing. Her voice sounded faraway, "It all started here."

Oh my God.

She was the angel that Clay had seen on this bridge. It hadn't been a hallucination. She had been the one to save Clay's life.

And now she would be the one to take it.

I bit my bottom lip with my teeth and tasted blood. "You don't have to do this."

She lifted her stormy eyes to me. They no longer glistened with anger but were muted and matte, painted with a deep sadness that caused a knot to rise in my throat. "Yes, I do."

I prayed that Clay wouldn't come. I prayed that he would figure out that this was a trap and call the police. I prayed for any number of things. For the moment that Clay stepped onto this bridge, he was as good as dead.

My heart began to race as I heard the hurried crush of dirt from behind me. As I turned I prayed in vain, *please don't be Clay.*

My heart sank, hope fleeing from the house of my soul as his familiar figure appeared through the mist from the other side of the bridge. I had never seen him look so unsure. That *he* would lose his confidence too…had we no hope left?

"Aria?" Even his voice had become thin and pallid.

"Clay, please go back," I cried.

"Shut up," Salem snapped behind me. "Come on, Clay, come a little closer so we can talk."

Turn around. Go back! Can't you see she's crazy?

But he wouldn't listen. He walked onto the bridge, his footsteps slow and uneven, and my heart thudded louder and harder at his proximity. He stopped only metres from me, his eyes focused over my shoulder. "Salem," his voice shuddered around her name. "Put the gun down. You don't want to hurt anyone." He took another small step towards me.

"Stop!" Salem yelled from behind me and I jumped at the sound, my nerves strung so tightly I was on the verge of snapping apart. "You come any closer and I'll shoot, I swear to motherfucking God!"

He froze, his palms going up as if to try and placate her. "Okay, okay. I've stopped moving."

"Why did you come, Clay?" I gasped, my chest squeezing out of helplessness. How the hell were we going to get out of this mess? "Why did you come alone?"

He didn't answer me.

I hated that I couldn't see Salem. I felt half-blind with my back to her. I hated that I could only see Clay while all he saw was *her.* He had barely glanced at me.

My stomach curdled. Was it true then? Did Clay love Salem? Olivia? Whatever fucking name she went by?

Or was he pretending not to pay me any attention to let her think that he didn't care for me as much as he did?

"Now show me your hands," Salem said. "Show them to me!"

Please Clay, I begged in my head, *just do as she says.*

"Okay, okay." He raised his hands, palms towards me, up to his chest height, his biceps tightening against his grey cotton shirt. "Don't do anything drastic."

"Drastic. Me?" Salem let out a sharp laugh. "Drastic is my middle name, don't you know?"

"Why are you doing this?" I dared to ask. "Do you want him back? Is that it?"

She laughed. "No, you stupid girl. This has all been for *you.* I know the truth about Clay, the truth he tried so hard to bury. I've been trying to protect you from him. To scare him off. But he won't leave us alone. Only one thing left to do."

My stomach tightened at her implication. *Only one thing left to do.* "You don't have to… We can run away. Just you and me, Salem."

"It's not enough. He'll come after us. He'll find us."

I shook my head. "There's been some mistake. Let's just talk about this."

She snorted. "Clay, tell Aria about how you've been trying to get rid of me. Go on, tell her."

Clay flinched. I studied his face, mouth pinched and a darkness clouding his eyes.

Oh my God. "Is it true? Are you trying to get rid of Salem?"

But he wouldn't look at me. He just stared at Salem, his eyes narrowing. "Aria, maybe once upon a time Salem was exactly what you needed. But now she's just holding you back. She'll never let you move on."

My head spun. My sister and my boyfriend, each trying to get rid of the other. The diary entries of Salem's I had read were all one-sided. What pieces was I missing? What had Clay been doing to try and get rid of Salem?

My vision shuddered and I felt something cracking inside me, like the tentative edge of a cliff finally buckling under the elements. I squeezed my eyes shut and tried to shake off the incoming headache. "This doesn't make sense. Both of you, just stop."

"Salem," Clay's voice echoed out across the gorge. "We need

to tell her. We need to tell her the truth."

My eyes snapped open. "Tell me what?"

"No!" Salem cried.

"She's stronger than you give her credit for."

Salem growled. "Don't you remember what happened that−?"

"That night. That night. You keep talking about *that night*. But that was then. This is now."

Once again I felt like an outsider. Watching this argument play out between them, stuck in the middle of them. *That night. What happened that night?*

"Aria," he called. "You're stronger than you know."

Salem had always been the strong one. I had to be strong like Salem.

The last few weeks fluttered inside my head like a bird taking flight. No, I realised, I had to be strong like *me*.

"I know you won't want to hear this, but you need to know the truth…"

"Don't you dare!" Salem pulled back the hammer and it made a horrible cracking sound. Just like my heart.

"Please, no," I begged, the tears forming in my eyes beginning to run down my cheeks.

"You won't shoot me," Clay said.

"I will."

"No, you won't. You care too much about me. But you're right about one thing. It's time to end this. Aria…"

"Stop! I'm warning you," Salem shrieked.

There was a bang as she fired. I screamed. The branches beyond Clay's head cracked as the bullet tore past it. He flinched but the determination didn't slip from his face.

"Stop it, Salem! Stop it!" I spun to stare at my sister. Her eyes were wild and deranged, the gun held in both hands pointed towards Clay. My muscles tensed, ready.

"I'm sorry, Aria…" Clay's voice cracked from behind me.

"No," Salem hissed and I felt rather than saw her finger move. I dove towards the barrel to smother the next bullet with my body.

"…you are Salem."

Chapter Seventeen

My vision shuddered as I flew through the air. I braced myself for a fall onto the bridge but I didn't hit the ground. Nor did I feel the pain of any bullets tearing through me.

You are… Clay's voice echoed in my head.

I felt the sensation of waking and I jolted where I stood. I swayed on my feet before my balance took hold. For a second my mind stuttered before all of my memories flickered back into place, organising themselves into a messy line like a long strand of broken dominos.

You are…

What am I?

Tell me.

I blinked as I stared around me. I was standing on the bridge facing Clay. How was I facing him? I was missing something. I tried to grasp onto more of my memories but they fluttered out of reach like black crows, cawing at me, taunting me with what I didn't know.

How did I get here? Salem had been standing here when I lunged for her.

My eyes found her, my twin, standing beside Clay, her body blurry as if my eyes just couldn't focus on her.

"You idiot," Salem cried. It took me a second to realise she was screaming at Clay. "Now you've done it. The fallout is all on you."

He didn't move. He just stared at me.

And Salem dropped her gaze to stare at her own empty, shaking hands.

Hands. There was something in my hands.

I was holding a gun.

What the hell was I doing with a gun?

The gun handle was smooth under my palm as I pointed it at *his* chest. Fear flashed across his face, causing a riot of power to flood through my veins. For once, he was scared of *me*.

My hands weren't shaking anymore.

"Sweetheart..."

"Go to hell." I squeezed my finger.

Bang bang bang the noise exploded through the room. My father's eyes bugged open as blood spread across his torso from the six holes that I had plugged into him. All six bullets that I had loaded. Now in his body. He made a strangling noise. "You will never hurt me again."

Then he collapsed...

I caught myself before I collapsed onto the bridge.

Salem had been holding this gun. How did I get this gun in my hands?

"Aria?" Clay was standing there, his eyes wide and on me, looking at me...like he was afraid. No, this wasn't right. He wasn't the one that I wanted to fear me. He... He wasn't the one I shot...

I shot someone?

I found my voice. "What's going on?"

"Please, put down the gun."

But a part of me didn't want to. I felt safer with it in my hand. Safer. I gripped the handle tighter. "Not until someone tells me what's going on." I turned my eyes to Salem. For once she was just standing there, mute, a look of absolute dismay on her face. "Salem?"

"Aria, listen to me carefully," Clay said, his voice firm. "Salem isn't real."

Clay's words from earlier finally came back to me. *You are Salem.*

You are Salem.

228

You are…

But the words wouldn't find purchase. They pinged off the inside of my mind like metal pellets.

I swung my eyes to Clay. He was relapsing. He was delusional. How had I not noticed the signs? The odd behaviour. The mess growing in his apartment. "Calm down, Clay," I said slowly. "Salem is right there."

He didn't even look. "No, Aria. She's not."

"Clay, Salem is right there. I can see her. Just look."

"Salem isn't real."

"Salem is right fucking there," I yelled, pointing with the gun at where she stood near him. "She was your ex-girlfriend, Olivia. You loved her and she loved you but when something happened… something that happened that night, she left you. And you came after me. To get her back. Or you used me as a substitute for her. Or…" This wasn't making any sense anymore. My skin started to crawl. What was happening to me?

"Don't freak out."

Anxiety rumbled through my body, shaking me from the inside. "I'm not freaking out."

"Olivia," he said slowly.

That name is cursed.

"Why are you calling me Olivia?" I lifted the gun automatically as Clay started forward towards me.

"Whoa," he raised his palms to me and flinched back. "You're freaking out."

"I'm not freaking out." I was freaking out. I inhaled deeply and loudly.

Don't freak out.

Rosey.

Olivia.

Salem.

Aria.

Don't. Freak. Out.

Salem isn't real.

Salem's words from earlier today came back to me.

Did you ever stop to think that perhaps it's you who is crazy? You're the one in denial?

"But Salem is Olivia," I said, but now I didn't sound convinced.

"*You* are Olivia." Clay was begging me now. "You *were* Olivia. Please, remember. We met right here on this bridge. You saved my life here."

My white cotton dress fluttered as I swung my legs over the railing to sit on it beside a dark-haired boy.

I shook my head and it was gone. "I don't remember. Why don't I remember any of it?"

"Salem's been keeping it from you."

"No," I screamed as something inside me battered against the lid of this box of unwanted things. I couldn't let them out. I couldn't. Keep it inside.

Salem was right. Clay was trying to fuck with my head. I'm not crazy. I'm not the crazy one. Salem is.

I am Salem.

I clutched the gun tighter. "What happened to me? Tell me what you did that night that made Olivia run away."

"I'm afraid," he said. "I'm afraid that as soon as I tell you... you'll run away again."

"If you don't tell me, I'll shoot. There are two bullets left in this gun. I will put one in your leg. It won't kill you but it will hurt. A lot."

I watched him swallow down, hard. When did I learn to use a gun? How did I know that there were two bullets left?

Because I loaded the gun. I loaded it with three bullets before I left my house.

And *I* had let off one shot over Clay's head so there were two bullets left.

I am...

"Your mother died when you were very young," Clay said. "And your father...he started to do horrible things to you. You couldn't cope so you created a sister, a twin sister called Salem who you believed took all the abuse for you. Your name was−"

But I already knew what it was.

Rosey.

Olivia.

Salem.

Aria.

"Rosa," I said. "My name was Rosa."

"Yes," Clay's voice cut into my thoughts. "I met you when you had become Olivia, after you had run away. After you killed him. You didn't remember any of it then. You were seventeen and I was eighteen. We fell in love. We were happy, so happy. Then on your eighteenth birthday, you decided…you wanted to lose your virginity. To me. I didn't know that it would cause you to flashback."

You're so tight.

"You freaked out."

Don't freak out, Olivia.

Clay swallowed. "And that's when I met Salem for the first time. That's when she told me…what had happened to you."

…And the Mirage Falls Mirage Falls Mirage Falls Mirage Falls

"Olivia, Salem, Aria…these are all just parts of you. Dr Bing says that you have Dissociative Identity Disorder. I took you to her because I wanted to know if you could be helped."

Dr Bing *had* been assessing me.

"You don't need help," Salem cried. "You just need me."

Suddenly the gun seemed too heavy. It hung by my side in my right hand like a dead weight. Suddenly it didn't seem safe anymore. It wasn't enough to keep away everything that was coming for me, and I could feel it all coming for me, like scuttling clawed creatures coming for me all at once. "What do I do?"

"I can help you," Clay said. "Give me the gun. We can go together. Dr Bing can help you. She's on her way now. I called her before I came. She wants to help you."

"No one can help you," Salem screamed. "Only I can. I've been the one protecting you all this time. Run with me. Just you and me." Salem held out her hand. "Give me the gun. Let me end this. I'll do what you can't."

Salem, what have you done?

I did what you couldn't.

"I promise," she said, "you won't remember anything about him tomorrow. Quick, before Dr Bing gets here."

"You have a choice, Aria," said Clay. "You can choose me, you can choose to…believe the truth. But it'll be painful. You'll start to remember everything."

Even from here I could smell the reek of alcohol reek of alcohol reek of–

I blinked and it was gone, the ends of it brushing against the tips of my mind.

I looked at him. "If I choose you then I lose Salem."

He nodded, his lips pressed in a grim line. "And you'll lose Salem."

I gazed at Salem, my sister, standing as real as Clay, standing so close to him that she could reach out and touch him if she wanted to. "But she's real to me."

"I know she's real to you."

"She was all I had," I spoke to Clay but stared at Salem. A tear began to fall down my cheek, and it was mirrored in hers. "I love her. I don't know if I can live without her."

"I know."

"Choose me," Salem said. "We can run again. I can make you forget him. Forget all this. We can become someone else again. It'll just be you and me. And you'll be protected."

I turned my eyes towards Clay. He was trying so hard not to show how much he was suffering, but it squeezed out in the creases of his face and was clear in his trembling chin.

"You won't lose me."

"Don't make promises you can't keep."

How could I do this to the man I loved? How could I give him up? "But if I choose her, then I lose you."

He nodded.

"I don't know what to do," I whispered.

I wanted to run and run and keep running until I was so far away that nothing could find me… I could forget Clay and become someone else again… It would be easy.

But I'd lose him. I'd lose who I was becoming, who I *could* become…

Pain shot through my head.

Even from here I could smell the reek of alcohol, the stink of him as he fell into the bed against me.

"Go away," I cried as he grabbed one of my wrists. I punched out with my thin arms but they just bounced off him.

That sick choking feeling rose up inside me to cut off my air as he slipped his hand down between my−

A moan ripped from my lungs. Bad things. Horrible things. Sticky turn-my-insides-out things. I had to keep it inside.

Keep it inside.

Salem and Clay both ran for me but I lifted up my gun and they froze. If either of them touched me right now I would fall apart. Don't touch me. Keep it inside. "Stay away. Both of you. Stay away from me."

"I'm sorry," said Salem. "I don't want to hurt you. But I had to show you a piece. Just a piece of it."

The last shred of doubt about Salem's existence fell away. All those memories I had of her, watching those things happening to her…they had happened to *me*.

"Aria, you can get through this," said Clay. "But you have to face it. It's the only way to start getting better."

Could I?

"Do you think for one second that you're strong enough to handle any of it?" Salem said.

Was I?

All I knew was, I had to choose.

Chapter Eighteen

In the end, my life came down to this. Two people – two faces, two pairs of hands that have pushed aside tears, two pairs of arms that have protected me, held me despite the darkness, despite the pain that threatened to pull me under. And now these two people, the two people I loved the most, were tearing me apart.

"Choose, Aria!" my sister cried at me, her sharp voice echoing over the expanse of the gorge and the sound of water crashing onto rocks.

My hand holding the gun felt heavier and heavier, the muzzle dipping, sweat rolling from where my palm wrapped around the grip, my tendons trembling and crying out in a discordant harmony along with the weighted, fractured wailing of my heart.

I shifted my weight, trying to stand in a way that would keep me upright, even as my legs were trembling so hard I thought I might collapse, my feet crushing dried broken leaves that had swept onto the bridge as if they were bones or pieces of my shattered self. The smell of my own sweat and fear mixed in with the pine and the tang of moist earth.

Choose. The rest of my life came down to this. One choice. Two faces.

In moments like these, everything slowed. Salem always joked that it was life's way of making sure you didn't miss the turning points, the important bits. As if gravity sank heavier and heavier with the weight of the moment until the world was too heavy to turn and everyone held their breath.

It certainly felt like that now. My next action, my next word, would change all of our lives.

"Aria," Clay's deep voice reached my ears. "Whatever happens…I love you." The usual assuredness and authority was gone. Instead, strain and hurt had crumpled up and shoved into his throat. *Choose me. Save me. Love me.*

Before him my life had felt like a stack of old movies: frames missing or out of order, muted crackling sound, flickering and shuttering away, unloved and unseen in an old unused cinema, dank carpets and the smell of stale cigarettes in the musty air.

Then I found him. Or he found me.

He created a warm shield around me where I could be safe. He coaxed away all my layers and shed all my masks and his love soaked right into my skin, right into the very soul of me. He pulled out the fossil buried inside that had been my heart and breathed life into me.

How could I give up the man I loved? The one who loved me with a fierce and unwavering passion, the man who made me feel like I could defeat demons as long as he was by my side.

Winking in the threads of sunlight piercing through the solemn grey clouds, seed fluff twirled about me like swirling, dancing couples. Spinning around like Salem and I used to do in our backyard, hands clasped together tightly, turning round and round, eyes to the sky, our twin voices giggling and floating into the air like dandelions.

She had been my shield before Clay.

"I'm nothing without you, Aria," Salem's voice trembled, desperation leaking into the breaths between her words. *Choose me. Need me. Love me.*

How could I end her? I just got her back. For so long we shared almost everything, and she protected me. Her whole life had been about protecting me. Because she loved me that much.

How could I turn against her, toss her away like an old broken toy?

But I had to choose.

Several weeks ago there was one small, stupid moment, after

I had her back and I had Clay, where I believed I could be happy.

Damn, girl, are you actually smiling?

Oh Flick, everything is just perfect.

One stupid moment.

But that's the thing about us humans: we're resilient. Hope is so hard to snuff out. Even if we've been kicked and beaten down and trod on, hope flares. It rises to the top like oil on water.

Even now as I stare between Clay and Salem, trying to digest our impossible situation, Hope is still there, that terrible pixie, fluttering on my shoulder, whispering.

Maybe it doesn't have to end this way?

Maybe Flick will show up and sort this out in the way only she could do, clear and stern but with a whole lot of sass.

Maybe the police will come storming through the trees, their flashlights and guns upon us, forcing us all apart.

Or a knight riding on a white horse...

Fuck you, Hope. Here's the truth.

Nobody is coming.

No one will save us.

And someone isn't going to make it out of this forest today.

I could see us now, the three of us making a chain like when I was a kid, folding pieces of coloured paper into rectangles, cutting out an arm, a leg, and half a head, and unfurling my new patterns in the light to reveal a line of paper dolls. Clay, Salem and I – we were all just paper dolls in a paper chain, me in the middle, each end pulling tighter and tighter until something had to tear.

Who would I rip apart?

"Choose," my sister screamed. "It's either him or me."

My fingers tightened around my gun in a reflex. This was it. I either ended her. Or destroyed Clay.

I squeezed my eyelids shut for a moment, just for a moment of peace. Just for an instant I could shut out the inevitable, and in this blessed darkness I believed I could conceive a way that both could exist in my life. A way that I could choose Salem *and* Clay.

You can't have both.

You tried.

You.

Can't.

Have.

Both.

Choose now.

But how?

What do you do when someone puts a gun to your head? Clay's words came back to me, echoing as loud in my mind as if he had just spoken them. *You refuse to bend. You push back. You find another way. You take that gun off him and put it back in his face. But you do* not *give in.*

Find another way…

I knew what I had to do. A kind of peace settled on my skin, as delicate as gossamer, as light as silk.

I opened my eyes to a world of bright light until my vision adjusted. The torn and pained faces of the two people I loved came into focus. The only two people I've shared air with while we slept, the same two people I'd crawl into Hell to be with, and the only two people I would die for. I forced the ghost of a smile forward.

And turned the gun on myself.

Chapter Nineteen

Salem stared at the barrel I pointed at her. At her. At me. At the part of me that had been protecting me.

"You're choosing him?" Salem choked out, her face twisting up, revealing her inner pain. A pain that I felt in my own stomach.

I lowered the gun. "I can run with you, Salem," I said, my voice shaking. "But then…we'll just keep running. But we can't outrun ourselves. I'm sorry. I can't go with you. I don't want to keep forgetting things."

"You fucking idiot," she cried. "These memories will destroy you."

Sometimes we need to crumble to nothing before we can rebuild ourselves into someone better.

"Maybe… Maybe not… But I have to try."

"No," she wailed. "You were supposed to choose me. *Me*."

I didn't know what to do, stunned into silence as she began to cry. Her voice trembled as she sniffed back sobs, my heart breaking as I watched her fall apart because a gun, a choice and the truth separated us.

"You want to get rid of me, even though I protected you from everything you didn't want to face. I took all of it just so you wouldn't have to remember it. I killed that bastard because *you* couldn't do it. When you had a breakdown because of him," she pointed at Clay, "I took you away from him, I hid him from you. And when he came back for you, I tried to stop him. I did all those things for you because I love you. I fucking love you, Rosey. And you're still choosing *him*."

"*What if that's not the choice you have to make?*"

"*What do you mean?*"

"*What if you don't have to choose between Clay and Salem?*"

"*Then what would I choose?*"

"*Choose* you*.*"

"That's not what I'm choosing. It was never a choice between you and Clay. Don't you see? I'm choosing me," I said. "I'm choosing *me*."

"No," slipped from Salem's mouth, disbelief clear in her wide eyes and hanging jaw.

"Please, Salem. I want to get better. But you're a part of me. *You* need to want to get better too."

"You're asking me to give up my existence…for you."

My shoulders dropped. "It's not like that…" I trailed off.

It was exactly like that. For me to get better, she would have to hand over all of the missing pieces of me that she had kept safe until now. She would have to eventually fade away.

Choose you.

I held onto these two words with every cell of my being, willing her to understand. I forced myself to stand strong. Salem stared at me, her sobs slowly abating, until two silent tears ran down her cheek.

I felt her tussle with this choice, her choice, my choice. I knew I could never move on unless we were both in agreement. Even though she wasn't *real*, she was to me. And she mattered so much.

Her fear shot through me because it was mine. Was I strong enough to face my past? Would I just break?

I felt her anguish because we shared it. How had she become redundant?

I tasted her hurt like sourness on my tongue. I didn't need her anymore.

"You're wrong," I said. "I need you now more than ever."

We inhaled.

We exhaled.

I felt the moment when she accepted it like a release inside of me. And underneath it all was a glimmer of hope as two torn paper dolls folded together to appear as one.

"Salem?" I asked.

"Do I have to sit around hugging other sweaty patients?"

"You'll only have to hug me, I promise."

"And no stupid blot pictures."

I managed a laugh through my tears. "No blot pictures."

She walked right up to me. I felt like I could really see her for the first time, shimmering and ethereal like my reflection in the lake that summer. How could I ever thank her for protecting me the way she did? How could I ever thank her now for what she was giving up?

"Thank you," I started to say. "Thank you for—"

She raised her hand to silence me. *I know*, she said, but only in my head. *We* are *the same person, you know?* She smiled.

I smiled back even though my heart was hurting.

Chapter Twenty

Day 1

"I'm not sure I want to stay here anymore."

"Angel, it's only for three months. I'll be waiting right here for you when you get out."

I looked back to the doctor and nurse waiting patiently for me and bit my lip. My stomach a jumbled ball of twine.

After our confrontation on the bridge Clay drove me back to his place, calling Dr Bing to let her know to meet us there instead. I had been so tired. Not physically but mentally, and my soul felt leadened by chains now that I had decided to carry my past all on my own. I knew I had a long road ahead of me. But first I needed sleep.

When Dr Bing arrived she offered something to sedate me. I accepted it. I slept for almost sixteen hours in Clay's bed. Every time I woke I found Clay watching me, fear shining in his eyes as he tentatively asked me if I knew who he was.

I always remembered him. When I said his name his face melted to relief and I felt safe enough to sink back down under.

Dr Bing organised for me to attend an intensive recovery program in Sydney to work through all of my repressed memories. They still hadn't pushed their way through yet. Not yet. Salem was still doing her duty, her last stand at guard, before I gradually took over.

I told Flick that I had to take some time off for personal reasons. I didn't explain why exactly but she didn't ask. She seemed to know not to ask.

Clay had flown down to Sydney with me. Last night he had rented a suite at a gorgeous hotel overlooking the Harbour Bridge. We hadn't made love. We just stayed up most of the night holding each other. It didn't matter how many times I had run my hands over his body last night, I still felt unsatisfied. I had been so scared to fall asleep because then our remaining minutes together would be gone.

Now we were down to our last few seconds and I didn't know if I could cope. "I won't get to see you at all. Or touch you…kiss you."

"I know. And I'll be missing you for every single one of those ninety days. But you don't need any distractions during your recovery. Remember, you chose *you*."

Sometimes it sucked doing the right thing. "I'll be all alone."

"No, you won't be."

I looked over his shoulder. Salem stood there, her arms crossed over her chest, a bored look on her face. "Will you two hurry it up already?"

I'm almost ready.

Dear God. Would I ever be ready for this? I tucked myself further into Clay, inhaling his scent as if holding it in my lungs meant that I could carry a part of him with me. I pulled back when something struck me. "There's one more thing that's been bothering me. I found a comic in your apartment…"

He was already nodding, a smile touching the corner of his mouth. "*Adventures of Aria.* I drew her based on you. You encouraged me to submit it to be published. I did. It was the break I needed." These were all things I hadn't started remembering yet. But I would.

"But you'd named her Aria. Aria hadn't existed then."

"I like to think that's why you chose the name Aria to take on after you left and forgot about me. A part of you still remembered. A part of you didn't want to forget me."

Another piece of the puzzle clicked into place. My eyes filled with tears as I clutched onto him. "I'm so sorry I left. I'm so sorry for everything I put you through."

He shushed into my hair and rocked me gently in his arms. "It's okay. Or…it will be."

"I can't believe how much you put up with for me. How much you went through for me."

He sighed and kissed my head. "The course of true love never did run smooth," he quoted.

Despite everything, I smiled. It surprised me. How could I smile again?

But I knew, deep down, even after I remembered everything I would smile again. I would laugh again. And I would make love again.

He leaned down and kissed me goodbye; it wasn't rushed. I tried to memorise everything about this moment. His lips were hard yet soft, sweet yet heated, but mostly this kiss was full of hope.

Finally he pulled away. He tugged a strand of my hair as if he was only leaving me until tomorrow. "See you around, angel." He turned and walked out of the lobby before I could change my mind.

I turned to face my waiting party, an older doctor with a full head of silver hair and a kind smile. Beside him was a younger nurse with a clipboard.

"Welcome, Aria," the doctor said to me. "Or would you prefer Rosa?"

I swallowed as the name I was born with echoed in my head. It still felt like a foreign object to me, like it belonged to a character in a novel instead of me. But apparently that's part of my way of coping. "I've decided to stick with Aria. It's less confusing that way."

He smiled. "Okay. I'm Dr Swanson and this is Nurse Dent." His brow raised in a question. "Is…Salem here with you?"

Salem stepped up to my side, took my hand and squeezed. "I'm here for you. Always."

I smiled at her before turning back to the doctor. "She's here."

"Okay, then let's get you settled and shown around the facility." He turned and walked down the hall and we followed, Nurse Dent taking up the rear.

Salem never let go of my hand. "Tell the doc I won't eat any of that wholemeal pasta shit. Hey, doc, where does a girl get a cup of coffee around here?"

I shook my head, biting back a smile.

She nudged my side. "Hey, sis."

"What?"

"Wanna play a game?"

Day 2

Even from here I could smell the reek of alcohol, the stink of him as he fell into the bed against me.

"Go away," I screamed as he grabbed one of my wrists. I punched out with my thin arms but they just bounced off him.

That sick choking feeling rose up inside me to cut off my air as he slipped his hand down between my skinny legs. Air, I needed air. Where's the surface?

"Stay with me, Aria."

"I can't."

"Sweeetheaaaaart."

"I can't. Make it stop. Make it stop."

"You're so tight you're so tight so tight fucking tight."

"Salem, come back," I screamed, my voice cracked and my throat scraped raw. "I was wrong. I need you, come back come back."

I heard a sigh. "Sedate her…"

Day 9

"Are you okay, Aria?"

Are you okay?

Okay?

No.

I'll never be okay again.

"Do you want to try again?"

I want to die.

Even from here I could smell the reek of alcohol, the stink of him as he fell into the bed against me.

"Go away," I screamed as he grabbed one of my wrists. I punched out with my thin arms but they just bounced off him.

That sick choking feeling rose up inside me to cut off my air as he slipped his hand down between my skinny legs. Air, I needed air. But I was a long way from the surface now.

"Sweetheart," he growled low in his throat. "Sweetheart. Sweetheart. Sweetheart."

He yanked my pyjama bottoms down and he climbed on top of me. Like always, that's when I froze, barely moving, barely breathing, holding everything inside. Keep it inside. But I never could. I felt the sharp rise of bile burning my throat. I shoved it back down. No. No no no. He climbed on top of me, made a shoving motion with his hips and I heard a small sob come from within me. It would be the only cry I made as he did what he did.

A low moan came from him. "You're so tight."

Sweetheart. Sweetheart. So tight sweetheart. The whole room, the walls, the mattress, shook, like the world was falling apart. For me, it was.

"Salem," I sob-whispered, over his grunting, tears squeezing out of my eyes. "What do I do?"

"Don't watch," Salem said as she gripped my face with both hands standing right in front of me so she was blocking Dr Swanson's face. "Just don't watch."

I buried my face in her shoulder.

Day 16

"I thought we'd talk about something else today."

He always wanted to talk.

I didn't.

I wanted to hide. I wanted to disappear into the blackness of an everlasting sleep and feel nothing, remember nothing. I wanted Salem. I wanted Salem here. But Dr Swanson never wanted Salem in here with me. He would make me leave Salem at the door before I came in. And as I closed the door between us, all I could see were the grey clouds of her eyes.

Salem came in anyway when I needed her. She was always there when I needed her.

"Tell me about Clay."

Clay.

At the mention of his name a thread of light found a way to cut through the darkness. Slowly I looked up from my fingers, my nails chewed back to the quick, and up, up to Dr Swanson's jaw. He had a deep dimple on his chin, which I sometimes stared at. It was always too much to look him in the eyes. I was afraid of what I'd see when he looked at me. Anger. Disgust. Pity.

"Clay," I whispered. A pang of longing clenched at my chest. Where was he? Did he think of me? Like I thought of him?

His name is Clay. Clay Jagger.

Is that it? All I get is a name?

What do you want to know?

Is he good to you?

He's wonderful.

So far.

What's that supposed to mean?

My eyes darted aside looking for Salem, always looking for her. But today she stayed away.

"Aria?"

My eyes went back to his chin dimple.

"Tell me about Clay."

Clay. Clay Jagger.

I licked my dry lips. "He makes me laugh. All the time."

"Good. What else?"

"He's brave and strong. He would go to the ends of the Earth for me, no matter what I did. And…"

"Aria, you're stronger than you know."

"And?"

I lifted my gaze to Dr Swanson's eyes. They were a light blue. Not as dark or as vivid as Clay's. But no blue was ever as vivid as Clay's eyes. "And he believes in me."

Day 21

"Can you go any further today?"
Aria, you're stronger than you know.
Clay believed I could do this. I could do this. I could.
I nodded.
Get off me.
I inhaled slowly.
He yanked my pyjama bottoms down and climbed on top of me. Like always, that's when I froze, barely moving, barely breathing, holding everything inside. Keep it inside.
And I exhaled.
I felt the sharp rise of bile burning my throat. I felt every outline of his fingerprints marking my skin. I felt every sticky inch of him as he violated my body. And his moan was a poisonous gas seeping into me.
You're
so
tight.
Every thrust, every thrust, piercing me, piercing me, leaving holes in my paper soul. Please, be quick. Please. Be over. I squeezed my eyes shut, fleeing as far away as far down into my own mind as I could go.
Down
down.
Down I go.
But it was never far enough down. I could never get far enough away. My body, my mattress, my whole room, shook, like the world was falling apart.
You're stronger than you know.
I won't leave you alone. I'm here.
I gritted my teeth and my fingers dug into the couch. And the world shook a little less. And a little less.

Day 89

"Last day," Dr Swanson said as we sat in his office.

I nodded. The last eighty-nine days had been some of the hardest and darkest of my life. As the truth about my past broke its way through like weeds in the cracks, there were two things that kept me going, two points of light, two faces in my mind that kept me fighting to push past the darkness when it threatened to swallow me.

I had good days and bad days in here. And I would continue to have good days and bad days. The bad days would come less and less and then they would become bad hours, then bad minutes... but I accepted that they may never really go away.

"Is Salem here?" he asked.

My shoulders wilted as a sadness rolled around in me. That was one thing I wasn't sure I had truly accepted. I shook my head, my eyes lowered to the latte-coloured carpet.

"When was the last time you saw her?"

I swallowed. "I haven't..." The doctor let me have my silence, perhaps realising I needed a moment. "I haven't seen her in weeks now." And I missed her so much.

I heard the sound of paper flicking as he closed my file. "Well, reviewing your file I think your treatment went well. I'll be happy to release you tomorrow. Well done, Aria."

It was you, Salem, I thought, wondering if she could even still hear me. *I couldn't have done it without you.*

At the door to Dr Swanson's office I paused and turned to him. "Do you think I'll ever see her again?"

He pressed his lips together. "Salem was a strategy for your adolescent mind to deal with something horrific happening to you. Something that no one should ever have to deal with. You've made the right steps to move past it. So, don't take this the wrong way but...I hope not."

Chapter Twenty-One

Day 90

My release day. As I walked down the hall from my room towards the lobby, my lonely footsteps echoed off the walls, my stomach tumbled over and over again like a half-empty dryer. Would Clay be there waiting for me? Like he said he would? We hadn't seen each other in ninety days. We hadn't even spoken in ninety days. But I'd thought of him every day. And I woke up every morning to his face on the backs of my eyes and the feeling of his ghost by my side.

Ninety days is a long time.

Anything could happen in ninety days.

We fell in love in less than ninety days.

And I forgot him in less than ninety seconds.

He could have met someone else. Moved away. He could have forgotten about me… Or chosen to try and forget about me. I wouldn't hate him if he did. I had already caused him so much suffering.

I held my breath as I rounded the corridor to the lobby. Would he be there? Please be there. Please…

There he was.

Waiting.

With a smile as radiant and wide as I had ever seen it. My breath released in a sob as my body flooded with cool relief.

I broke into a run. Even as my vision blurred behind my tears I found my way back into his arms. And his lips were on mine. And his arms were around me, crushing me, and I was being lifted, and I was weightless. And I was flying and I never wanted to come down.

"Aria," my name broke in his voice as he leaned his forehead on mine, his smell of musk and cedar and his warmth making a home all around me. "God, I've missed you."

"You came."

"Of course I came."

"I'll come for you. I'll find you. No matter where you go, I'll find you." Now that I remembered everything, I felt our love stretching back to the day we met on that bridge, a thick, rich tapestry of him and me. Even though I ran from him, he searched for me and found me and waited patiently for me to fall in love with him again. He never gave up on me. Which is why *I* could never give up on me.

"I love you," I said without hesitation.

"I love you, too, my indestructible angel." He kissed me, his lips hot and fierce, a promise for what was to come. I didn't even flinch as whistling and claps sounded out around us; they all sounded so far away to me.

Not everyone gets to find a love like this. I'm a very lucky girl, very, very lucky. Although I didn't always feel that way.

I'm lucky because Clay Jagger loves me. Unconditionally. All of me. Even the torn or folded pieces of me.

Epilogue

I watch you and Clay walk from the facility lobby to the taxi he has waiting for you. I watch from a distance, always at distance, never too close to you, but never too far away. He has his arm slung over your shoulder and your hand is travelling across his back as if you're trying to remember every part of him. And you don't sense that I'm here.

You should know I'll never really leave you, sis.

Never.

I love you too much.

I told you I'd always be here.

Watching.

Waiting.

Even if you don't think you need me anymore, I know you do.

Or you will.

The End

Paper Hearts
A Paper Dolls Novella
By Sienna Blake

This is a prequel novella told from Clay's perspective. Please finish reading Paper Dolls before you read Paper Hearts as it contains spoilers.

My name is Clay Jagger. And I have a secret. A secret that I just couldn't live with…

Until an angel came along and saved me with her light and her laughter. And for a while we were happy.

But my angel has a secret too. A dark secret that if exposed would tear us apart.

Please continue reading to find out how to read Paper Hearts…

Dear Readers,

Schizophrenia and Dissociative Identity Disorder are real illnesses and a lot of the elements of this book are factual. However, I made some creative decisions in regards to some aspects of this story (like the ending. Contemporary therapy encourages DID sufferers to live alongside their alters as opposed to giving them up). I hope I haven't offended. It was certainly not my intent. My heart goes out to the brave souls who live with mental illness every day.

At the request (demand, haha. I bend easily) of one of my early readers, I wrote Clay's novella, Paper Hearts. It will *not* be for sale anywhere. It is a labor of love and a 'thank you' that I will be giving out (for free) to my VIP Romance Readers. My VIPs get access to VIP-exclusive giveaways, freebies (like Clay's novella) and get an occasional newsletter when I have a new release or sale. If you'd like to read Clay's novella, please join my VIPs (either Romance or All Genres) at:

www.siennablake.com

I also hold weekly giveaways on my Facebook page so go and give it a "like" and see you there!

https://www.facebook.com/SiennaBlakeAuthor/

Did you enjoy the book?

Please support me as an indie author by posting a review where you bought this book. Even one or two quick sentences is so helpful to me! Send me a message through my website or Facebook page so I can thank you personally! You can help by recommending me to a friend. Word of mouth is still the best way for new readers to find me.

Books by Sienna Blake

ROMANTIC SUSPENSE

Bound by Lies (Bound #1)
Bound Forever (Bound #2)
Paper Dolls

Dark Romeo series ~ coming soon

www.siennablake.com

Acknowledgments

Firstly to Emma. This book is already yours but I just wanted to say thank you (again) for cheering this project on even before I had written the first word. And for early reading the hell out of this book. Love you, my little padwan.

To Terrie from Just Another Book Bitch, my social media guru, marketing madam, and all round badass. Thank you for handling all that boggy day to day crap done, for being a friend, for making me laugh, and for pretending I'm funny when I send you dirty jokes. (Wait, wait… what's long and hard and has the word 'cum' in it? …A cucumber! teehee).

To Kathy Newton from Just Let Me Read. Bless you, woman, for your encouragement, support and for being one of the Dolls early readers. I'm so glad Sammy pointed me your way!

To Dani, thank you for reading that awful first draft (sorry) and helping me to fix that beginning section (aka cut it all out, lol).

Thanks to Sonja T from Migrating Miss, for your beta edits and for help with that Prologue.

To Christie, my editor. You really went above and beyond for this one. Damn technology fails! *shakes fist* haha, it all worked out in the end, right?

To Romac Designs for that gorgeous cover! *wistful sigh* One day all these other authors are going to realize how awesome you are and I'll have to fight them off with sticks to get into your schedule. And you'll deserve it too ;)

Thanks to J for answering my questions on Schizophrenia and

Dissociative Identity Disorder. And to the scores of anonymous forum posters with these actual illnesses. Thank you for being so open and frank about what living with a mental illness entails.

To my writing gals: Mounia & Elly. Thank you for the endless cups of coffee, laughs, and letting me hash out the plot twist(s) so hard it made all your heads hurt, lol.

Thank you to Aisling O'Shea for answering some hospital procedure questions ;)

Finally to my darling. Who puts up with my crap when I'm soul-deep in a writing project. And for making me laugh when I was tearing my hair out over the ending by telling me to "just kill everyone like you normally do". (I don't do that, do I?) Volim te.

About the Author

Sienna Blake loves all things that make her heart race — rollercoasters, thrillers and rowdy unrestrained sex. She likes to explore the darker side of human nature in her writing.

Sienna is a pen name for a bestselling fiction author. If she told you who she really was, she'd have to kill you. Because of her passion for crime and forensics, she'd totally get away with your murder.